From *The Spirit of the Dark Island*

Bam! Bam! Bam! Polly woke up to a heavy pounding on the cottage door. Who could be knocking at this hour? She slipped out of bed and crept to the bedroom window. She cracked the curtains, but could not see the door; the three-foot sill was too deep.

Bam! Bam! Bam! The knocking came again.

She tiptoed cautiously to the door. Could she see anything through the keyhole? Carefully she removed the key and bent to look through the hole, and almost collapsed from shock when the knocking erupted a third time just above her head, even louder and more vigorous: BAM! BAM! BAM!

Shaking, she made a decision. She was a woman all alone in the middle of nowhere, and she was not going to open the door to someone knocking in the middle of the night. The knocker might be a burglar, a rapist, a vampire, even a zombie. Or a werewolf. The idea of confronting a werewolf in this desolate house on this deserted road made the hair on her neck prickle.

A sudden light shone through the keyhole, and she shrank back in alarm until she realized the moon had come out. It was full tonight and would illuminate brightly the land below. She crept back to the bedroom window and pulled the curtains slightly open so she could peek out. She saw nothing. She was almost sure there was no one there, and the last knock had come some minutes ago.

Did she dare open the door?

By the same author:
Westering Home
The White Rose of Scotland
The Devil and the Dark Island
Rosie's Cèilidh
Magic Carpet Ride
Down by the Salley Gardens
The Woman Who Loved Newfoundland
O'Leary, Kat and Cary Grant
O'Leary, Kat and the Fairy from Hell

The Spirit of the Dark Island

A Ghost Story

A Scottish Island Novel

Audrey McClellan

AMBER SKYE
PUBLISHING

ISBN: 978-0-9894003-3-6
Library of Congress Catalog Number: 2015930131
Cover art by Carla McClellan
Eilean Dubh map by Jane Gordon
Book design by Chris Fayers
All musical selections in this book composed by and copyright to
Sherry Wohlers Ladig and used by permission.
Scottish country dance, "The Spirit of Eilean Dubh," devised by and
copyright to Lara Friedman-Shedlov and used by permission.

1935 BERKSHIRE DRIVE
EAGAN, MINNESOTA 55122
AMBER SKYE   651-452-0463
PUBLISHING   www.AMBERSKYEPUBLISHING.COM

Printed in the United States of America
First Printing: January 2015
To order, visit Amazon.com or ScottishIslandNovels.com

Dedication

Dedicated to the memory of our beloved late brother and sister-in-law,
Steve McClellan and Joan Whitney-McClellan

To love is to place our happiness in the happiness of another.

—Leibnitz

From ghoulies and ghosties
And long-leggedy beasties
And things that go bump in the night,
Good Lord, deliver us.

Scottish prayer

Prologue

Enter the Spirit

Let us go in, the fog is rising.
Emily Dickinson

*I*n daylight Eilean Dubh, the Dark Island, seemed very much like any other part of the Scottish Highlands. It looked, in fact, like a scene out of a tourist brochure. Rolling fields of green gave way to rocky outcroppings that gave way to more green fields, all liberally criss-crossed by sparkling clear streams called burns. Bright patches of wildflowers popped up here and there. A craggy mountain hovered in the background, several smaller peaks crouching at its foot like bear cubs around their dam.

At twilight Eilean Dubh lay serene beneath a purple sky, its fields, rocks, flowers and burns touched with gold by the rays of the majestically disappearing sun. *Beinn Mhic-an-Righ*, the high western mountain, stood like a sentinel, its peaks blazoned across the sky in red and orange. A more peaceful scene could not be imagined.

At night Eilean Dubh was a land of darkness and shadows, almost impenetrably so, as streetlights were found only in the towns of Airgead and Ros Mór, at opposite ends of the island. Not until the full moon was there light upon the land.

In fog Eilean Dubh was altogether different. It was not the least bit serene or peaceful; it was downright eerie. Menacing, in fact. White mist rose in clumps from the fields and drifted to hover over the rocks. Burns floated in midair and disappeared into bottomless caverns to trap unwary walkers. A cold damp wind prowled, moaning low in its throat and chilling all it touched.

An old Eilean Dubh saying, "where the mist hangs low ye dare not go," warned of the dangers of being abroad when the fog was out for it always hovered thickest over the Island's deadly bogs and haunted spots, writhing in clouds, dipping low to the ground, and rising like a spectral dancer.

Over Cemetery Hill the heavy serious layer was pierced now and then by a faint laugh or a baby's despairing wail. On the mountain *Beinn Mhic-an-Righ* the silhouette of the Great Gray Man moved in and out of foggy patches, scattering wild rabbits, alarming voles, and terrifying the tiny burrowing owls.

Eilean Dubh in fog, at night, was a bad dream, especially on the two-lane road connecting the towns of Airgead in the north and Ros Mór in the south. The gray mass swirled over the pavement, shifting the verges out of their proper spots and into the center of the road, hiding the dangerous cliff edge. A particularly persistent patch hung in midair at the bottom of the road's lowest spot, down the road from a decrepit old stone house.

This was the most dangerous part of the road. It swerved perilously close to the edge of the cliff and the rock-strewn shore a long, long way below. There was no guardrail. The Council had debated its installation for several years, ever since the Laird's Bentley nearly went over in the Great Blizzard of '03. But somehow, it was one of those things that never got done, largely because of budget constraints.

Ian Mór MacDonald, one of the Island's two doctors, was speeding down the road in his little blue Austin, his headlights reduced to candles against the fog, his head nodding in the first tremors of sleep as he approached Cemetery Hill. He knew he was driving too fast, he knew he was approaching the curve, but he couldn't seem to do anything about it; doziness held him in too tight a grip. He'd been up at six to assist a mother in a difficult birth, worked his regular shift at the clinic, come home for dinner, and was settling in to watch a DVD with his wife Sally when the telephone rang.

The caller's voice unsuccessfully masked panic. Her four-year-old had a very high temperature, had vomited, and was now rolling in his crib in terrible pain, wailing desperately. Could the doctor come, please?

Ian Mór came, and diagnosed acute appendicitis. The child was in hospital and in the operating room in forty-five minutes. Ian operated successfully, and after seeing his patient stable and comfortable, was on his way home when the fog came down, fatigue took hold, and the inevitable happened. The Austin, feeling its owner's hands slackening on the wheel, drifted to the left, towards the cliff edge.

A full moon emerged, scattering the clouds. Abruptly a figure loomed up on the car's left front fender. Ian's head jerked in shock. He swerved right round in a tire-burning full turn, slammed on the brakes, screeched to a stop, and flung the door open to discover that he was teetering on the edge of nowhere. Terrified, he clutched the door to save himself.

Under his sleepy guidance, the car had wandered from the road onto the verge and beyond, and was now perched on the edge of the cliff rearing above the ocean. Two more feet and it would have been over and down, into the deep, deep water far below, a fall no human could survive.

Shaken, Ian settled back, started the engine, and backed onto the road. When all four wheels were safely on the pavement, he dropped his head on the steering wheel and gave himself to the luxury of an old-fashioned full-body, teeth-chattering, shuddering fit.

Suddenly he remembered the figure that had loomed up in front of him. Where had it gone? Had he hit it and knocked it over the cliff? Was it lying lifeless and bloody in the wildflowers filling the verges? He grabbed a torch from the glove box and steeled himself to go and look. He climbed out. Swishing the light in a wide arc in front of him, he examined with care the area from across the road to the cliff edge. He peered over, and saw nothing. He stood for a moment, thinking in his logical way about what had happened.

What was anyone doing out on the road at this time of night? Where had he, or she – Ian really wasn't sure which – gone? Why couldn't he bring into focus what the figure had looked like? All he could remember was a tall wraith in raggedy clothes and a seaman's cap, with what looked like seaweed dripping from its shoulder.

Seaweed?

His father, Jamie MacDonald, would have understood right away. He had the Sight, that ability of some Highlanders to anticipate and understand mysterious events, and in his almost fifty years he had encountered enough spooks, fairies, misty wisps, and Great Gray Men to satisfy the imagination of a dozen Stephen Kings. Jamie would have recognized the fortuitous intervention of *an spiorad*, a spirit, in human affairs.

Ian Mór MacDonald, with no trace at all of the Sight in his practical, scientifically-trained brain and no patience at all for supernatural happenings, decided he had fallen asleep at the wheel and been wakened by a nightmare.

They were both right.

Part I

The MacDonalds of California

One

Father calls me William,
Sister calls me Will,
Mother calls me Willie,
But the fellers call me Bill.

Eugene Field

William Wallace MacDonald had never had the slightest desire to visit Scotland. His world was bounded by his parents' home in California, a sprawling ranch-style mansion on thirty acres south of Ventura Boulevard in the San Fernando Valley, by Princeton University, where he'd gotten his undergraduate degree, and by the offices of his father's business in a suburb of Los Angeles.

He functioned quite nicely within these geographical limits, bouncing from one corner of the triangle to another as was appropriate to the time of the year. After he graduated from Princeton, he narrowed his range to include home and the firm. In his tidy, well-organized way he had set himself the goal of joining the family business as his two siblings had done.

His older brother, Robert Bruce MacDonald, was already an executive with the family firm and his father's right hand man. He had not been required to start as an office boy as his father thought that was nonsense. "Boy's going to be an owner of the firm one of these days, so he might as well start learning the business from the top down, not waste time sharpening pencils," said Robert Burns MacDonald, the patriarch.

Sister Flora had signed on after graduating from Vassar and now headed the marketing department. She was a perfect example of a marketing executive; she could sell sand in the Kalahari. She could quote by heart the ABC figures for the forty largest United States magazines and newspapers, she knew which advertising agency had the best track record for increasing sales in her company's NCAIS code, and she was on socializing

13

terms with three governors, five governors' wives, one governor's husband, and a handful of highly-influential senators, male and female.

William Wallace was the little brother, the odd man out, not because of any perceived deficiency, but because he hadn't identified the niche for him to fill. He fully intended to slot himself neatly into the firm once he had completed his education and decided what sort of work he wanted to do. He had taken a management degree and gotten good grades, but his studies had not interested him; he'd slogged through them successfully only by determined hard work at which he excelled. His family often said, "Once William Wallace gets his teeth into something, he doesn't let go till it's mastered." "Like his namesake at the Battle of Stirling Bridge," his father proudly declared.

Next he'd decided to try the legal division, and to that end had obtained a law degree from Harvard, but found corporate law unutterably boring even for his methodical self. His current plans were to obtain an MBA in business, specializing in international trade, since the firm was expanding into overseas sales thanks to Flora's marketing efforts; they had a foothold in France now. He had been accepted for the highly regarded graduate school of his choice and expected to matriculate there in the fall.

His plans to spend the summer learning the business at his brother's side were abruptly terminated when his father announced that he was going to achieve a cherished dream, visiting his old friend, Darroch Mac an Rìgh, laird of tiny Scottish island Eilean Dubh.

"I've been promising Darroch a visit ever since we first met, when I got a bunch of our California Scottish-American guys together to cough up big bucks to support the Eilean Dubh Trust. They've been contributing ever since that night. Darroch keeps writing me that I've got to come to the Island and see what the Trust has accomplished with the help of our dough, and by jinks, I'm going to do it this summer." Robert Burns MacDonald nodded his head in that determined way that made wife and children uneasily aware that his mind was made up and would not be changed. The family considered him to be even more doggedly tenacious than the legendary Scot, William Wallace.

The family was sitting on the patio so Louise MacDonald, mother and wife, could indulge in one of the four cigarettes daily she allowed herself; she never smoked inside the house. The cigarette was an expensive English brand, imported especially for her by a high-end tobacco and liquor firm that imported the three single malt whiskies Robert Burns favored. She lit up, her long-fingered hands shaking a little with nerves as she considered her husband's decree. She knew there was no point in arguing with him, so she agreed instead, hoping by stealth to undermine the project. "Of course, darling, you should pay them a visit, after the long connection you've had with the Island."

The entire family knew that Scotland was the senior MacDonald's obsession. Had he not insisted that all three of his children be named for Scottish heroes? Had he not served as president of every major Scottish-American organization in California and two national ones? Did he not own the finest collection of Scottish-themed books in the United States outside of a library, and moreover, had he not read every one of them, even the boring ones?

Had not his genealogy been researched back to the Scottish immigrant who had come from Nova Scotia to California during the Gold Rush and founded the proud family he now headed? And before that, to humble origins in the northernmost Highlands.

And did he not own not one, not two, but three of the finest kilt outfits in America, with handsomely-jeweled *sgianan dubha*, the little black knives that resided in the socks knitted for him in an exclusive design by an Edinburgh firm catering to wealthy Yanks. The man was a walking, talking example of a proud Scottish-American.

Of course Robert Burns MacDonald must go to Eilean Dubh, but he could not be allowed to go alone. The family had had a scare a year ago when they'd come close to losing him to a very serious heart attack. He had taken excellent care of himself since then, following his specialists' instructions to the letter, but his wife and children, who adored him, were unwilling to let him out of their sight for fear he might become ill again.

Louise stubbed out her cigarette and picked up her knitting; she always had to have something to do with her hands. She said, "I'd love to go with you, dearest, but would you mind delaying your trip a bit? I've been asked to serve on the hospital's board." There were oohs and ahhs of congratulations from her family, who knew how dedicated she was to the local children's hospital, how hard she'd worked as chair of its volunteers, and what an honor it was to be asked to be a board member. "They want me to be in charge of our next fund raising drive. It'll take all summer to plan. If you could wait till autumn. . ."

Robert Burns MacDonald had the look on his face and the jut to his chin that wife and children both recognized and dreaded. He was a reasonable man much of the time, but he had a certain Scottish stubbornness that meant that all decisions were carefully considered and, once made, were unshakable. "Nope. The best weather is in summer, Darroch says, so that's when I am going. Don't worry about it, Lou. I'll go ahead and get the lay of the land, and you can join me when you've got time. The hospital fund-raiser comes first."

Worried looks were exchanged. *He can't go by himself*, signaled Louise with her eyes, and the children nodded in agreement. Flora said coaxingly, "Daddy, wouldn't a tour be better? Think of those heavy suitcases you'll have to drag on and off planes and through airports. And the hassle with tickets and foreign money and going through customs. It'll be an enormous amount of work and stress and ..."

She stopped, knowing better than to mention his heart attack; it would only make him more determined to prove that he was completely well and fit again. He'd always prided himself on his stamina and vigorous health and his illness had been a blow to his ego and his self-image.

Robert Burns shook his head. "Tours don't go to Eilean Dubh. I've done – well, my secretary's done – the research, and I've talked to my travel agent. It takes a special itinerary and she's working on it for me. She thinks I'll have to hire a guide."

William Wallace sighed and did what he had to do. At twenty-six years old he was more than aware of his duty to his family and of the importance of his siblings. He knew his brother's expertise and managerial skills were absolutely necessary to the firm if its founder and leader were to be gone. Flora was commanding a huge new marketing effort designed to keep the company's industrial fastener products foremost in their customers' thoughts, always a challenge with so much competition these days.

He was the little brother, the expendable one, the fifth wheel, with nothing to do all summer but watch his brother make decisions and his sister manipulate the media, and wonder why he was wasting his time sitting passively in Robert Bruce's office. Surely there was more to life and work than that. And he couldn't let his father go off three thousand miles away in the care of a professional guide who didn't know his tricky health history or what symptoms of illness to watch for. He said in a falsely cheerful voice, "Say, I've got a great idea. I'll go with you, Dad."

"Will you, son?" said Robert Burns, delighted.

"Oh, sure. I've always wanted to visit Scotland." Everyone but Robert Burns knew this was an out-an-out lie. The MacDonald children had been enmeshed for years in their father's obsession with a small country three thousand miles away. They'd had been dragged to every Scottish festival and Highland games in California (and there were many), had been to more Burns' Night suppers and been forced to eat more haggis than even a Scot would consume in a lifetime.

They'd taken Scottish dance and music lessons and participated in competitions. They'd been fitted yearly with new kilts and (for Flora) kilted skirts with the ones they'd outgrown being donated to less fortunate young American MacDonalds. They knew they were children of the proudest and most numerous clan ever to originate in the Scottish Homeland and they knew they were named for great heroes of that country. And frankly, they no longer gave a damn.

It was great to have all that history and tradition in their family, but what possible relevance did it have to their lives? They were Americans. Go to Scotland? And beyond that, to a tiny island, where they probably couldn't recharge their iPods and smartphone batteries or access their laptops by wi-fi? Maybe there weren't even computers on Eilean Dubh. Or wi-fi. Or cell phones. Yikes. For himself, William Wallace MacDonald would rather walk three miles with his shoes full of tacks all pointed straight up.

But he knew what he had to do. He took a deep breath and said, "So, Dad, when would you like to leave? And how long are we going to stay?"

"Soon as possible and we'll stay two to three months, I reckon."

William Wallace sighed again, quietly. Three months! he thought. What the hell would he do in Scotland for three months? He'd better pack plenty of books in his suitcase; he'd have a ton of time to catch up on his reading.

Robert Burns was warming to his subject. "I want to settle in and experience the flavor of Eilean Dubh. Of course, we'll first spend a few weeks touring the rest of Scotland. Have to find our roots, you know. Ancestral graves, old records, that sort of thing. Maybe meet a cousin or two." Robert Burns rubbed his hands together in glee. "Good job we all got passports two years ago when we took that trip to Guatemala for your mother's well-baby project. Just need to book tickets and pack and we're off at last! I want you to know, William Wallace, how proud I'll be to have you by my side."

"Thank you, Dad. It will be my pleasure to accompany you." Just as it had been the pleasure of each child to accompany Robert Burns to his many events until each had gotten old enough to be bored and clever enough to think of an excuse not to go with him. Such was the power and magnetism of his personality and their pride in his majestic kilted figure that the boys had not done this until they'd reached their late teens, and Flora still went with him whenever her schedule allowed. Being forced into Scottishness was one thing, but standing proudly by the side of Robert Burns MacDonald as he presided over yet another event was quite another.

So they went to Scotland, father and son, and spent an exhausting three weeks touring the Highlands. They met the Chief of their Clan and his Lady, kinsmen and kinswomen galore, and visited ancestors' graves on the Isle of Skye and in the Highlands.

They stood silent and grim in Glencoe, thinking of the treachery that had violated MacDonald hospitality and resulted in bloodshed and death. They stood silent and grim on the battlefield of Culloden, where Stewart hopes and loyal clansmen alike had perished. They peered out over a silent and grim Loch Ness looking for the monster, and climbed the crumbling stairs of more silent and grim ruined castles than either of them could have imagined existed.

At last, when both had had their fill of Scottish history and the silence and grimness that William Wallace MacDonald was beginning to think was the hallmark of Scotland old and new, they came to Eilean Dubh.

Two

Now's the day and now's the hour . . .

Robert Burns

*W*illiam Wallace was the one designated to drive the treacherous, winding, mountainous roads of Highland Scotland on what he obstinately persisted in referring to as "the wrong side of the road." Now it was his responsibility to drive the rental car off the Cal-Mac ferry, something he dreaded, but his father insisted he would first touch the soil of Eilean Dubh with his shoes, not with the tires of a car.

So the older man rode the ferry into the harbor ensconced on the passenger deck, peering worshipfully as the Island's dark *Beinn Mhic-an-Rìgh*-dominated silhouette came into view, grew larger, and at last presented itself as the sturdy, business-like dock of the port of Airgead. So enthralled was he to at last behold the Island that had occupied his thoughts and dreams for nearly ten years that he scarcely noticed when his son slipped from his side into the ferry's innards to resume the driver's seat of the rental car.

This was fortunate, for thus William Wallace did not have to witness his father awkwardly getting down on his knees and bending to kiss the soil of Eilean Dubh. Ferry passengers and *Eilean Dubhannaich* alike stared in shock.

"Let me give you a hand up, Robert Burns MacDonald," said Darroch Mac an Rìgh, stepping forward from the crowd as he recognized his old friend.

"Thanks. Knees aren't what they used to be," said Robert Burns, rising unsteadily with Darroch's firm hand under his arm for support.

"You're looking well," began Darroch, just before the older man folded him into his embrace. Darroch responded with a hug of his own, heedless of what onlookers might think of this distinctly un-Scottish mode of expression. He knew there'd been suppressed grins at the ground-kissing and he was frankly irritated at the reaction of the watchers. They had no need to poke fun. After all, they'd seen Americans before and knew what their reaction to their first step on the sacred Auld Sod would be and they should be used to it by now.

Now Robert Burns drew back and regarded his friend fondly. "Here I am on Eilean Dubh at last!" he said.

"Aye, and damned near about time," said Darroch, his blue eyes moist with threatened tears. He was fond of the older man and genuinely delighted to see him.

"Aye," said the American, who'd adopted years ago the Scottish word for *yes*. In others it might have seemed an affectation; in Robert Burns it seemed perfectly natural. "That's God's own truth, but here I am, after dreaming of it for so many years."

"And most kindly welcome you are. You'll remember my wife Jean; you met when we were in California while I was there to film a commercial," Darroch said, as a pretty brown-haired, green-eyed woman stepped up to his side and extended her hand to the visitor with a smile.

"*Ceud mille fàilte*," said Jean, knowing that the older man would enjoy the sound of the Island's native language.

He chuckled. "*Tapadh leat*, my dear," he said, and bent to kiss her cheek.

"Do you have the Gaelic?" she said, surprised.

"Oh, just a wee word here and there."

"By the end of your visit we'll have you speaking it like a native," promised Jean, a bit of exaggeration for which she trusted she'd be forgiven by the gods of linguistics.

William Wallace had maneuvered the rental car off the ferry, parked it carefully on the dock, and now stepped forward to be introduced. "My son, William Wallace MacDonald," announced his father.

To the younger man's relief, neither Darroch nor Jean commented on his name. He had gotten used to exclamations about it from people throughout Scotland who'd remarked about his being named for Scotland's greatest hero, and he had despaired of ever persuading his father to introduce him simply as William. Why, he wondered, did fathers make it their life's work to embarrass their sons?

"Will you ride with me to the Rose Hotel, Robert Burns? Jean can go along with your son to make sure he doesn't get lost," said Darroch, suppressing a chuckle at the thought of anyone getting lost on the one and only road that led from Airgead to Ros Mór. He had suggested it because it did not seem kind to leave the young man alone in his car to follow the Bentley's stately progress.

"Certainly. The car's right over here, Mrs. Mac an Rìgh," said William Wallace, his tone correct and formal, so unlike his father's American friendliness.

"It's Jean, please," she said.

"Please call me William Wallace," he said, opening the car door for her.

Jean settled in, wondering what on earth she was to talk about to this imposing young man on the ride to the Hotel. A twenty-minute drive had never before loomed so long and she envied Darroch his passenger, whom she'd already sized up with relief as quite a talkative and friendly gentleman, unlike his starchy son. Neither she nor her husband had been able to visualize what William Wallace would be like, as Darroch had not seen him since their first introduction years ago. "He was a nice wee lad," Darroch had remembered. "A bit shy, but he had a wonderful boyish grin."

That grin was not at all in evidence now and Jean wondered if it had ever existed outside of Darroch's fond memories. She tried valiantly to bring the mythical smile to the young man's lips with cheerful chat as she pointed out the sights of Eilean Dubh, its glorious mountains, rock-strewn pastures, sparkling burns, the view of the cerulean sea on the left of the road, the picturesque cottages on the right.

William Wallace's only comment was, "There seems to be quite a lot of sheep."

"Oh, aye," babbled Jean. "Our crofters raise them." Even ten years on Eilean Dubh had not made her fluent about sheep. They had wool, four legs, large ears and big wet noses, and what was there to say beyond that? She doubted that William Wallace would have much interest in the market for lamb or wool or the variety of disgusting diseases to which sheep were prone, although she was tempted to babble about those subjects just to have something to say. Long conversational pauses made her nervous.

But defeated at last, she fell silent. When the younger man said suddenly, "It's quite beautiful here," she jumped in surprise and could only manage a weak, "Aye, it is." He must believe that I'm an idiot, thought Jean, but reminded herself that it takes two people to make a conversation.

They arrived at last at the Rose Hotel, to their mutual relief, and pulled up just as Gordon Morrison, owner of the Hotel, was being introduced to his new guest. Robert Burns had insisted on a slow drive so that he could take in the beauty of the Island. He became almost poetic when he spotted a rippling burn with a tiny waterfall and a clump of yellow flag on its banks, and he was delighted into chuckles by the quaintness of the town of Ros Mór and the multicolored shop fronts around its tidy little square.

Now he was prepared to be equally enthusiastic about the rambling old Rose Hotel and his accommodations therein, and he shook Gordon's hand with fervor. "Fine looking place you've got here," he said, as Gordon led them through the lobby and up the stairs to a comfortable pair of rooms overlooking the sea front. The connecting door had been left open, so that Robert Burns and William Wallace had the pleasure of adjoining rooms like a suite, and the convenience of a bathroom and a separate entrance apiece.

"We start serving the evening meal at seven," began Gordon, but Darroch interposed, "The MacDonalds will be dining at home with us tonight. I'll come and get you and the lad at six-thirty, Robert Burns, so you'll have time to unpack and perhaps have a nice wee lie-down. You must be tired after your weeks of adventuring around Scotland."

Robert Burns admitted that a few minutes of shuteye would be welcome. Darroch noted the relieved expression on the younger man's face and wondered if William Wallace was tired, or if he was happy that his father was willing to take a break, however short, from his exertions. Darroch knew about the heart attack and had put two and two together when he'd heard that the son was accompanying the father to Eilean Dubh. To look after him, he'd assumed, and a jolly good idea it was, too.

He'd invited the MacDonalds to stay at *Taigh a Mhorair*, figuring they could just manage to accommodate two guests with the room addition and the new second bathroom, but William Wallace, who was making the arrangements, had politely declined.

It would be more restful for his father to stay in a hotel, he'd written to Darroch. He did not mention that he, William, would also have the privacy his restrained soul required. It gave him the shudders to think of being crammed into a cottage with a family that included two small children and a Dandie Dinmont terrier and her newborn puppies. Not that he had anything in particular against children or dogs, but they demanded a certain level of social interaction that he dreaded. Smiles at breakfast, mindless comments on the weather, multiple iterations of "have a nice day," to say nothing of being expected to make a fuss over the puppies.

Dinner that night at the Mac an Rìghs was a merry event, full of good food and laughter; even William Wallace relaxed and enjoyed himself in the cheerful company of Darroch and his family. Jean had invited her daughter Sally, son-in-law Ian Mór and their twins, and next door neighbors and best friends Jamie and Màiri MacDonald. She set up her dining table (using both leaves) in the sun room instead of in the cozy but smaller kitchen so there was room for everyone, and a view out the huge windows for the assembled company to enjoy as the sun set in splendor behind *Beinn Mhic-an-Rìgh*.

Looking happily at her dinner arrangements, Jean completely forgot the weeks of disruption that had accompanied the remodeling, and thought only of how pleasant it was to have enough room to entertain a dozen people for a meal. Worth all the dust and noise and smells of construction, she thought. And that's saying a lot, because there were times she'd thought she'd go bonkers from breathing in paint fumes.

And now she also had a bathroom on the first floor! An extra bathroom was one of the few things she missed from her years in Milwaukee with her former husband, Russ, in their five-bedroom house with its view of Lake Michigan.

Robert Burns, rested, refreshed, and trading stories with everyone, was tickled to death to meet the Island MacDonalds, and persisted in addressing them as "Cousin Jamie" and "Cousin Màiri," which amused both the reserved Scots immensely.

"But it's Jamie who might be a cousin," Màiri said, "since I'm a Ross of Eilean Dubh by birth, and only a MacDonald by marriage. Jamie's from the Isle of Skye."

"So was one of my ancestors!" exclaimed Robert Burns. "From a little village called Achnacloich. Emigrated from there after the battle of Culloden and settled on Cape Breton Island in Nova Scotia. Several generations later a branch of the family moved down to Pennsylvania and a son of that branch came to California in the Gold Rush. He was my great-great-great-great grandfather."

"You certainly know a lot about your ancestry," said Darroch, privately wondering, as always, why Americans set such store by genealogy.

It seemed at odds with the accepted idea of the United States being a land of self-made people who didn't give a hang about where they came from, only about where they were going.

"I should," said Robert Burns. "I hired the best genealogist in Scotland to research it all for me. It took him months and a lot of that time he was working in my library so I hadn't its use, but it was worth it. I've got a complete chart of my family that goes back to the fourteenth century in Scotland, with a couple of barons and earls in the line-up, and an illegitimate king's son."

The assembled company made polite noises of interest. The Scots didn't need to research their genealogy; they knew who they were and who their ancestors had been, and the other Americans, Jean and her daughter Sally, kept in mind the fact that genealogies were not infallible. Jean's great-grandmother had been adopted, a fact kept secret as was customary in the past and only whispered about. But it meant that the lady's bloodline remained a mystery and had nothing to do with the family of MacCriathars (anglicized to Greer) from whom Jean was descended.

"I have family in Achnacloich," observed Jamie, "so maybe we truly are related, away back in the past."

"Let's find out. I'll give my genealogist in Edinburgh a call and have him look into it."

"Of course," said Jamie, startled. He'd had no idea that Robert Burns was serious about a family connection; he had just been making pleasant conversation when he suggested it. But the idea tickled him; what would it be like to be related to this affable American with whom he had nothing else in common?

Robert Burns said, "Wonderful dinner, Jean, I enjoyed every bite. Could we have a wee bit of music now? Perhaps a tune from our fiddling cousin? I've been waiting all evening for it."

Jamie, pleased to be asked, went to get his fiddle, thinking perhaps he did have something in common with Robert Burns MacDonald, after all: a love of Scottish music.

Part II

The Perils of Pauline

Three

She wondered why it had never occurred to her before that you cannot successfully navigate the future unless you keep always framed beside it a small clear image of the past.

Jan Struther

Eilean Dubh: Celebration of a Small Island. It was the book that would bring Polly Gillespie to the Dark Island.

She'd ordered it from the Internet after seeing the small ad in one of the Scottish heritage and travel magazines that she subscribed to and mooned over, visualizing a land of heather, dashing heroes and romantic music that called to her soul. She'd had a quiet obsession with Scotland for years, but reading about the country was the closest she'd ever come to visiting it.

She'd never had the money to travel until now, when she had ten thousand dollars, meant for her baby's support for six months, from the child's father. Now the baby was gone, lost to a miscarriage, and the father was gone, too; where, she had no idea. Nor did she care.

"I don't want to get married, Polly," Duane had said, when she'd told him about her unexpected pregnancy. "I think it would be a mistake. And I don't think you want to marry me, either. Or do you?"

Did she? Emphatically not. The pregnancy had been a mistake; whether hers or his, she didn't know. Perhaps the condom had been faulty or put on incorrectly; Duane had been in a hurry. He was always in a hurry.

At any rate, it was a lesson to be more careful in the future. She'd gone out with him for several months, and when he'd said that he wanted their relationship to include sex and had awkwardly begun to make love to her, she'd assented. She'd been a virgin long enough, she thought; at the age of twenty-six it was time to learn what lovemaking was all about.

She'd liked Duane, sort of, but she wasn't in love with him. Sex would be an experiment to see if the relationship would mature into something serious. To embark upon sex without love and especially without marriage was not something a nice girl would do, and it would have shocked her mother, who was obsessively religious and unforgiving, but Polly decided to do it anyway.

Sex with Duane turned out to be unutterably unfulfilling, but she'd tolerated it well enough to acquiesce several times, and one of those times, an unplanned, impulsive one, had resulted in pregnancy. But the relationship had not developed enough to result in marriage. Duane was too footloose and immature to be what he'd called "tied down" in a lifetime relationship, and to Polly that's what marriage meant: a lifetime of commitment. She had no interest in flitting from man to man like a movie star or rock singer. She expected she would know true love when she encountered it, and that it would result in marriage.

It was a simplistic point of view, but Polly was like that. She prided herself on her down-to-earth attitude, never realizing that other people sometimes viewed her as cold-blooded. If anyone had called her that, she would have been astounded, for she considered herself as tender and caring as any other woman. She cried during sad movies, for example, or when she read touching books, and sometimes even stories on the television news could make her eyes spill over.

Duane told her, "I'm opposed to abortion, so if you try to get rid of it I'll fight you tooth and nail. And I won't wiggle out of my responsibility. I'll provide you with enough money so you won't have to work for six months, and you can stay home with the kid and give it a good start in life. After that you can go back to work, and I'll chip in for child support from then on. Sounds fair to me. What do you say?"

It sounded fair to her and was probably the best deal she could expect from Duane. The pregnancy had scared her until she'd got used to the idea. She'd always thought she'd enjoy being a mother, as part of a husband and family package. Those dreams had disappeared with Duane's blunt rejection. But single mothers managed somehow, and surely it would be better to be a single mother than to be tied to an unwilling man in a relationship that to her spelled long-term disaster. And time was moving on; even at twenty-six she was aware of her biological clock.

Duane was a nice enough guy but he wasn't the sharpest tack in the toolbox, and the thought of living with him for the rest of her life was not something that she could consider seriously. His idea of a good life – partying, a big fancy car, sports events, a high-status, high-pressure job – was not one she could share. She'd never even considered the possibility of living with him; in fact, it made her queasy to think about it. He'd certainly be boring and bossy, and have obnoxious habits like expecting her to do all the housework and cooking, leaving the toilet seat up, and scattering piles of dirty laundry around. One look at his bedroom had convinced her of that.

There had been times in their dating association when he'd been callous and unfeeling, and she'd wondered why she was bothering with him at all. Perhaps it was because a good man was hard to find, especially if you were a lanky five-foot-ten dishwater-blonde woman without much to say for yourself, no sparkling conversation, no winning smile, no flirtatious manner. She had a good sense of humor, but was too shy to try to say funny things. She thought them, but she didn't say them out loud.

She'd been told once that she had pretty eyes – they were hazel – but that was hardly enough to overcome a case of terminal shyness. Even if it wasn't the romance of the century, Duane was reasonably good company, and she liked having a man to escort her to movies and shows and restaurants, since she was timid about going out at night by herself. So she hung in there with him. Better a bird in the hand than no bird at all.

As the baby grew inside her, she began to look forward to its arrival and to raising it on her own, visualizing it as a sweet little companion to assuage her loneliness. A child to nurture and teach, someone that belonged to her and her alone; somehow Duane didn't fit into the picture at all. A little hand to hold hers, and only hers, as they took walks in the park or visited the zoo or the playground.

She had no experience with children; her neurotic, over-protective mother had never even allowed her to baby-sit. So she knew nothing of the sleepless nights, the expense, the endless drudgery of laundry and meals, the relentless quest for good, inexpensive child care, and exactly how irritating small children could be. She was as innocent about babies as a baby.

She told herself that lots of kids these days grew up without a father. She could raise it by herself. She was a mature adult.

She started reading parenting books and magazines and taking an interest in the things that interested parents, like good schools, appropriate television, and homes in nice neighborhoods. On her lunch hours she walked through the children's department in the department store close to her work, fingering baby clothes and looking at furniture, deciding what she would buy for the new arrival. She checked out her firm's insurance coverage and maternity leave policy, preparing herself mentally for the moment when she would disclose her pregnancy at work. She was going to keep it a secret until she showed.

Then the check arrived in the mail. Ten thousand dollars and a sticky note from Duane, telling her he'd accepted a transfer with his firm to another city. He'd be in touch about the child support, he'd written, after he got settled. That was a disappointment for Polly; she'd expected him to be around to ask for progress reports on her pregnancy and to provide emotional support, to his limited ability. She did not expect him to take pre-natal classes with her, but she did harbor a hope that he'd be present at his child's birth. That did not seem too much to ask. And maybe, after the baby was born, he'd make occasional visits to check on it since it was, after all, his flesh and blood. Regardless how she felt about Duane, a baby should certainly have the chance to know its father.

Several weeks passed after she received the check and the sticky note, and she'd had no further correspondence from him, not even a note with his new address. She called the advertising agency where he worked.

"I want to get in touch with Duane Redmond," she told the receptionist. "I believe he's transferred to another branch of your company. Can you give me his work address?"

"I'm sorry, Mr. Redmond is no longer employed by Wheaton Advertising."

"Are you sure?" she stammered, taken aback.

"Quite sure. He left us in March." The voice was professionally pleasant, brisk and businesslike. This was not the first call about the elusive Mr. Redmond she'd fielded.

March! That was two months ago. "But I understood that he'd transferred to another city . . ."

"Wheaton Advertising does not have branches in other cities."

And that was that. Duane was gone, leaving no forwarding address, taking with him any hope of child support and paternal interest. She was on her own, with ten thousand dollars to cover raising a child to the age of twenty-one. That was less than five hundred a year. It probably would not cover the cost of a year's worth of clothes and shoes for a growing child.

She was frightened, panic-stricken and angry. She had not exactly been played for a fool but she'd certainly been bought off cheaply. She was too attached to the baby now to terminate it, if she'd been of a mind to do that; she'd gotten used to its presence inside her. She'd even begun to talk to it. She'd declined when her obstetrician offered to tell her its sex, preferring to be surprised, but she was getting a "little boy" feeling about the fetus.

At last she came out of her fog of fear and made a decision. She'd never shirked responsibility, and she'd always handled her life by herself, without help or counsel. She could and would go it alone.

But one morning late in the third month of her pregnancy, she woke up and noticed splotches of blood on her sheets. Not a lot, but worth calling the obstetrician about. He wanted her to come in at once. A little worried, she dressed and called a cab. On the way to the doctor's office, she began to experience cramps and back pain, and by the time she arrived, she was seriously uncomfortable and seriously alarmed.

The obstetrician was alarmed, too. He took her straight into the examining room and after poking and peering, said gravely, "I'm sorry, Polly. You're going to lose the baby. Your cervix is fully dilated and that means the uterus is getting ready to expel the fetus."

The next several hours passed in a haze of pain and, at the end of it she was no longer a mother-to-be; she was back to plain old all-by-herself Polly. Her intuition had been right; it was a boy, whom she would have named Walter, after her late father. She wasn't allowed to see him; the obstetrician said it would be better that way. Polly was too groggy with shock to argue with him, and would regret forever what might have been.

She'd stayed home from work for a week, telling her boss that she had the flu. She'd not confided in a single soul about her pregnancy, and she certainly did not intend to tell anyone about the miscarriage, dreading the idea of sympathy for her lost baby and curious, disdainful pity for her unwed status.

Her physical recovery was quick, but it was a difficult time for her emotionally. She'd been so focused on the coming child she could not help but feel lost and empty without it, unable to plan for the future.

Everything in her present life seemed irrelevant, and work seemed the most irrelevant of all. She was a claims adjuster for a large insurance company, and it was boring work at best and unspeakably tedious at worst.

One night, after an irritating day spent trying to do her best to extract money from her reluctant company for victims of a particularly unpleasant tornado in out-state Minnesota, she sat down with a bottle of wine and assessed her life.

She had no baby, no boyfriend, no companion animals. She had no close friends; she was too shy to make friends. She'd always been a loner and never minded it until now when she wanted someone to talk to. She couldn't tell her mother about the baby; the woman was too emotionally distant. She lived in a small town in western Minnesota, in a sort of religious commune, and Polly's contact with her was limited to occasional telephone calls, which always involved queries and reproaches about her non-existent churchgoing habit. The idea that Polly had been pregnant out of wedlock would probably shock her into hysterics. At the very least it would mean tears, reproaches, and predictions of eternal damnation.

What were the other pros and cons (mostly cons) of her life? Her apartment was nothing special, in a nondescript old brick building in south Minneapolis. She had no hobbies or special interests. She spent most of her free time reading – she was a voracious reader – or watching public television. Sometimes she went to the local two-dollar movie theater, but usually she waited for films to be released on DVD so she could watch them at home on her lumpy old sofa with a bowl of popcorn and a chocolate bar.

She was unhappy, and she thought she might be on the brink of becoming seriously depressed. Part of her depression was hormonally-induced from the loss of the baby, but most came from realizing that at the age of twenty-six she was leading a totally pointless, bland life, and would likely continue living that kind of life if she didn't do something about it.

She had ten thousand dollars that she could not return to the giver, who had disappeared to God knows where. She could spend that money for her own benefit; she could do something to lift her spirits and raise her from the depths. She had no close ties to bind her down, she was free. What should she do to save herself?

It was a unique opportunity.

She didn't like her job. Should she go back to college? The money would pay for a year of training to prepare her for a new career if she could think of anything that she wanted to study. That would be the sensible thing to do, but her head was empty regarding future goals and future jobs; she simply could not make herself focus.

She could buy a small house or a condo with the money as a down payment, and get out of her dreary apartment and into a big mortgage that would trap her forever at the insurance company. Or she could fling caution to the winds and splurge on a cruise or spend a week in New York or San Francisco or Hawaii or some other glamorous place she'd always wanted to visit, sleeping on linen sheets and gorging on *haute cuisine*. Which she would be eating alone, her brain reminded her. What fun would that be? If she was going to fritter away all that money, she wanted to enjoy every minute of it.

Her head whirled, too full of possibilities for her to decide anything. To clear her thoughts, she put down her wineglass, picked up one of her Scottish magazines, and leafed through it idly, enjoying the pictures of beautiful scenery, charming lochs, stately homes and cozy cottages.

Of such casual gestures come great decisions. It was like the proverbial light bulb going off over her head. She would go to Scotland. At first she rejected the idea as crazy. What would she do in Scotland all by herself?

The answers came to her so quickly that she was overwhelmed. There was plenty that she'd always dreamed about doing. She would hike up mountains and visit castles, museums and ancient cemeteries. She would shop in curious little bookstores and buy books about Scottish history and culture and authentic Scottish music CDs. She would sit in front of a cozy fire in a quaint little hotel, and sip whisky while chatting to the friendly proprietor and petting his huge furry dog, her shyness with strangers completely vanquished and her conversation charming and delightfully funny.

She would rest and recuperate and get her life together and then she would be able to chart a course for her future. A trip to Scotland would help her sort out her life.

Resting and recuperating sounded the best of all, something she owed to herself after her miscarriage. But where in Scotland should she go? Not to a city, the idea was a real turn-off. She didn't think she was emotionally ready to cope with city life; even the traffic and hustle of medium-sized Minneapolis got on her post-pregnancy nerves. Nor did she want to rent a car and cope with driving on the wrong side of the road. What she needed was a place that was quiet and pretty, where the pace of life was easy-going and relaxed and the inhabitants were friendly but minded their own business. Where she could fit in without having to explain to anyone why she was there.

Her eye fell on the book that was a permanent resident of her coffee table, the beloved tome entitled *Eilean Dubh: Celebration of a Small Island*, by Jean Mac an Rìgh and Sally MacDonald, both residents of the Island they were writing about. The book was full of anecdotes about Island life, recipes, sheet music and photographs, that painted a picture of a place that was quirky, cozy, and friendly, full of people who were gentle and laid-back.

That was what she wanted. Eilean Dubh, the Dark Island.

Why couldn't she go there? But how? In a fever of excitement she opened the book and found the pages that described how to travel to Eilean Dubh. By plane to London or Edinburgh, then by train to Oban and take the Caledonian-MacBrayne ferry, or by train to Inverness and take the helicopter service operated by someone called Murdoch the Chopper. The authors made it sound like a long, involved journey, to be sure, but indicated that it would be well worth it, since it ended on the Dark Island. It would be an adventure, and it might even be fun. Just what she was looking for.

She'd need a place to stay, but both Eilean Dubh hotels looked expensive in a boutique sort of way, and besides, a hotel would mean taking all her meals out. That would use up her money in a hurry and rich restaurant food day after day would surely upset her digestion.

No, she wanted – had always wanted, she realized suddenly, was a cottage. Preferably one like the little thatched cottage pictured on the cover of the book, in which one of the authors lived. If she found one with a reasonable rent, she could stay there for several months, economizing by cooking her own meals and doing her own laundry. Much cheaper than a hotel and her ten thousand dollars would last much longer. And it would be fun to putter around in a cottage that was like a doll's house. Maybe she'd even get a copy of Julia Child or Betty Crocker and teach herself to cook.

There must be zillions of darling thatched cottages on Eilean Dubh, just waiting for her to grace them with her presence.

She was so excited her heart was pounding and her brain was in a dither. She was on the brink of making her newly awakened dream of Scotland come true, thanks to Duane's money. She'd find a little house to live in comfortably, while she thought about what to do to create a new life for herself.

Maybe she had talents she hadn't yet discovered. She'd gotten good grades in English in school; maybe she'd write a book. Or poetry. Or learn how to play a musical instrument. Or study Gaelic, the ancient Scottish language that was spoken on Eilean Dubh, and write poetry in it. Maybe she'd meet a tall handsome Scotsman and have a passionate romance with him; that sounded like the best idea of all. The possibilities were enormous, and once she was on the Island, her future would at last be revealed to her. Polly was a romantic, and an optimist as well.

She'd once seen an old movie called *Lost Horizon*, about an idyllic valley in the Himalayas, a paradise where people lived happily ever after, forever, in beauty, youth and peace. It was called Shangri-La.

Eilean Dubh could be her Shangri-La.

She turned on her computer and checked airfares to London. They would take a large chunk of her cash, she realized. She'd have to budget money for the train and the ferry, too. But once her travel expenses were taken care of, she'd have the rest of Duane's money to live on. It felt like a fortune to her.

Where to stay was the biggest question. How could she find her dream cottage? Search as she might on the Internet, she could not find any listed for rent on Eilean Dubh. Then she thought of newspaper ads. According to the book, *The Island Star* was the local newspaper; surely someone with a cottage to rent would advertise it in the paper.

She took a deep breath, called international Information and got a phone number for *The Island Star*. The simplicity of the act astonished her. The next problem was the six-hour time difference between Minnesota and Scotland. The earliest she could call the newspaper would be three in the morning Minnesota time, and it was now only ten. If she went to bed right now, she could get up early, phone and ask the newspaper editor – the book said her name was Anna Wallace – for suggestions on finding a cottage to rent.

She'd be drowsy all the next day at work, but she didn't care. It would be worth it. She flung off her clothes, showered and jumped in bed and was, predictably, too excited to sleep, her mind going over and over her splendid plan.

When she finally did fall asleep, she had a disturbing dream. She had fallen over the edge of a cliff and was clinging to its breast, thousands of feet above a rocky coastline and the raging waves of a cerulean blue sea. When she tried to struggle upwards, the ground beneath her crumbled into lumps of golden-brown dirt that were an unstable combination of sand and clay. She dared not move for fear of collapsing the cliff face and plummeting downwards onto the rocks. A small faceless child appeared at the top of the cliff, and she heard herself say calmly, "Get your father and tell him to bring a rope."

In the unknown space between waking and sleep she was conscious of a blurred figure of a tall man throwing her a rope, and she realized as she knotted it around her waist that she was saved.

The dream and its resolution disturbed her so much that she got up, wide awake, at 3:00. She didn't believe in signs and portents, but thought the dream must be her subconscious telling her she was out of control and in danger of sliding into hopelessness and depression. The child in the dream must have been her baby, she thought, and it was telling her that she could no longer look to him to affirm her life.

The man with the rope she discounted entirely; he was simply a *deus ex machina* created by her subconscious to reassure her that there was a way out of her predicament. Nothing in her believed, had ever believed, that she must have a man to make her life complete. If one came along, that would be great, but she could manage alone, just as she'd always done. She was used to being a loner; she even enjoyed it, in a peculiar way. Most of the time, anyway.

She would take the dream's advice and create a new reality for herself, and she would begin it with a fun, carefree adventure in Scotland in a cozy cottage. With that decided, she made a cup of cocoa, drank half of it, and, her hand shaking, dialed the phone number for *The Island Star*.

Four

Blessings on the hand of women!
Angels guard its strength and grace,
In the palace, cottage, hovel,
Oh, no matter where the place . . . .

William Ross Wallace

The voice that answered said something in a language she didn't
understand. Gaelic, of course, the language of Eilean Dubh. Polly
said, "Hello. I'm calling from the United States. Do you speak English?"

"Of course. How may I help someone in *Ameireaga?*"

Polly took a deep breath and replied, "I want to find a darling cottage to rent on Eilean Dubh." "Darling" slipped out, a fugitive from her
daydreams, and she realized it made her sound like she had a mental age
of twelve.

Anna Wallace put down her morning cup of Earl Grey and sighed. It
was not the first time that she'd had a call from an eager American who
wanted to come to Eilean Dubh and rent a "darling" little cottage to stay
in. It was that book, of course, and Sally MacDonald's articles in travel
magazines, and last year's Folk Festival, which had aroused interest in the
Island in a number of far-flung places. Most of the callers were conven-
tional travelers, happy to be referred to the Rose Hotel in Ros Mór or its
counterpart in Airgead. Others she had put in touch with a B and B owner.
A cottage dream was much harder to fulfill and it was difficult to explain
why to an outsider. She said carefully, "I'm afraid there aren't any available."

Polly saw her bright dream evaporating, and she felt as though she'd
been stabbed in the heart. She said desperately, "Oh, are they all rented?
Are you sure?"

"Quite sure. This is a small island without much tourist trade and
without unused housing, so we don't have cottages to rent. Visitors stay
in the hotels or B and Bs."

"But I want a place where I can cook my own meals and live economically and independently."

"That's what we call self-catering. Are you sure that's what you want? Most people prefer to take their meals out when they're on holiday; they don't want to fuss with cooking and washing up."

"I'm not exactly taking a holiday and I want to stay longer than I can afford to stay in a hotel." She might as well be perfectly frank.

"Ah. Well, let me think a moment." This was hopeless, Anna thought; foreigners, Americans especially, all had dreams of adorable thatched cottages with rosebushes twining round the door, walled gardens, plus all mod cons like dishwashers and fancy bathrooms. They did not understand that such homes were largely extinct, if they had ever existed at all outside of a novel writer's imagination. She covered the mouthpiece of the receiver and said to Zach, her husband, who'd just come downstairs, "I've got an American on the phone wanting to rent a 'darling little cottage' on Eilean Dubh."

"So?" Zach picked up a copy of yesterday's *Island Star* and glanced at it.

"There aren't any cottages for rent, especially not darling ones."

He turned a page in the newspaper. "The old Ferguson place, up near the archaeological site. It's vacant."

"That old granite monstrosity? It's a rubbish tip. The roof leaks and I'm not even sure it has an inside loo. And besides it's haunted."

"It has an inside loo, the roof was fixed and it's not haunted. What a ridiculous notion, there's no such thing as ghosts. Megan Barry and Stephen Carson were living in it up to three weeks ago and they never complained about leaks or about spooks."

"Megan and Stephen were two of your student diggers and you worked them so hard they only had energy left to flop into bed at night, let alone have a cuddle, and never mind their surroundings." Zach, a transplanted Cornishman, was an archaeologist, excavating the Mesolithic site that he and Anna had discovered several years ago near the scenic lookout. He'd had enough imagination to visualize an entire Mesolithic settlement in an area where one had never even been thought of before, but not enough imagination to believe in ghosts.

He shrugged. "It's a cottage, it's for rent, and that's what your caller wants."

The voice on the other end of the phone was making agitated noises, fearing that it had been cut off. Anna uncovered the mouthpiece and said, "Hullo again. My husband has just suggested a possibility, an old granite block cottage that his student archaeological assistants were living in three weeks ago. But you know students; they'd stay anywhere. I must warn you it's not terribly attractive and not in very good shape."

"Oh, that's wonderful. Do you have a phone number I can call to ask about it?"

"One moment." Anna turned to Zach. "So who's in charge of the tip?"

"It's Council property."

"I repeat, who's in charge of it?"

He gave her a wide grin. "Since I booked the last tenants, I suppose I am."

Anna put out her tongue at him, then turned back to the phone. "Ms . . . uh . . ."

"Gillespie, Polly Gillespie."

"Ah, a good Scottish name."

"Is it?" Polly had never made the connection, despite her long obsession with Scotland. She had no interest in her ancestors; her notions were more romantic than family-oriented. But she filed the comment in her pre-trip "to do" list: investigate self's possible Scottish heritage.

"Aye, it is. Well, Ms Gillespie, it turns out that my husband has some information about the property, so I'll just put him on." She handed the phone to a reluctant Zach, hissing, "Be sure and tell her it's a tip. No, Americans would call it a dump, and an American won't want a dump; they like everything new and shiny and smelling of flowers and disinfectant."

Anna went upstairs to refill her cup of Earl Grey, which had gotten cold, and when she came back down Zach was concluding the phone call. "Right, then, Ms Gillespie, I'll take a few snaps of the cottage and post them off to you, and I'll tell the Council that you want to rent the place. If you like what you see in the photos, we can talk about a deposit and the length of your stay."

The voice at the end of the phone was pathetically grateful.

Anna said, "Did you tell her it's a dump?"

He shrugged. "I tried, but I'm not sure I got through to her. I'm going to send her photos and she can make up her own mind. But I rather think she's going to want it. She sounds like she's got a bad case of Scotland-itis. Sometimes I think it's endemic in Americans. They read too many travel magazines and romantic novels with brawny half-naked guys in kilts on the cover."

Anna said fatalistically, "She'll want it, if she's someone who fantasizes about bagpipes and thistles and heather and cozy cottages with peat fires. You'd best get on to Barabal Mac-a-Phi at once and get her to have things repaired and the place cleaned up. We can't have an American living in a dump; she'd whine, whine, whine all the time and complain to the Scottish Tourist Board, and there'd be no end of bother. And for heaven's sake don't mention ghosts."

Zach grumbled, "Superstitious nonsense, why should I mention it?" But did as he was told. He rang Barabal and arranged to have the cottage's worst deficiencies seen to. But she warned, "We can make it habitable but there's no money to tart it up for a visitor who's only staying a month or two. Make it clear to her that she'll have to rough it."

Zach promised to include pictures of the unprepossessing interior of the cottage in the packet he would send. When he came out to take the promised snaps with his digital camera, though, it was too much to expect of his romantic Cornish soul that he would not be swept away by the building's dramatic location on the cliff above the wild sea, and the backdrop of majestic mountain *Beinn Mhic-an-Righ* in the opposite direction. He concentrated on photographing the scenery instead of the inside of the dreary old place, which he didn't consider the least bit photogenic or romantic. He was right about that.

Anna clucked in dismay when he printed out the pictures but could not persuade him to go back and take more. He was too busy, he said; in reality he'd lost interest in the whole project and considered that he'd done his duty.

When she received the photos in the mail, Polly was enchanted, and predictably preferred, like Zach, to moon over the scenery instead of peering too closely at the two dark, drab interior shots. She put the scenic photos on her refrigerator where she could look at them whenever she got the urge, which she did, frequently, hugging to herself the knowledge that she was going to Scotland to live in a cottage. It wasn't the thatched cottage of her dreams, but the location was charming and beautiful, so the cottage must be the same.

She told herself that all she really needed from a place to stay was a fridge, a stove, a comfy chair in the living room and a lamp for reading, a bed and a bathroom. The rental was very reasonable, which was her main concern, and she could manage otherwise. She wasn't expecting anything fancy, after all. Or so she told herself.

Her excitement grew, bubbled and seethed inside her and swept her along in the days that followed. She was going to Eilean Dubh and that was all that mattered.

Five

Anna Wallace's inborn sense of Island hospitality told her that she should meet Polly Gillespie at the ferry and drive her to the old Ferguson cottage. Public transport on the Island was not at all what an American would be used to, even though Murdoch the Taxi would have his mini-bus at the dock when the ferry arrived, and would be quite willing to drop Polly off at the cottage and carry her bags to the door, and not charge her tuppence extra for the courtesy.

Anna dithered and tried to talk Zach into meeting Polly. "Sorry, got a deadline on an article for *British Archeology Today*," he proclaimed cheerfully. Zach was very adept at getting out of things he didn't want to do, and this was one of them.

Anna tried again. "But you're the one she corresponded with and you made all the arrangements."

"I've done my bit, then, haven't I? Besides, she arrives on a Wednesday, and you put the paper to bed on Monday, it's out on Tuesday, and you don't have another issue to get out before Friday. So you've got bags of time on Wednesday. She'll be more comfortable with a woman meeting her and she might think I was up to no good. And if she's pretty, I might be."

He ornamented that remark with a lustful leer and a wink to let her know he was just kidding. No reason to raise jealousy in the breast of the trouble-and-strife, he thought, although a little bit kept the home fires burning brightly. He gave her a quick kiss and escaped upstairs after saying, "Pick her up, there's a good lass, and I'll take you to MacShannock's for pizza as a reward."

"'If there is anything disagreeable going on, men are always sure to get out of it,'" Anna quoted Jane Austen to his retreating back and decided she was stuck. She thought wistfully of sending the American directions on how to recognize Murdoch the Taxi's mini-bus at the dock so that she could do for herself, but that seemed like a lot of work. She hated writing letters even more than she hated interacting with foreign strangers. And maybe it would be a little cruel to expect the visitor to fend for herself right away.

So Anna equipped herself with a hand-written sign that displayed Polly's name and went off to meet the ferry, grumbling under her breath. At least it wasn't raining, as it had been for the last three days; this afternoon was bright, sunny, and almost warm for Eilean Dubh.

The American woman was easy to recognize amongst those departing the Cal-Mac ferry; she was the one who stepped ashore with the awed look customarily found on the faces of those arriving on Eilean Dubh for the first time. She also looked baffled, until she saw the sign. "Hi, I'm Polly," she said shyly to the sign-holder.

"Anna Wallace. *Fàilte gu Eilean Dubh*. That means . . ." Anna began.

"Welcome to Eilean Dubh," said Polly eagerly. "That was in *Celebration of a Small Island*, and I learned it by heart. I wasn't sure how to pronounce it until now, though. I read your piece in the book about the wildflowers. They sound wonderful and I'm looking forward to seeing them. I love flowers."

Meeting a fellow flower fanatic always warmed Anna's heart, and she shook the young woman's hand enthusiastically. "My car's just over there on the street. May I help you with your bags?"

"Thanks. I'm afraid I brought rather a lot," said Polly, indicating the two large suitcases and the backpack she'd dragged, with difficulty, through two changes of flight (excess weight charges), two train changes (sweating and cursing under her breath), and onto and off of the ferry (struggling not to fall overboard).

"Well, you're staying several months. Might as well bring enough bits and bobs to keep yourself comfortable," said Anna, trying to conceal her grunt as she lifted the heaviest suitcase and carried it to her car. She moved the front seat forward, stowed the luggage in the boot and the tiny back seat, and motioned to Polly to climb in. The girl complied, folding her legs carefully in front of her in the small space left.

Anna made polite conversation at first, until she realized that Polly was too absorbed in what she was seeing to do more than nod and murmur in response. She obligingly fell silent and contented herself with occasional sly glances at her passenger, registering her as a person of ordinary appearance, with nothing unusual about her shoulder-length mousy blonde hair, tall lanky figure and undistinguished features; although she'd noted on first acquaintance a pair of large, attractive hazel eyes.

She'd made up her mind that she was going to leave her guest at the door of the old Ferguson cottage and not go in herself, so she would not be subjected to any gasps of disappointment or recriminations when the American got a good look at the tip. Drop her off, and scarper, as cowardly as that was. At least she knew what the cottage looked like from the outside, thanks to Zach's pictures, so she couldn't complain about that. But something in her character made Anna unable to just dump the visitor and drive away, and she ended up accompanying Polly inside.

Anna had done her best to add a touch of home beyond Barabal's, Zach's and the carpenter's and plumber's repair efforts. She'd scrounged linen and towels, borrowed a floor lamp and Sheilah at the Rose Hotel's spare mattress, donated an afghan from her own household, and spent her own money to stock the fridge with essentials for supper on the evening of arrival and breakfast the next couple of mornings.

She'd written out instructions giving the location of the Co-Op market in Ros Mór and put by them the daily schedule of Ian the Post, whose mail bus served as Island transport between Eilean Dubh's two towns. She'd also left her phone number at *The Island Star* in a note indicating her willingness to field questions, hoping inwardly there would not be too many inconvenient ones. She was uneasily aware that she was putting herself *in loco parentis* to the newcomer, and wondered however she had gotten into that position. It was all Zach's fault, she groused, and promised herself a wee chat with him on the subject of responsibility. She was always having wee chats with Zach about his failings, and none of them did any good.

Despite Anna's interior cheer-up, the cottage was still cold, dark and depressing which was not lost on Polly at first sight. In fact, she felt a distinct bone-rattling chill as soon as she approached the door, before she was even inside the plain grim building, which was made of ugly stone blocks and did not have a thatched roof or rambling roses. It was not like the picture in her mind. It was reality, and she did not like it one bit.

But she could not say so, not with Anna chatting cheerily at her side, making a gallant effort to stress the good features of the cottage. The trouble was, she couldn't think of many good features, and fell awkwardly silent after her reference to the easy chair and the lamp, "so nice for reading," and the afghan, "in case your legs are cold; it gets chilly at night even in summer." Anna grew even more eager to escape this difficult situation.

So she showed Polly how to unlock the door and lock it again, without mentioning that most Islanders never locked their doors, and helped carry the bags inside. Then she said, "That's you settled, and I'll be on my way. Supper's in the fridge, a nice pan of lasagna that's a welcoming gift from Jean Mac an Rìgh."

"The Laird's wife," whispered Polly, awed. "Only I'm not supposed to talk about him being the Laird, am I? There was something about that in the book."

"Quite right," said Anna, nodding approvingly. "He prefers to be thought of as one of the gang, as Jean would say. Now just give me a ring if you've a question or problem. The phone's in that red box just down the hill where the road dips and turns."

So there wasn't even a phone in the place, and she'd noted with regret the absence of a television set. Polly stepped out onto the chilly front door step and quickly off of it, and waved a polite goodbye. Then she turned around and stared at her new home. It was one story high and built of blocks of a particularly depressing shade of gray granite peculiar to Scotland, and used in much of the country's construction. The front windows were small and deep-set, one on each side of the door and one in the bedroom, and the slate roof sat stolidly on top of the building like a flattened hat.

Polly sighed, bidding farewell to her dreams of a cheerful, cozy, welcoming-arms-extended cottage like the ones in romantic novels. Anna Wallace had been right about the American's expectations, but wrong about her ability to bear disappointment: not a hint of a whine had surfaced yet.

She walked slowly around the building and came face to face with a splendid sight visible down the cliff at the back, the cerulean-blue ocean with its white-topped waves sparkling like diamonds in the afternoon sun. She crept cautiously to the edge of the cliff, remembering her dream and wondering if it had been a presentiment. Shuddering, she stepped back a few paces, thinking that the cliff edge might be unstable, which it was, and wondering if the cliff was faced in golden-brown clay, which it wasn't.

Thinking of the dream made her nervous, and a brisk little wind off the sea had picked up, chilling her through her light jacket. It was a cool day even if it was June. She completed the circuit around the cottage, noting the clothesline, several scraggly bushes, and a discouraged-looking tree with bare branches on the left front corner, and hopped nimbly inside to escape what she now thought of as the Frozen Zone. She felt both elated and apprehensive. But once inside, elation disappeared and apprehension triumphed, as the full force of what she'd gotten herself into struck her.

The interior was nothing like she'd hoped and imagined. It was excessively plain with thick whitewashed stone walls. The furniture was old and showed it, despite the hand-knitted afghan that Anna had conjured up to cover the dismal sofa and the bright blanket she'd flung over the chair which had a sagging seat and a footstool with a leg missing. Polly snapped on the floor lamp by it and was slightly cheered by the warm circle of light it cast. Anna, herself a great reader, had made sure that the bulb was the highest wattage the lamp could stand without blowing one of the ancient fuses.

A huge fireplace loomed, dark and empty, at one end of the room. Approaching it, Polly found logs and peats stacked inside, and a paper attached giving instructions for lighting the fire and keeping it burning that were so complicated her head began to ache reading them. Was there another way to heat the place? Anna had said something about night storage heaters, but added, "You won't need those, now that it's summer. A light blanket will be all you'll need." Polly, shivering from the chill of the stone walls, was starting to doubt that statement.

She went to the two larger windows on the back wall, opened their curtains, and felt her spirits lift higher at the view of the sea visible through the dust-filmed panes. Barabal, Anna and Zach, in their tidying work, had none of them thought to wash the windows. Concerned as they were with making the place livable, there was not much time left to make it hospitable. I'll wash them first thing tomorrow, thought Polly; the idea of a housekeeping chore in her new home lifting her spirits.

She took a quick peek into the bedroom, which had a front window, the required bed, a dresser, and a large old-fashioned wardrobe. The bathroom had a toilet, sink and tub. Nothing fancy, just sparkling clean, and adequate.

Her optimism soured and her spirits plummeted when she went into the kitchen. The first thing she saw was a dreadful old sink that consisted of a cement trough perched on four sturdy posts with a wooden drain board for dishes slung across one end. She'd never seen anything so ugly, not even in her first and most horrible apartment. She tore her eyes from the monstrosity and began to catalog the rest of the kitchen's deficiencies. An elderly three-burner stove, perched on spindly legs. A minute refrigerator of unimaginable age. A kitchen table with a top scarred and battered from use, and two wooden chairs of a deliberately uncomfortable type that she vaguely remembered from her great-grandmother's kitchen on her Minnesota farm.

Overwhelmed and shivering, Polly sank into one of the chairs, bruising her bottom on its uncompromisingly hard surface. She burst into tears of frustration and disappointment, a stream of despairing emotions running through her head: I can't stay here, I can't bear it, it's too dreary, it's too old, it's too cold. And that Frozen Zone outside the front door is just too freaky for words.

"I'll call Anna and have her tell Zach that I won't take the house. I'll ask for my deposit back and then I'll make a reservation in one of those nice hotels, stay as long as I can afford to, eat gourmet meals out, and then go home. It'll be fun," she declared out loud, noting unhappily how her voice echoed against the high ceiling of the miserable room, and how unconvincing her words sounded.

It came to her then that she had nothing to go home to. She'd given up her apartment and put her few possessions in a storage locker. She'd quit her job and had been given a farewell party by the staff in the office break room, a pen and pencil set for a leaving gift. She'd canceled the newspaper, stopped her mail, paid her bills and fled.

To what? To this dismal, drab cottage that reminded her of something out of a Dickens novel about poor people, with a cliff behind it that reminded her of her worst nightmare. Fatigue, hunger and depression hit her like a blow and she put her head down on the table and sobbed and howled her grief to the cottage's unhearing rafters.

Once she began crying, she couldn't stop; it was as if a spigot had been turned on full blast. She wept for all the awful things that had happened to her over the last six months: the pregnancy, horrid Duane and his defection, the baby's death, and her realization of the utter futility of her life. She cried for five straight minutes for her child, knowing dimly that she'd never truly, deeply, mourned his loss.

After a while, completely spent, her forehead aching from the table's unyielding hardness, she lifted her head and looked around for something with which to wipe her swollen, streaming eyes. There was a box of tissues sitting on the table. She seized one, blew her nose, sniffled and felt extremely sorry for herself.

Then she realized that she was starving and a thought of the Laird's wife's lasagna swam into full view in her mind. She could almost smell it cooking. She looked around for a microwave, and then realized what a ridiculous idea that was. There was not the slightest hint of a modern appliance like a microwave in the kitchen, except for a grizzled old toaster glowering on a counter beneath the rickety wooden cupboards.

Very well, she'd have to heat the lasagna in the oven. She stood, wearily aware that she was worn out after the long arduous trip from Minneapolis to Edinburgh to Oban the day before and this morning's travels. She encouraged herself with the thought that if she could get her meal cooked, she could gobble up a hot meal and go to bed to overcome her jet lag and depression, and that gave her just enough strength to tackle the oven.

It was a box-like affair on one end of the three-burner stove, and inside it was cold enough to serve as a second fridge. It had no pilot light and would have to be lit by hand. She'd had a brief encounter with such a stove at great-grandmother's farm and had nearly set herself on fire, escaping with a hand that bristled with singed hairs on the back.

Matches were the next problem, but thoughtful Anna had left a box of long wooden ones on top of the oven and had written careful instructions on how to light the oven. Reading them, Polly had a cowardly thought about eating the lasagna cold and raw, thus avoiding the conflagration that was sure to erupt when she tried to light the stove.

What a ridiculous idea; only a loser would think of doing such a thing. She pulled herself together and took her dinner-to-be out of the tiny thigh-high fridge for courage. The Laird's wife's lasagna looked delicious in its cheerfully decorated glass dish and it deserved a better fate than to be gobbled without being cooked to its full perfection. She re-read the lighting instructions, braced herself, turned on the gas and stuck a match by the gas outlet. After five matches and a matching number of curses, it caught with a terrifying whoosh. The oven was successfully lit.

A small but important triumph. She peered at the rickety oven gauge and set it at what she estimated to be about 350 degrees; the gauge called it Mark something-or-other. If the oven actually worked, didn't explode or self-extinguish, she would have a lovely dinner. It was a wonderfully warming thought.

She went back to the fridge and pulled out a bunch of lettuce, a small tomato and a bottle of salad dressing, and approached the sink. She turned on a faucet, which creaked grouchily in response but poured forth a stream of icy-cold water, and washed the lettuce.

Next she opened cupboard doors and drawers, found a bowl for salad and a plate for lasagna, and located cutlery. She set a place for one at the kitchen table. She decided the oven had preheated long enough and put the lasagna in. There was no timer, of course, so she glanced at her watch to estimate the cooking time.

A loaf of what looked like homemade bread sat on the kitchen table, with a knife beside it ready for slicing chores, a large pat of butter on a saucer, and a bottle of red wine, a corkscrew and a glass. Whoever had left the makings for supper had thought of everything, and Polly grew tearful again, thinking of how kind that person – Anna, presumably – had been.

She pulled herself together, opened the wine, and poured a glass. She wasn't much of a drinker, but the wine was delicious and it gave her a warm, optimistic glow. She drifted back into what Anna had called the lounge, and what Polly thought of as the living room, and stood looking out through the dirty windows at the gorgeous sunset over the gently rolling sea, which was now tinted pink, orange and violet. She finished the wine staring at the glorious view, her head empty of everything but the struggle to get to Eilean Dubh and to fix dinner.

The setting sun reminded her that quite a bit of time had passed and she glanced at her watch. The lasagna should be ready by now if the oven had functioned properly. Wobbly from wine, an empty stomach, and fatigue, she staggered into the kitchen, found battered oven gloves, and pulled out the pan.

The lasagna smelled delicious and bubbled away in an appetizing manner. She put it on the table, found a knife, and cut herself a large piece, forgetting to wait the fifteen minutes lasagna requires to set up. It oozed sloppily all over the plate, but Polly didn't care. She was suddenly ravenous. She hacked off a slice of bread, buttered it, poured herself more wine, and dug into her meal. Everything tasted incredible, like fairy food.

She won her first battle with her new home.

Perhaps she should give this cottage a fair trial.

Six

Human beings, by changing the inner attitudes of their minds, can change the outer aspects of their lives.

William James

After two good nights of sleep on a surprisingly comfortable bed, and two days of relaxing with the quaintly Scottish and extremely elderly collection of books and magazines from the bookshelf, Polly felt recovered enough and brave enough to think about exploring her surroundings.

She'd discovered a box of cereal in the cupboard to go with the milk and orange juice in the fridge, so she had the makings for breakfast. The lasagna lasted through her second day and for lunch on the third, but now she was out of food. She had to venture out to search for supplies. This would be the ultimate test of her courage: interacting with strange Scottish storekeepers in strange Scottish stores. She dreaded the idea.

How was she to get around the Island? She remembered that the post office bus provided transportation but she'd lost track of where she'd put the schedule. Perhaps there was another alternative.

Someone had left a copy of the Friday edition of *The Island Star* on her doorstep that morning. She'd snatched it inside, shivering from contact with the Frozen Zone, particularly chilly this morning, and she'd read it from front to back with great interest. This was the newspaper mentioned in the *Celebration* book, edited by Anna Wallace, who had met her at the ferry dock and escorted her to the cottage. The last two pages of the newspaper were want ads, and one was an ad for a bicycle. "No use for it now – free to the first taker," the ad said.

Polly read the ad and sprang to her feet. Outside and a short ways down the road was the old-fashioned red phone box Anna had mentioned, and that Polly recognized from hours of watching British programs on public television. She snatched up a handful of coins from her purse, hoping some of them would work, ran down the road to the box, and pushed her way into the cobwebby interior, causing several spiders to scuttle away in alarm. She experimented with coins and finally selected the right ones, popped them into the slot and dialed the number in the ad. The phone rang, a peculiar burring noise.

Of course the bike would be gone by now, she thought, someone would have claimed it. But it wasn't. The woman's voice on the other end of the line said cheerfully, "It's yours, but you'll have to come and get it if you want it. I can't leave the kiddies."

"I'll walk over right now if you're not too far away," said Polly, bemused by the fact that the woman had an American accent.

"Where are you?"

"North of a place called Cemetery Hill, I think."

"That's not far. Walk south towards Ros Mór until you come to a lane on your right. We're in the thatched cottage, first house down the lane. My name is Sally and I'll be incarcerated here all afternoon, thanks to my offspring."

Scarcely able to believe her luck, Polly tramped down the road until she came to what was unmistakably a thatched cottage. It was adorable and it raised a storm of envy in her breast, and made her think sourly of her own cold stone shanty. A large brown cat sat like a sentinel on the doorstep. It observed Polly suspiciously and she approached with caution, as it seemed like the type of animal that might make a sudden lunge with bared fangs at her ankles. She loved dogs, but cats made her nervous; they were unpredictable. Polly didn't like unpredictable, and in the last two days she'd encountered more than her share.

The door was ajar. Polly knocked and heard, "Come on in," in the distinctly American voice of the telephone. Carefully skirting the cat, she entered.

Two babies lay on a large blanket in the center of the floor, kicking, cooing and laughing at their mother, a pretty blonde woman in her late twenties who sat cross-legged beside them, opening up a diaper.

"Oh, you've got twins!" exclaimed Polly, forgetting her shyness at the sight of the babies.

"Yep. The Dynamic Duo, or the Terrible Two, or if they're having a particularly busy day, the Why Me, God pair." Sally smiled up at her visitor. "Hi. You're Polly? I'm Sally MacDonald. Nice to meet you. Take a seat, I'll be right with you as soon as I'm done with diaper duty."

To Sally's surprise her visitor sank down on the floor next to her and the twins. "What sex are they?"

"One of each. This is the girl, obviously," Sally said as she wrapped the baby in front of her into a diaper. "Her name is Fiona. The other one is Hamish, named for his grandfather Jamie. Sometimes known together as Ham and Fee. Sounds like breakfast, doesn't it? If they'd been triplets, we'd have had to name the third one Toast."

Polly chuckled. "How old are they?"

"Six months. Finally big enough to be interesting, my husband says. He's kidding, of course. He's been keeping a diary of their every burp and wee since they were born. He calls it research for an article on child-development that he plans to write but I think he's just a doting daddy. Say, would you like a cup of tea, um, Polly?" For an embarrassing moment she was afraid that she'd forgotten the other woman's name.

"That would be great, if it's not too much trouble."

"None at all; I just brewed up a couple of moments ago. Keep an eye on the kiddies for me. Make sure they don't escape." Sally unfolded her long legs, rose and moved to the kitchen area at the far end of the room.

Polly eyed the babies, who wore identical expressions of dismay now that their mother had disappeared. They craned their necks left and right, trying for a sight of her. Fiona puckered up and seemed about to burst into tears. Feeling an obscure urge to keep them happy, Polly put out a tentative hand and tickled the little girl's exposed belly.

Distracted, Fiona giggled.

Delighted by her success, Polly tickled the soft skin while the baby kicked and gurgled. Her brother watched curiously, then began to wriggle, competing vigorously for his share of attention. Polly put her free hand on him and soon she was completely absorbed in baby tickling.

An unexpected, uninvited feeling overcame her as she bonded with the twins. *Walter would have been like this*, she thought, like Fiona and Hamish, pink and soft and warm, trying out sounds of communication, kicking in excitement.

Without realizing it Polly began to cry. Silent tears formed in her eyes and began to course uninvited down her cheeks.

"Milk and sugar?" called Sally from the kitchen. Receiving no answer, she piled the whole tea set onto a tray, carted it into the lounge, and put it on the floor. She settled down beside the other three. It was only after she'd arranged herself into a sitting and serving position that she noticed the tears. She froze, the teapot suspended in mid-air. "Oh, hell. What's wrong?" she whispered.

"I lost a baby."

"So did I." Sally's hand trembled, and she set the teapot down, afraid of dribbling hot liquid on the children's exposed legs. For a long moment the two women looked at each other. Then Sally said, "Miscarriage?"

"At two and a half months."

"I was about three months gone."

"What sex?"

"A girl. I named her Carol."

"Mine was a boy, named Walter. Did you get to see her?" said Polly wistfully.

Sally shook her head. "Ian, my husband, wouldn't let me. It happened here in the cottage, late one afternoon. I'd had a backache all day; then my pains started in earnest just as the sun was settling. It was all over by sundown. I always have thought that if only I'd paid more attention to that backache, told Ian about it, gone to the hospital right away, we might have saved her. But Ian said no, that her heart was malformed; it was outside of the chest wall. That's why he wouldn't let me see her.

"He said nothing could have saved her. He's a doctor so he should know." She was crying now, too, which surprised her for it had been three years ago and she hadn't thought she had any tears left.

Polly said in surprise at her similar experience, "I had a backache, too, and bleeding and cramping. Serious enough to make me call the doctor. He said to come right into the office. I terrified the cab driver with my moans, I'm afraid."

"Did you go into hospital?"

"No, I lost the baby in the doctor's office. He was whisked away before I knew what had happened. I didn't get to see him, either."

"Male doctor?"

"Yes."

"Guys," said Sally. "What do they know?" She looked at Polly, and alarmed by the tears that still flowed like a rippling waterfall, murmured what she'd realized instinctively she shouldn't say. "How did your husband take it?"

Polly lifted her head and looked the other woman straight in the eye. "I wasn't married. I've never been married," she said and waited for some sign of condemnation.

But all Sally said was, "I'm sorry for your loss."

To her bemusement Polly found herself relating in a dull voice the whole story of Duane, his reaction to her pregnancy and his ultimate betrayal. Sally put a comforting hand on her shoulder. "What a rat. Sounds like you didn't lose much when he scarpered."

"Yes." Polly sighed and straightened up and the other woman withdrew her hand. "You're the first person I've talked to about this," she said in wonder. "My mother is very religious and she would have been horrified at my being pregnant out of wedlock, and I have no close woman friends."

Sally looked at her in genuine, heart-deep pity. She was remembering how husband, mother, stepfather, family-in-law and friends had closed protectively around her like a cocoon and treated her like the most fragile of butterflies until she'd healed. To have to go through that experience all alone was an appalling idea. "Well, any time you want to talk about it, I'm here," she said awkwardly and wondered if she was inviting long dismal afternoons of tears and self-reproach. She'd gotten over her loss and she had the twins for comfort. But if the other woman needed to talk . . . she straightened up and prepared to do her womanly duty.

But Polly said, "Thanks, I'll be okay. I'd not allowed myself to think much about it until now, and seeing your babies brought it all out at once. There's no need to indulge myself in orgies of grief. I appreciate your offer, though; it helps to have someone to talk to." She brushed tears away and fumbled in her pocket for a tissue.

Sally pulled one from her own pocket and handed it over. Fiona was a watering pot, always needing her tears dried for some baby woe or other, and Sally was always prepared. She turned to the tea tray and took the cozy off the pot. She poured Polly a cup and added milk and sugar for comfort, wishing she'd remembered to put some of her mother's chocolate chip cookies on the tray. Cookies were good after tears.

Polly took the cup and sipped without enthusiasm, longing for a good American cup of coffee. British people were nuts about tea, she thought, then realized that the disdained beverage actually tasted good. It was subtler than coffee and left a comforting taste in her mouth. She drank with renewed enthusiasm, remembered at what point she'd left her story and felt impelled to finish it. "I had ten thousand dollars and no baby to spend it on, so I decided to come to Scotland instead."

"How did you find out about Eilean Dubh?"

"It was a book called *Celebration of a Small Island*."

"No kidding! My mom and I wrote it. You actually got our book there in . . . ?"

"Minneapolis, Minnesota." Polly nodded. "I discovered the book on the Internet and ordered it. It's wonderful. It made me fall in love with Eilean Dubh." She stared at Sally. "Wow, I've never met a real author before."

The twins had been suspiciously quiet during the tear episode. Fiona had fallen asleep, her hands thrown up on either side of her head in classic baby pose, and Hamish had been investigating his toes. Now he suddenly threw out arms and legs in a burst of excitement and struck his sister on the side of her head. She woke and wailed.

Startled by the sound, Hamish began to cry in sympathy.

"You take her, I'll take him," ordered Sally and scooped up her writhing son.

Polly cautiously slipped her hands under Fiona and lifted her to her shoulder. "There, there," she said awkwardly, rubbing the baby's soft plump back. She had the satisfaction of having the child quiet beneath her hand as she rocked and crooned.

Sally undid her blouse and bra and put Hamish to her breast. "I'll feed him if you can keep Fiona distracted for a few moments. Can you reach that pillow? Thanks," and she tucked the baby into the curve of her arm, using the pillow for support.

The baby nursed happily and fell asleep at the breast. Sally got up, Hamish drowsing on her shoulder while she pressed against his back till he uttered a heart-felt, melodious burp. Then she disappeared into the bedroom next door.

Fiona, as if sensing that she was next in line for a feed, grew wiggly and began to mewl like a starving kitten. Her mother reappeared, scooped her out of Polly's arms and settled into the rocker that sat nearby. "Fiona always takes longer," she said, rocking contentedly while the baby nursed. "Hamish just sucks it up like a vacuum cleaner and passes out. Then he wakes fifteen minutes later with wind. Sounded like I got the bubble out of him this time, though."

Polly rose, picking up the tea tray. "Would you like your cup?"

"Yes, thanks. Got to keep up the vital bodily fluids."

For a few minutes there was silence, Sally absorbed in the baby and Polly unable to think of anything to say, now that the twins had broken the thread of conversation. At last Sally looked up from her contemplation of her daughter's fuzzy scalp and said, "After I put Fiona down for her nap, I'll get the bike out for you."

"I appreciate your letting me borrow it. I could pay you for it," began Polly.

"What? Charge you for a bike I have no use for, now that I'm tied down with the twinnies? Don't be silly. It's not like you're going to tuck it into your suitcase and disappear, is it. When you're done with it, you can hand it on to someone else here. Or maybe, oh frabjous someday, I'll have Ham and Fee tamed and can get back to biking, before my legs get too old to crank the pedals."

Polly nodded her thanks. "Any time you want it, let me know."

They drank their tea without further talk. Sally rose, tucked her daughter into her cot and came back, sighing. "If I'm lucky, a blissful hour to be someone other than mommy milk cow and chief baby minder," she said without a trace of resentment. "My mother-in-law Màiri was the mother of twins; my husband's one of them. She said that if a daughter of hers got preggers with two she'd rejoice, but if she herself ever fell with twins again she'd jump off *Rubha na h Airgid* into the sea." She chuckled.

"Come on out to the shed and we'll get the bike. Have to warn you that I don't have a helmet to lend. They're virtually unknown in Eilean Dubh. But people respect bikes because so many of us use them, and drivers are careful. Just don't get going too fast down Cemetery Hill, though. There's a sharp curve at the bottom and a ditch, and beyond that a one-way ticket to the ocean."

She opened the shed door and wheeled out a scarlet-painted woman's bike. "This is Bouncing Betsy. She's nothing fancy but she gave me good service and great exercise," Sally said, patting the handlebars fondly and giving the bell a jingle.

"I hope I can remember how to ride," said Polly in some anxiety.

"Take her for a trial spin down the lane," advised Sally, and Polly complied. It took her a bit of time to learn again how to balance but she at last caught on.

"Right," said Sally, suddenly remembering the dozens of baby-related chores ahead of her and ready to draw this pleasant but vaguely distressing episode to a close. "Good luck with her, and watch the hills, especially by Cemetery Hill."

"Okay. Thanks for the bike and tea and especially for listening. I enjoyed meeting you and your kids."

"Stop by any time," said Sally, and realized that she meant it. It had been fun talking to a fellow American her own age, somebody who wasn't a stiff upper lip Scot; it had been a while since she'd had that pleasure. She waved goodbye as Polly wobbled to the top of the road, then went inside to start yet another load of baby laundry, and maybe, just maybe, if she was lucky, to snatch a few moments with the new Nora Roberts novel her mother Jean had loaned her.

Polly turned Bouncing Betsy toward her cottage and though she found the steep road daunting, managed to make it around the dangerous curve and all the way up the hill without having to get off and walk. She went inside her cottage, feeling she'd had an afternoon of modest triumph, and collapsed into a chair to ease her throbbing legs. After a bit, she remembered that she hadn't put the bike away and dragged herself outside. Where to store it? She didn't really want to bring it inside because its wheels bore the imbedded dirt of previous adventures. Nothing occurred to her. Finally, she parked it against the side of the cottage, forced to rely on the honesty of the *Eilean Dubhannaich*.

It did not occur to her that no *Eilean Dubhannach* would ever think of stealing someone else's primary means of transport.

Seven

Happiness comes of the capacity to feel deeply, to enjoy simply,
to think freely, to risk life, to be needed.

Storm Jameson

Now that she had acquired transportation, Polly began to view herself as a person of independence. She could go sightseeing, purchase groceries for the next week and maybe grab a bite of lunch someplace. From *Celebration of a Small Island*, which had been her bible before she left Minneapolis, she had learned that the Co-Op was the Island grocery store and that there were two branches, one in Ros Mór, one in Airgead. The former was closer and she knew how to get there – just follow the road that led past Cemetery Hill – so that would be her destination for shopping.

She pedaled down the long slope, negotiating the tricky bend in the road with care, remembering Sally's warning, and wheeled into Ros Mór. The road took her directly into the High Street square with its rows of shops, each shop front painted a different softly faded color, pink, peach, yellow and one lilac. She parked the bike against the cool blue wall of the Co-Op, thinking ruefully that she didn't have a lock for it, and hoping it would still be there when she came out.

The Co-Op's interior was like that of an old-fashioned general store of years gone by with groceries on one side and a wide variety of merchandise on the other, ranging from sewing supplies to hardware to clothing. It smelled like dusty fabric and fresh food mixed. She wandered through the groceries, marveling over the unfamiliar names of some of the products. Demarara sugar – what was that? What were Marmite and Bovril? What were rock and tablet and golden syrup?

And where was the bakery section? Polly did not realize that the Island had independent bakeries, so there was no need for the Co-Op to

stock much in the way of baked goods. She finally settled for a phenom-
enally expensive loaf of organic bread full of nuts and weird seeds from
the frozen food cases. She also found a frozen pound of something that
looked like hamburger but was called mince, and added it to her shopping cart, wondering if it would thaw in time for her dinner.

Her cart was getting full, but it was the potatoes that tipped the
balance from necessities to excess. Polly loved potatoes and these were
tiny new local ones, each perfectly round, each with a dusting of good
black Eilean Dubh dirt clinging to them. With visions of dainty boiled
potatoes swimming in butter to compliment her hamburger meal, she
selected each one carefully, dropping it into a paper sack, feeling like a
real Eilean Dubh housewife, and enjoying herself immensely.

When she took her purchases up to Flòraidh Ross, the cashier, she
had gained self-confidence as a shopper and conquered her shyness
enough to inquire about bread, having decided that the frozen loaf she'd
selected cost too much and was too peculiar. She'd read the label and had
no idea what half the ingredients were.

"Most people go to one of the bakeries on the square so we don't carry
fresh bread," said the cashier, eying Polly with barely disguised interest.
Strangers were rare enough to excite curiosity in any *Eilean Dubhannach*,
and tourists seldom found their way into the Co-Op, so this was a unique
and exciting opportunity to gather gossip for the Island grapevine.

"A bakery! Would it be all right if I put this back? I'd rather have a
fresh loaf."

Flòraidh whisked the bread away. "I'll re-stock it, never you mind.
And I'll pop the frozen mince back as well, since you can step next door
to Murray the Meat and get it freshly ground."

It was not until her groceries had been rung up and she'd carted them
outside that Polly realized her mistake. She had five paper bags full of
groceries and one bike basket and two saddlebags in which to stuff them,
and she still had to stop by the bakery and the butcher. Try as she might,
she could not get everything packed in the limited space available. She
stood on the sidewalk beside the bike cursing her imprudence in allowing
herself to be coaxed by the lure of exotic food and a wallet full of what
seemed like play money into buying far too much.

At last she gave up. She loaded the groceries back into the bags and
carried them into the Co-Op. Flòraidh was between customers, so Polly

approached her. "I've only got a bike for transportation and I can't carry all these packages," she confessed. "I'll have to make two trips. Is there a safe place where I can leave my bags until I come back?"

"Wouldn't you rather have them delivered?" asked the cashier in surprise. She had watched, amazed, through the Co-Op window Polly's struggles with the saddlebags, and wondered why the young woman was making so much work for herself.

"Delivered? Really? Can you do that?"

"*Ceart math*, sure thing," said Flòraidh, proud of her knowledge of American slang; she'd quickly pegged the young woman in front of her as the new Yank on Eilean Dubh that she'd been hearing speculation about. "Let me get your particulars," and she launched happily into the interrogation she had been dying to conduct ever since the stranger had come into her domain. "Name, please?"

"Polly Gillespie."

"Oh, a good Scottish name. By any chance would you be related to the Gillespies in Aberdeenshire? My second cousin married into a Gillespie family there."

"I don't think so," said Polly dubiously. "At least, I don't know if I am, because I ran out of time to work on my genealogy before I came to Scotland. I'm from Minneapolis, Minnesota, in the United States." Then, as the other looked puzzled, she added, "It's in the center of the country, about 400 miles west of Chicago."

"Oh, that would be near Milwaukee. Our Laird's wife is from there and her daughter too, Mrs. Sally, that's married to our young doctor Ian Mór."

"That's Sally's bike I'm using."

"Aye, aye, I thought I recognized Bouncing Betsy. Now then, I'll just mark your bags with your name, and where is it that you are staying?" She knew the answer already from the gossip about the visitor; her rental of the Ferguson cottage was one of the few things the Islanders knew for sure.

"In a little old stone cottage halfway up the road from Cemetery Hill."

"That would be the old Ferguson place, then. We'd heard someone had taken it. Bit decrepit inside, isn't it?" That was an understatement; the cashier had heard that it was hardly fit for an animal to live in, let alone an American woman whom everyone knew would be very particular in her tastes. There was also a rumor that it was haunted, but as a good churchgoing woman she did not believe in spooks. What she believed as an *Eilean Dubhannach* was another matter entirely, and not something she'd care to discuss with the Minister, who frowned severely on speculation about the supernatural.

"It's not so bad. The kitchen's old and creaky, but I've learned how to operate the stove, which was a real challenge. I'm still working on how to build a fire, though."

Flòraidh rolled her eyes sympathetically. She would have continued this fascinating conversation, offered suggestions, and ferreted out even more information to be shared Island-wide, but two customers were wheeling their carts into line. She said, with a sigh of regret for the wasted opportunity for gossip, "Oh, aye, you have to pay heed to the downdraft. Now then, that's your groceries sorted, and you can expect young Artair Mac-a-Phi with them this afternoon."

"What's the delivery charge?" asked Polly, reaching for her purse.

"Not a ha'penny, although some folks like to slip a shilling or two to Artair since he carries the groceries right into the kitchen so you don't have to take a bit of trouble with them yourself. You don't have to give him anything, of course," she added hastily.

"Oh, I will. Thank you so much for your help," Polly said, and turned to leave.

"It was my pleasure and my name is Flòraidh Ross, so grand to have met you. Goodbye then, and take care on that bicycle until you're more at home with our roads." The cashier smiled and turned to her other customers, who had been listening to the conversation shamelessly, and rather regretted its ending.

Polly headed for the bakery and the butcher, pleased with her grocery-shopping experience, and totally unconscious of the fact that she had been examined, interrogated, identified, sized up, and filed in the appropriate niche for Island reference. American, like Mrs. Jean and Ian Mór's Sally, and friendly like all Americans seemed to be. Free-spending; she'd bought over a week's worth of groceries in one trip instead of doing her shopping a day or two at a time, like the *Eilean Dubhannaich* did. However was she going to fit all the cold stuff into her fridge?

And she was from a big city and not used to Island ways, but not the least bit high-nosed about it. Polite and properly grateful for help. Friendly and talkative, with a little encouragement, of course.

Polly had passed the first stage of the audition.

Eight

Cèilidh: A party, gathering or the like, at which singing and storytelling are the usual forms of entertainment.

Random House Dictionary of the English Language

*G*iddy with her success as a shopper, a couple of days later Polly decided that she could venture out even more. She biked into Ros Mór, bought an egg and cress sandwich, which she assumed was like egg salad, from the bakery, ate it on a bench in the square, and then wheeled her bike around the tiny shopping area, which she'd categorized to herself, not without irony, as "downtown." She found a fishmonger's and the second of the town's two bakeries, both of which were having sales on luscious day old pastries. Next she walked to the end of the street and discovered the Citizens Hall.

It was an Edwardian-era building constructed from the same blocks of dismal gray granite as her cottage, and was obviously a venue for public meetings and events. A yellowing poster outside advertised that it housed on alternate Fridays a *cèilidh*. Whatever was that? The word looked familiar. She peered more closely at the poster.

It said that the program would feature a bagpiper, Highland dancers, Scottish country dancing, a storyteller, and *Tradisean* folk music group with Darroch Mac an Rìgh, and that supper would be served at intermission. Ah, now she remembered the chapter in *Celebration of a Small Island* about the *cèilidh* every other week. That was the Gaelic name for a party with music and dancing and food, and it was pronounced kay-lee, according to the book. Pleased to have recaptured the memory, she murmured the word under her breath, and realized she'd spoken her first word in the Gaelic.

This was the appropriate week, so she'd go to the cèilidh. She could slip in, take a back seat and enjoy the music without anyone noticing her. She did not know the Co-Op cashier, Flòraidh Ross, had speedily shared what she'd learned about the newcomer with her friends and relations, who'd just as speedily shared it with their friends and relations, and that their curiosity had only been whetted to a sharper point.

Polly was unaware that all the Eilean Dubhannaich would have their eyes on her, because everyone was consumed with curiosity what had brought yet another American to their shores. The place was on its way to becoming a wee New York City, they all agreed, and wondered, with a touch of smugness, what magic Eilean Dubh exerted to lure Americans from their earthly paradise to a small insignificant island.

Polly thought about riding her bicycle to Ros Mór for the cèilidh but decided against it, because she would have to ride home in the dark on a road still unfamiliar to her, and uphill, besides. It wasn't more than a mile or so into town, and she could walk there and back. The exercise would do her good.

Her plan to slip in unnoticed received a severe setback when she saw that Sally MacDonald was at the admissions table, a twin in a baby bucket on either side of her, and next to her an older woman with lively green eyes and hair the reddish-gold color of a fine whisky. "Hi, Polly!" chirped Sally. "Welcome to your first cèilidh. At least I assume it's your first. First one on Eilean Dubh, at any rate."

"Yes. I'm looking forward to it."

"You'll love it. Ma," she said, turning to the woman beside her, "let me introduce you to our newest American resident. This is Polly Gillespie from Minneapolis. Polly, my mother, Jean Mac an Rìgh."

"Oh, wow!" exclaimed Polly, shyness forgotten, taking the other woman's hand and shaking it enthusiastically. "You're the other author of my favorite book."

Jean said, "My, that little book has certainly gotten around. Wherever did you pick it up?"

"From the Internet."

Jean might have replied to that, but a large family arriving to buy tickets to the cèilidh diverted her attention and Sally's, requiring both their efforts to handle the mob. Sally said, "We'll have a chat later. I'm dying to know how you're getting on with the bike and the cottage. Go on in and get yourself a good seat, Polly."

She did, congratulating herself that she'd arrived early enough to get a desirable place. Chairs were set up in neat rows facing the stage, and she picked an unobtrusive one near the back. Then she decided she wanted to be closer to the stage and gradually edged up, forgetting her resolve to be unnoticed, until she ended up in an aisle seat in the third row. She peered over her shoulder nervously at the large noisy family, hoping they wouldn't sit behind her, and didn't relax until they had seated themselves on the other side of the aisle back in the sixth row.

The Hall began to fill up with people, but the two places next to her were empty until two men appeared at her elbow. "Are these seats taken, love?" asked the older of the two, a tall, dignified gray-haired man in a beautiful kilt and jacket that even Polly's inexperienced eyes recognized as an expensive outfit, tailored to fit perfectly.

"No," said Polly, scrambling up out of her seat and stepping into the aisle to let the two by her. She turned her head away shyly and out of the corner of her eye took a peak at the second man. He was wearing a kilt of the same tartan, and a blue crew neck sweater over a white shirt and tie. He was younger and taller, well built, with light brown hair, large bright gray eyes and a look of bored dissatisfaction on his handsome face. Very dashing, except for the look of ennui.

"Thanks," he mumbled as he moved past her into the third seat.

"There we are," exclaimed the older man, settling into the chair next to Polly. "Thank you, miss, for letting us disturb you."

"No trouble at all," said Polly and suddenly recognized his accent. "Are you an American?" she asked.

"I am, and if my ears aren't deceiving me, so are you. I'm Robert Burns MacDonald from Los Angeles, and this is my son, William Wallace MacDonald."

"Polly Gillespie from Minneapolis, Minnesota," said Polly, shaking hands with them both, and noting that though the younger MacDonald had a firm handshake and had said, "Pleasure," he had not lost his bored expression. For some reason that annoyed her. She spoke directly to him, hoping to provoke a reaction. "You're a long way from home."

"So are you," said William Wallace accusingly.

His father ignored him and said to Polly, "Yes, we're here fulfilling a dream of many years duration, visiting Eilean Dubh. How about you?"

"Same thing, I guess, because I've always wanted to see Scotland. Eilean Dubh was sort of an afterthought that was inspired by a book."

"Ha! *Celebration of a Small Island*, is it? Did you know that the two authors are at the ticket desk tonight?"

"Yes, I met them both. I know Sally from earlier in the week; she's loaned me her bike."

"Staying here for a couple of weeks, are you?" said William Wallace, in a tone that insinuated *you're a tourist, and I'm not*.

"Several months, actually," said Polly with dignity. Until my money runs out, she thought to herself.

"That's the spirit," said Robert Burns. "We're here for the summer and enjoying every minute, aren't we, William Wallace?"

"Yes, Dad," replied his son in a resigned tone.

It did not sound to Polly as though the young man was enjoying himself at all but it was none of her business. What a misery-guts, she thought, and turned to respond to Robert Burns, who had asked her what interesting things she'd found to do on the Island.

"I'm just getting settled in," she said. "I arrived less than a week ago. On Wednesday I went to the Co-Op and bought so many groceries that I couldn't carry them home on my bike. Luckily, they deliver."

"Groceries! So you're not staying at a hotel, then."

"Nope," said Polly proudly. "I'm self-catering. That's what they call it here. I've rented a cottage up past Cemetery Hill."

"Good girl. Excellent way to get to know the Island and its people. Visit the shops, take walks, come to the *cèilidhean*, talk to folks."

William Wallace looked more jaded than ever, and concealed a yawn behind a large hand. Whatever was the matter with him, Polly wondered, but had no more time to think about it because the *cèilidh* was getting started with the traditional opening act, Raghnall Wallace, a large blond-bearded piper who played stirring tunes on his bagpipe. Everyone, even the large noisy family, quieted and settled down to listen.

She could not resist slanting occasional glances at William Wallace MacDonald throughout the program. He seemed to enjoy watching the young Highland dancers and bent occasionally to whisper a comment or two into his father's ear. Then she forgot about him and allowed herself to get caught up in the music played by the folk group *Tradisean*. Jean Mac an Rìgh was one of the group, and assumed that the tall, attractive black-haired singer was Darroch Mac an Rìgh, the laird, Jean's husband. He looked like a laird, Polly thought, very upright and commanding of mien, though he had a friendly smile. The other two in the group were an astonishingly handsome blond man who played the fiddle, and a plump and pretty pianist with long red hair rippling down her back nearly to her waist.

Introductions and songs were all in the Gaelic language until near the end of the program, when Jean Mac an Rìgh sang a medley that Polly recognized from her college folkie days as Appalachian Mountain tunes. The music made her wistful and just the tiniest bit homesick. She sang along under her breath, mouthing the words to herself so as not to disturb her companions in the next two seats.

At the end of the program the audience called out their approval instead of applauding, then rose and bustled about folding up the chairs on which they had been seated, carrying them to the sides of the Hall, chatting happily as they did so.

"I'll take your chair, Dad, and yours, too, Ms Gillespie," offered William Wallace, in what Polly recognized as a ploy to get out of the center of the action. But she didn't object. If he wanted to help her with her chair, more power to him. She said to his father, "It was nice talking to you, Mr. MacDonald."

"Call me Robert Burns, my dear. There's more than one Mr. MacDonald on Eilean Dubh; you have to differentiate amongst us somehow. I've enjoyed talking to you, too. Will you partner me in the first Scottish country dance?"

"I don't know how, so I'll just watch, but thank you anyway," said Polly nervously and slipped away to the sidelines with a polite nod.

She was too timid to expect anyone to ask her to dance, but she was especially glad she had declined Robert Burns's offer, because she'd never seen anything like this kind of dancing. Groups of eight people gathered in two lines, males on one side, females on the other, and took turns executing a series of formations using complicated footwork. It would have been totally beyond her, she realized. She was so engrossed in watching the dancers that she only dimly registered someone standing at her side.

"Do you mind if I sit down?" said a familiar voice. "Unless you'd like to dance, of course," William Wallace added in a voice that very much hoped she'd say no. His father had ordered him to ask the young lady to dance but he didn't have to like it.

"No," she said. She should have been shy with him, but something about his attitude roused her combative spirit. "I don't mind if you sit down and I don't want to dance. I don't know how to do it, whatever it's called."

"Scottish country dancing," he offered, folding his tall frame into a chair.

"Whatever. I suppose you know how."

"Oh, yes," he said in a resigned tone. "Highland dance lessons from age six, Scottish country dance from age twelve. They're dancing a strathspey now, 'The Lea Rig.' That formation they're dancing now is called a petronella and the dance finishes with a half-diamond poussette."

Polly stared at him. "Why aren't you out there dancing?"

"Don't want to. I've had over twenty years of Scottish dancing and I've had enough. I've also had enough of bagpipers, thistles, mountains, castles, *Scotland the Brave*, and haggis." He shuddered. "Especially haggis."

"What is haggis?"

"Oatmeal, lamb's heart and liver, suet and onions, boiled in a sheep's stomach," he said with ghoulish relish, enjoying the horrified expression on her face.

"You're kidding."

"I only wish I were," he said. "I've eaten enough haggis to stuff a mattress, which would be a good use for it, except it would smell awful. It's traditional Scottish fare, served on all festive occasions, especially at Burns Night suppers and Hogmanay."

Polly sent an alarmed look over at the refreshment table. "Will they be serving it tonight?" she whispered.

"Probably not. It's a lot of trouble to make. I should know; I've watched our cook fuss with it any number of times."

Cook, thought Polly. His family had a cook. Were they rich? She glanced at him. The moody, disinterested expression had vanished from his face, leaving it alert and mischievous; he was really quite attractive in an irritatingly self-assured sort of way. His gray eyes, she thought in surprise, were sparkling, unlikely as that seemed, revealing a hint of violet in their depths. Then she understood: he was teasing her, and enjoying it. She felt a little thrill of female triumph, that she'd managed to get his mind off of whatever had been bothering him. She decided to encourage the trend. "How do you know so much about this Scottish stuff?" she asked.

"My dad. He's a nut on his Scottish ancestry and has inflicted it on all of the family. None of us want to hurt his feelings by telling him we've had enough, though." He gazed moodily out at the dance floor, where

Robert Burns MacDonald was leading Jean Mac an Rìgh into a set with courtly grace. "Silly old man," he grumbled.

"You shouldn't call him that," said Polly, shocked. She was sensitive on the subject of fathers and the respect due them, since her own had died when she was twelve, and she had missed him desperately ever since then.

"I will call him silly when he's out there getting ready to dance 'Màiri's Wedding.' It's his favorite; he never misses it. But he's got no business in a dance that vigorous. He had a heart attack last year and he's supposed to take it easy, not dance forty bars straight without a chance to catch his breath and then dance another thirty-two in the second repetition."

He was looking grim again and now Polly understood. He was worried about his father's welfare. She said helpfully, "He'll probably be all right."

That was the wrong comment. His previous persona was back in a flash, and he looked at her scornfully. "And if he's not? What am I to do then, doctor? Ship him back to California in a coffin?"

Shocked, Polly could think of nothing to say.

"I've got to go. Excuse me," he snapped, and headed out around the edge of the dance floor, looking for someone more responsible with whom to discuss his father's transgressions. She watched him as he strode up to Darroch Mac an Rìgh and began to speak, waving an arm vigorously, the grim expression back on his face.

A little miffed at being brushed off so abruptly, Polly stood up from her chair and headed for the door. It had been a long evening and she had lost interest in watching the dancing. She didn't dare go near the refreshment table for fear of haggis, and besides, it was surrounded by a crowd of laughing Islanders. She'd had enough for one night of watching other people having a good time. Besides, they would all stare at her covertly since she was a newcomer.

And especially, she'd had enough of the brusque Mr. William Wallace MacDonald. Cranky men were a right bloody nuisance, as the folks around here would probably say, just like they did in her favorite Britcom back home on public television.

On her way out she passed by a room that appeared, at first glance, to be full of babies. A longer look told her there were also several toddlers, two of whom were asleep on cots, and a little girl playing with a set of blocks. An even longer look had her recognizing Sally MacDonald's twins. Fiona was asleep in her bucket, Hamish was wide awake, waving his arms and legs and chortling to himself in his inimitable manner. She could not resist stopping in to see him.

"Hi, Hamish," she whispered, sinking down on her knees in front of the baby, who responded with an eager smile and a stream of babble. She shook his hand solemnly, which made him laugh, and said, "How nice to see you again."

A voice from above said, "Do you know the twins?"

She looked up. A lovely blonde woman cradling a small child in her arms stood there, smiling. "I met them at Sally MacDonald's house the other day." Then, feeling that she needed to introduce herself, she said, "My name is Polly Gillespie. I'm a visitor from the United States."

"Oh, yes, I've heard about you."

Surprised, Polly said, "Good things, I hope."

The other woman laughed. "You've got courage enough to stay in the old Ferguson place; that's one thing I heard."

"I don't know if courage is the right word. Maybe fortitude and patience, especially when it comes to dealing with the stove and the fireplace. I still haven't figured out how to keep a fire burning for more than half an hour."

"You need someone to give you a lesson. It's to do with proper stacking of the peats and warming the chimney first." The child in her arms had begun to wiggle with impatience so she put her down, saying, "Go play with your blocks, Marsaili, *mo chridhe*. Mama's arms are tired from holding you." The child ran off and the woman knelt by Polly, extending her hand. "My name is Catrìona. I'm wife to the postal carrier."

"Ha! You're Ian's Catrìona."

"That's what they call me," said the other woman. "It differentiates me from all the other Catrìonas, since that's a popular name here. How did you know that?"

"I read about you in *Celebration of a Small Island*. This is great; I keep meeting people from the book, and I didn't entirely believe you all were real before I came here."

"Oh, we're all too real," said Catrìona, laughing. "How odd, that you got hold of that book in the United States. What brings you to Eilean Dubh?"

"I've wanted to visit Scotland for a long time, and I had a sudden . . .

financial windfall . . . that made it possible. Renting the old cottage helps me to stay here longer because self-catering is cheaper," she said, a little surprised at her own frankness.

"More fun, too, I should think, doing for yourself and setting your own hours without being at the whim of a hotel or B and B owner. Sleep as late as you like, cook the food you prefer. But then I like being independent."

"So do I," said Polly, realizing to her surprise that it was true. At a loss for anything else to say, she ventured, "Who are all these children?"

"This is a *crèche* we've organized to care for Island children so that parents can come to the *cèilidhean*. We take turns staffing it."

"It's a lot of work for one person," said Polly sympathetically.

"I'm not really alone. The middle Mac-a-Phi girl is helping tonight, but her boyfriend came up a few minutes ago and asked if she could dance. I didn't want to stand in the way of young love so I sent her off with him. The other mothers keep an eye on this room. If I need help, I go stand in the doorway with a screaming baby and its owner will come running. Where it gets tricky is if more than one scream at the same time. I once had five yelling all together, and I nearly threw off my pinnie and ran out the door."

Catriona chuckled. "It got so noisy they had to stop dancing in the middle of 'Machine without Horses' because the dancers couldn't hear the band."

"I'm not surprised." Looking at little Marsaili, now happily involved in building a block tower, she asked, "Is she your only child?"

"So far. I lost two before her so we were over the moon when she was born."

Polly whispered, "I lost a baby, too," and wondered why she kept confiding her sad secret to strangers. Was it something in the Island air or was it the friendly frankness of Eilean Dubh women?

"Hell, isn't it," said Catrìona matter-of-factly. "Did this happen recently?"

"About three months ago."

"Oh, poor you. How are you feeling?"

"Better since I had a talk with Sally MacDonald. She's had a miscarriage, too."

"Yes, I know." Catrìona sighed. "It's sort of like a sisterhood, isn't it.

Only women who've been there know what it's like."

Polly nodded in agreement, grateful that this time she hadn't indulged herself in an outburst of tears. She must be getting over her sorrow, she thought; the distractions of the Island were doing that for her, and the kindly sympathy of Island women.

As though driven by some universal signal, two babies woke up and began to fuss, and Hamish, unhappy at being ignored by Polly for the last few moments, was gurgling and fussing, percolating himself into joining them. Catrìona sprang to her feet and hurried to the baby crying the loudest. Polly gave Hamish the rattle that was at the bottom of his bucket, heard his chortle of pleasure, and got up to go to the other child.

"What do we do now?" she asked.

"Mine wants changing so I'll tend to that. Yours needs a feed; take her up and go stand in the doorway until her mother sees you and comes to the rescue. She'll know that bright red baby blanket. We put all the babies in colorful blankets so their parents can recognize them at a distance."

"Good idea," said Polly. She scooped up the baby and the blanket and headed for the doorway.

Across the room a young woman sprang to her feet and headed for the *crèche* in a determined fashion. She arrived and took the baby from Polly with a murmured, "*Tapadh leat,*" and a quick smile. "I don't know you, do I?" she added in English, recognizing a stranger. "We'll get acquainted after I give the wee one what he wants."

Two more women came in and after them William Wallace MacDonald. "I was looking for you," he said accusingly.

"Now you've found me, what do you want?" Polly snapped, annoyed at his bossy tone of voice.

"I was told you ride a bike everywhere, so I've come to ask you if you need a lift home because it's too dark to bike. We can put the bicycle in the back seat of my car."

Polly said curtly, "I walked."

"I'll give you a ride anyway; you shouldn't be walking the streets at night. I'm glad you didn't bike because the car's a little small to put a bicycle into. But Dad never thinks of things like that."

"Giving me a ride home was your father's idea?"

"Yes," he said and stared at her defiantly. "Is there anything wrong with that?"

There really wasn't, although she couldn't help wishing that William Wallace had thought of the idea himself; he was an attractive guy and it would have been nice to have piqued his interest enough for him to offer the ride. "No, of course not. It's very kind of him – and you – but you needn't take the trouble to drive so far. I can walk."

"How far is it?"

"Oh . . . I don't know . . . I walked it in fifteen minutes. Maybe a mile."

"That's not far. Our driveway at home is longer than that. I walk it every day for exercise."

She stared at him in shock. Surely he was exaggerating?

"We have a ranch in southern California," he said. "Are you ready to go? I think this party is about over."

A ranch, Polly thought, and a cook, and Robert Burns' expensive kilt outfit. These guys must have money. The idea made her a little more standoffish than usual because something in her rebelled against the idea of cozying up to rich people. But a ride home would be nice; the evening had been tiring, even though she hadn't danced. She tried for a casual tone and said, "Sure, I could leave anytime."

The drive to the cottage was mercifully too short for much conversation. When William Wallace pulled up in front, he squinted at the old house dubiously. "This is it?"

"Yes. Thank you so much for the ride," she said, opening the car door.

"You're welcome." He was still studying the cottage. "The place looks really run down," he said.

"Well, it's not. It just seems that way in the dark. It's quite nice inside," Polly snapped, far enough at the end of her tether that she didn't mind stretching the truth.

"If you say so."

"I do say so." The devil got hold of her tongue and she blurted defiantly, "If you don't believe me, why don't you come for tea and see for yourself?" She slipped out of the car without waiting for an answer and was dumbfounded when one came.

"Sure. When?" William Wallace seized the opportunity to break the monotony of everyday Eilean Dubh life and the Islanders, all of which were beginning to get on his nerves. It was nice to have a fellow American to talk to, even if she was sort of a dork.

Absolutely astonished at herself for having made such an impetuous offer and even more astonished to have it accepted, Polly wanted to stall, or even better, back out, but she was trapped. One couldn't rescind an invitation however hastily it had been given, and besides, she wanted to assert herself with this officious young man. She stood thinking, her hand on the car door. "Ummm . . . how about Monday? No, Tuesday would be better, because I have to go to the Co-Op for food and it's not open on Sunday."

"Okay. What time?"

"About two-thirty?"

"A proper tea is served after three-thirty."

"All right, three-thirty," snapped Polly, thinking what a pain in the neck he was.

"I'll be there. Good night." He grinned in a self-satisfied way, started the engine and looped the car into a U-turn to head back to the Citizens Hall.

The doorstep was particularly cold this evening, so she scampered inside in a hurry, wondering what she had gotten herself into. She'd had enough problems trying to think of something to talk to William Wallace MacDonald about at the *cèilidh*, where there was plenty of distraction if she ran dry, but now she'd condemned herself to a *tête-a-tête* that would probably last an hour and a half or more.

What could she say that would interest him? She'd better prepare a list, she thought, wishing she had access to her favorite magazine, *The New Yorker*, its articles invariably a fount of unusual and interesting ideas for chat. She'd read somewhere that a person should have three topics in mind when going to a social event so as to have something to talk about if conversation flagged. She'd better come up with twice that number, and hope that William Wallace wouldn't dismiss all her gambits with curt responses, as seemed to be his habit.

Nine

We don't get offered crises; they arrive.

Elizabeth Janeway.

The more Polly thought about the invitation during the weekend, the more apprehensive she got. She'd never invited anyone to tea before; in fact, she'd never even been to a tea. What sort of food was she supposed to serve? Did she have nice dishes to serve it on? And – yikes! – did she have a teapot? She'd bought tea bags at the Co-Op and had been brewing them in one of the two mugs the cottage possessed. Both had slight chips and neither was suitable for company, especially not snooty company like William Wallace MacDonald. She ransacked the kitchen cupboards and came up with two each of cups, saucers, plates, and a matching serving plate, all dusty but otherwise in good shape. But no teapot.

By Monday morning she was in a state of despair. She couldn't cancel the invitation; she had no idea where the MacDonalds were staying or how to reach them. What was she going to do? Why, of course, call Sally MacDonald and ask her all these questions. Without hesitating, shyness forgotten, she ran down the road to the red telephone box and dialed Sally's number. "Hello, this is Polly Gillespie. May I please speak to Sally?"

The cheerful man's voice on the other end of the line said, "Aye, she's just coming back into the room. Hang on a tick while I relieve her of a baby."

Sally said, "Hi. Who's this?"

"It's Polly Gillespie and I need some help."

"Fire away," said Sally in her friendly American fashion.

"I've invited someone for tea. What should I cook, how do I cook it and can you suggest a place in Ros Mór where I can buy a teapot?"

Baffled by the barrage of questions, Sally seized on the last thing Polly had said and responded to that. "Isn't there a teapot in the cottage?"

"No."

"It must be the only house in Eilean Dubh without one. I have an extra I can loan you; we got two as wedding presents years ago and we already had one so we've never used the others. You can pick whichever you like best. You'd better come over."

"When?"

"How about now?"

"I'm on my way." She ran a comb through her hair, exchanged slippers for shoes and dashed outside to her bike. She remembered to slow down at the sharp curve just in time to avoid a spill, and arrived at Sally's to see her exchanging kisses with an extremely tall, Greek god-handsome man at her doorstep.

"Bye-bye, sweetie," said Sally. "Oh, hold on a sec. Polly, this is my husband, Ian Mór MacDonald. Ian, Polly Gillespie from Minneapolis, Minnesota. In the U.S.A."

"Hullo." Ian Mór thrust out a huge hand.

"Hi." Good heavens, he was large; he towered over both women, and neither Sally nor Polly was short. He must be six foot five or six, thought Polly, and he was so good-looking that she was momentarily tongue-tied. Luckily there was no need for conversation, for he smiled, strode off and inserted his enormous self with agility into a miniscule car parked by the cottage. Sally waved as he drove away.

"Off on his rounds. He's one of our Island doctors, and they both do house calls, unlike in the States," she said, and led the way into the cottage.

"Where are the twins?"

"Down for naps, both of them at the same time, a new Olympic record. Pray it lasts for a blessed hour or two and don't mind me if I carry on organizing the laundry while we talk. The teapots are there on the table. Choose your favorite."

Polly's favorite was a pretty blue one decorated with pink flowers with a matching sugar bowl and cream pot, sturdy enough that she needn't fear breaking it as much as she might the other one, which was delicate. That one appeared to be either Wedgwood or Belleek; she wasn't sure which, but she knew it was expensive. "I'll bring it back as soon as my tea is finished."

"Keep it while you're here. You might develop a habit of giving tea parties."

Polly shuddered. "I don't think so because this one has me tearing out my hair."

"Take a seat and tell me all about it. Who are your guests?"

"Just one. His name is William Wallace . . ."

"MacDonald. Whyever did you think of inviting him to tea? Excuse my saying this if he's a friend of yours, but he's a bit of a stick. His father is darling, but wee Willie is a drag. Although he is cute, if you like the type of guy who looks most comfortable in a smart suit, hand-knotted designer tie and button-down shirt."

"He is a drag and I haven't the faintest idea what I'm going to talk to him about."

"Let me repeat: why did you invite him?"

"It sort of slipped out. He gave me a ride home from the *cèilidh* on Friday night and he insulted my cottage, so I invited him to tea to show him how nice it is. Which it isn't, of course, so he'll probably make fun of it and stalk out."

"I don't think so," said Sally thoughtfully. "He's reserved and what we in Scotland call dour, but he's always been perfectly polite when I've been around him. So I doubt he's into gratuitous insults."

"He'll turn his nose up at my cottage, I just know it. I think his family is rich so a broken-down little hovel of a house will not be his cup of tea, so to speak."

"Is your cottage really that bad?"

Polly hesitated. "Well, I've grown to like it so I don't mind its faults, but even I have to admit that it's scarcely something out of *Martha Stewart Living*."

"You'll just have to make up for it with your charm and your fabulous food. He'll be too dazzled to notice his surroundings." Sally gave her an encouraging smile.

The other woman looked dubious. "Start with the fabulous food. What do I serve at a high tea?"

"To begin with, since it's in the afternoon, it won't be 'high tea.' That's what we in the States call supper, eaten around five or six, and meat is served so it's a proper meal. For afternoon tea, it's finger foods like cucumber sandwiches or bread-and-butter or savories, and scones, cakes and pastries. And perhaps fruit. The idea is to eat just enough to hold off starvation until it's time for dinner." She grinned at Polly's anxious expression. "You can buy the fixings at Beathag the Bread's bakery shop in the Square. Unless you bake?" She paused.

"Not on that oven in the cottage, I don't. I'm not much of a cook, anyway."

"Don't worry. Beathag has wonderful pastries and teacakes are one of her specialties. And I have a great recipe for savory sandwiches I can give you. It's got cream cheese, bacon and slivered almonds. Spread it on thin slices of Beathag's wheat loaves and cut them into triangles. Be sure to remove the crusts; it looks more dainty and lady-like that way." She chuckled. "It's really fun to see guys eat dainty sandwiches. They don't know whether to gulp them all in one bite or nibble at them. Sometimes I fix finger sandwiches for Ian Mór just to watch him grapple with the idea."

Polly took a deep breath. "I'll go to the bakery tomorrow and stock up. I think I can handle that. Just one more question: how do I make tea?"

"What?"

"I've been making my tea by the cupful using tea bags from the Co-Op. I don't know how to make it by the pot."

"You really are a newcomer to things British, aren't you. Okay, the first thing is to warm the pot by pouring hot water into it, then dumping it out. Use about one spoonful of tea per cup, and make sure the water is boiling when you pour it on. Brew for three to five minutes, depending on the tea and how strong you like it, and use a strainer – I'll lend you one – when you pour so you don't get leaves in the cups. And stir the tea once or twice while it's brewing.

"If you make a second pot, clean out the used leaves and start all over again; don't just add more water. Use fresh water each time because once it's boiled the oxygen is out of it, and the tea will taste flat."

"Hold on, I want to write this down." She fished a notepad and pen out of her purse. Sally repeated the instructions and Polly took careful notes. "I'd better practice this tonight," she muttered. "Wouldn't it be easier to use tea bags?"

"You can do that if you want. Personally – and don't quote me on this I prefer tea bags because you can take them out and you don't get that nasty bitter taste tea gets after it has sat in the pot and brewed too long.

But don't tell a Scot that. They get all hoity-toity about tea bags. I doubt that William Wallace will know the difference."

"He probably will, because he seems to know everything else about Scotland."

"That's from his father, who is more Scottish than half the people on Eilean Dubh. And much better dressed. His kilt and Prince Charlie jacket are fabulous and those are real jewels on his brooch and *sgian dubh*. Nobody here can afford an outfit like that. Anyway, I wouldn't worry about it. Wee Willie is a guy and he's probably never paid any attention to how tea is brewed."

"Probably his family cook always made it for him."

"Cook? Really? His family has a cook?"

Polly nodded. "He mentioned it when we were talking the other night."

Sally sighed. "Wish I had a cook. Especially now," she added, as a piercing cry erupted from the vicinity of the bedroom and the twins. "Wonder which one that is?" She left and returned with Fiona, whose little face was red with misery. "Bet it's a sore butt," Sally murmured, and put the baby down on the changing table. "Yep, that's what it is, poor sweetie. That awful nappy rash is starting again." She smeared white goo over the baby's bottom, lifting her legs in the air with one hand in a practiced motion.

"I should go; you're busy. But thanks for all the help."

"Let me get her nappy on and I'll pack up the teapot and cream pitcher and sugar bowl for you. Can't just shove them in a saddlebag."

Polly, who had been planning on doing just that, nodded meekly.

Ten

*Another novelty is the tea-party, an extraordinary meal in that,
being offered to persons that have already dined well, it supposes
neither appetite nor thirst, and has no object but distraction, no
basis but delicate enjoyment.*

Jean-Anthelme Brillat-Savarin

Polly was too nervous to sleep in on Tuesday morning, as she had been doing ever since she came to Eilean Dubh's relaxing surroundings. She gobbled breakfast, flung on her clothes, and jumped on the bike to pedal rapidly down to Ros Mór to buy supplies before the bakery was sold out of its best products. "The tea cakes go first, then the nut breads, so if you want those, get there promptly," Sally had advised.

She loaded up with a wheat loaf, a walnut loaf, two dozen tea cakes and a dozen adorable miniature cream puffs that made her mouth water just looking at them. She hoped they would have the same effect on William Wallace MacDonald.

At the Co-Op she shopped for loose tea, bacon, chopped nuts and cream cheese for Sally's sandwich recipe. She'd wondered how she'd to recognize the cream cheese, but to her relief it appeared in the dairy case in the familiar foil package she knew from the United States. Not every grocery product was different over here, thank goodness.

Cucumbers were not in season, so she'd have to skip the cucumber sandwiches, to her regret; she'd been looking forward to tasting them, the idea of using the familiar long green vegetable as a sandwich filling having piqued her curiosity. But there were strawberries, small, luscious, bright red and expensive, since they came all the way from Cornwall. They were called Rhapsody. She bought them as much for the name as for the idea of having them. Polly tended to romanticize food.

Clotted cream, also from Cornwall, was displayed next to the strawberries, but she passed on that, not knowing how to implement the "serving suggestion" pictured on the sign. Did one mix the strawberries into the cream, or put the cream on top of a bowl of berries? Another mystery she'd have to run by Sally MacDonald.

Remembering that she couldn't wait for her groceries to be delivered, she forced herself to stop shopping before she exceeded her carrying capacity. Both saddlebags were full of bakery goods so whatever she bought at the Co-Op would have to go into her basket as she didn't want to risk squashing any of her expensive and highly squash-able pastry purchases.

On the way home, lighter of heart and of purse, she had a devastating insight: what on earth was she going to wear for her tea party? Jeans and a tee shirt, her usual garb, didn't seem appropriate; something more formal was definitely required. Were the few skirts and shirts she'd brought with her all hopelessly wrinkled, and if they were, did the cottage have an iron? She became so agitated that she pedaled furiously and the bike flew up the usually daunting hill.

Panting and overheated from the effort of pedaling, she darted inside the cottage so fast she scarcely felt the cold of the Frozen Zone, to paw frantically through her meager wardrobe. The knit skirts were fine, their packing wrinkles having shaken out, but it was a warm day in June and knits would look ridiculously out of season and be hot and uncomfortable. Ah, there on the closet shelf was her red pleated cotton skirt, of the type that's stored tied in a knot. She untied it, shook it out and decided that though it was rather oddly creased, it would have to do. Did she have a clean blouse? Why hadn't she thought about clothes last night so she could have rinsed out something?

She found a short-sleeved white blouse that looked clean, but carrying it out to the window to view it in sunlight revealed a spot on the front that she had meant to treat when she last wore it, but had forgotten. There was only one thing to do. She would wear the blouse and pull on a cotton sweater over it. Sweaters were always appropriate in Scotland, she'd learned. She might be warm, especially drinking tea, but she would have to endure it and hope she didn't develop a sweaty forehead, so un-ladylike. For some reason she wanted to appear as a perfect lady, self-contained and self-controlled. It must be the influence of William Wallace MacDonald's cool formality, she thought.

It was now one-thirty. Polly flew at her preparations. She made sandwiches, washed and hulled strawberries, tidied the cottage and moved furniture in the lounge to make a conversational grouping of chair and sofa around a low table she'd rescued from the side wall, where it had been buried under a pile of old magazines, games and books. Those she hustled out of sight into a pile in the bedroom, and closed the door.

By three-ten her work was done, and it was time to turn attention to her appearance. Luckily she didn't have to worry about make-up because she never wore anything but a dab of lipstick. She washed up, pulled on her clothes and brushed her hair furiously, trying to tame the flyaway ends, then swept it all back into a ponytail, fastened with a rubber band and decorated with a ribbon. Then she took a final look in the mirror.

She thought somberly that she was nothing fancy, unlike the tea fixings now elegantly displayed on the low table. Just a plain dishwater-blonde female with ordinary features in an old-fashioned coral sweater and pleated skirt, socks and loafers. Miss Everyday America, ca 1990, complete with ponytail. Barbie, without the bosom and the spectacular body. With a list of seven topics (she'd over-achieved) that she could introduce if conversation lagged. She took a deep breath and walked to the front door to wait for her guest.

William Wallace MacDonald arrived promptly at three-thirty, clutching a bouquet of flowers. He was nicely dressed in a white shirt, black trousers, and a green cashmere pullover sweater; apparently he wasn't worried about getting too warm. His shoes looked as though they'd been freshly polished. She was touched at the signs he'd chosen his wardrobe with care, but would have felt more relaxed if he'd been wearing a sweatshirt, jeans and sneakers. Maybe he, too, thought a tea invitation deserved a touch of formality.

"Good afternoon," he said, and bowed slightly, extending the flowers.

"Good afternoon, and thank you for the lovely bouquet. Come in out of the cold."

"Cold? It must be sixty-five today. Unseasonably warm, I'd call it, knowing Scotland."

"Oh, I meant come in off the step, it's freezing there." That sounded silly, but she meant it. The chill was particularly active today; a blast of cold had hit her in the face when she'd opened the door.

"What?" Still puzzled, William Wallace stared at her.

"Never mind," said Polly, resigning herself to the odd notion that only she felt the frigidity of the Frozen Zone. Whatever did that mean?

Putting the idea out of her head, she waved her hand and urged him in. "Do sit down," she said, but he was walking about, his gray eyes sharp with interest, examining the cottage with great care. She wanted to ask him what he thought, but she was not going to be drawn into a verbal dueling match about her home's deficiencies, as he perceived them.

He came back to plant his long lean self on the sofa. "You were right. Your cottage is much nicer inside," he announced, and gave her a winning smile.

She felt as though she'd passed some kind of a test. "Thank you. If you'll excuse me a minute, I'll go and make the tea. Help yourself to the sandwiches and pastries."

"Sandwiches first," he said. "Sweets come last."

Polly ground her teeth. Heaven help her, he was familiar with all the niceties of a proper tea and wasn't shy about sharing them. How could she hope to measure up? She slunk into the kitchen and lit the fire under the teakettle with a match. While she waited for it to boil, she reviewed her notes from Sally. "Warm the pot first," she muttered. "Let the water come back to a boil before making the tea." She talked herself through the routine, then brought the teapot into the front room and set it down on the table.

William Wallace had taken two sandwiches, put them on a plate and was nibbling at one of them, quite unfazed by its dainty size. "This filling is quite good," he said.

"It's Sally MacDonald's recipe."

"Hmmm . . . cream cheese and bacon, I think. With nuts. Very similar to one our cook makes, which is my favorite. I believe she adds a touch of chili powder."

That cook again. "Do you have tea every afternoon at home in California?"

He grimaced. "Usually. Mom and Dad like it. It's a little fussy for me. And lots of extra calories between lunch and dinner which no one needs, especially not my father who should be following doctor's orders to avoid fat and sodium, and trying to lose weight."

"Can't your cook prepare low-calorie food?"

"She could but Dad prefers fatty, salty crunchy things and gooey sweets, and makes a fuss if she doesn't offer his favorite pastries. He's hopeless," he said, and sighed.

"It must be quite worrying, his having had a heart attack. My father died of one when I was twelve."

"That's reassuring," he snapped, looking down his long straight nose at her.

"I'm sorry," she said, and meant it. How tactless could she get? "Nowadays many people survive heart attacks. Perhaps you shouldn't worry so much, especially if you can't do anything about it."

"It's easy to tell someone not to worry, and hard to take that advice."

"I'm sorry," she said again. This was not going well. She tried to think of one of her conversational ideas so that she could change the subject, and failed utterly. Her mind was a blank, perfectly empty of thought. She turned to the teapot and carefully poured two cups, using the strainer to trap loose leaves. She handed one to her guest.

There was a moment of silence, as strained as the tea.

William Wallace said suddenly, "I believe this cottage was a *taigh dubh*."

"A what?"

"A *taigh dubh*, Gaelic for 'black house.' It was called that because in the old days fire was laid in the middle of the floor, not in a fireplace, and the smoke went upwards and out through a hole in the roof. The smoke spread all over the ceiling, which was the underside of a thatched roof, and coated it with soot, hence the term 'black house.'"

"So this once was a thatched house?" said Polly in excitement, harking back to her original cottage dreams before they were vanquished by this stone monstrosity.

"Yes. The granite blocks on the outside were added to the original stone walls; that's why those walls are so thick. Haven't you noticed that the inside walls are stone?"

Polly confessed that she hadn't paid much attention to the interior construction.

He was now in full lecturing mode. "And the stone floor slants towards the far end. I assume that's the bedroom? – because that once was the byre where the animals lived and the slant was to drain their waste away from the humans' living area."

Her eyes were enormous. "Animals lived in the house with the people?"

"Yes, of course. Very practical, saved the expense and work of having to build a separate barn. These were poor people, remember. The animals were secure inside and it wasn't necessary to go outside in bad weather to care for them. They also provided warmth with their body heat."

"It must have been smelly," said Polly, wrinkling her nose.

"No doubt. But it was very efficient. The roof thatch was recycled every few years, torn off the taigh dubh and put in the fields where it made very good fertilizer. And meat and fish were hung over the fire to smoke, making additional use of the flames."

"How old is this, umm, ty doo, do you think?"

"One hundred and fifty years old, or more."

Polly looked at her surroundings with new respect. She had a sudden idea. Was her house haunted? Were houses ever haunted on the outside and not on the inside? It would explain the chill of the Frozen Zone. "I wonder if it has any ghosts."

William Wallace gave her a pitying look and said, "There are no such things as ghosts. You want to be careful not to fill your head with Scottish superstitions. That's a common failing of tourists."

What business of his was it what she filled her head with, and what made him such an expert on the common failings of tourists? Besides, she was no more a tourist than he was. Annoyed, she tried to think of an appropriate response that was not downright rude, and failed. She snapped, "Don't forget that you're a tourist, too."

"I'm not. My father and I – well, my father anyway – are honored guests of Darroch Mac an Rìgh, the Laird."

"Who doesn't like being called that," she retorted, remembering a fact from *Celebration of a Small Island* and unable to think of anything else to say.

He shrugged his shoulders. "That's his opinion which I consider rather juvenile. I have always found that it's best not to deny reality and by simple reality, popular acceptance and hereditary principle, he is the Laird."

He really was the most opinionated man she'd ever met. Imagine him criticizing the Laird, she thought indignantly, lapsing unknowingly into a traditional Eilean Dubh attitude. Unwilling to continue an argument about which she knew nothing, she said, "How do you know so much about house construction on Eilean Dubh?"

"My father's library is full of books about Scottish subjects and occasionally I pick up one of them." That was a lie; he'd read many of them cover to cover with great interest. "Besides, I once wanted to be an architect so houses interest me."

"What do you do to earn a living, since you didn't become an architect?" Assuming he had to earn a living, that is, and didn't survive just on his father's bankroll.

"I'm training to join the family firm. I majored in management in business school, then took a law degree and I'm going back to school this fall for my MBA." Adroitly switching the subject from himself, he asked, "What about you?"

"I was an insurance claims adjuster but I quit that job when I came to Eilean Dubh. I'm trying to decide on a new line of work."

He said in a surprising burst of confession, "So am I. Management is boring, law is boring, but I can't think of anything else to do that will fit in with Dad's business."

"Do you have to join his business? Maybe you should strike out on your own."

"Why on earth would I do that?" he said, astonished at her perspicacity and quick to deny her suggestion. She had tapped into one of his private fantasies, one that could never be realized. Robert Burns MacDonald expected all three of his children to join him in his business. William Wallace had every intention of doing just that, as soon as he could think of some way to fit himself in that didn't involve being under his elder brother's thumb every day of the week, and probably on Saturday and Sunday, too. Robert Bruce loved bringing work home on weekends, and sometimes even went into the office.

Polly said, "Don't you want to do something you really enjoy?"

He said stiffly, "I plan to enjoy Dad's business, once I get into it."

"I want to do something else, something new and different," Polly said with conviction. "I want to strike out in a whole different direction. I just don't know what it is. I think I'd like to go back to school and get an advanced degree so I could get an interesting job, but I can't decide what I want to study. I loved going to the University of Minnesota; I think graduate school would be really cool."

William Wallace thought in envy of his own college days which had been slog, slog, slog. Why hadn't he had fun at the university, like Polly obviously had?

A silence fell, as both contemplated their teacups. Then she said,

"Why did you decide not to be an architect?"

"Oh . . . it didn't fit in with the family business."

"That again. What is it, anyway?"

"My father's company makes industrial fasteners."

"What are they?"

"Things to hold other things together." He realized now the vast gap in his knowledge. Robert Bruce knew and Flora knew what the firm made, but he had never understood nor considered it necessary that he understand. Things were manufactured and things were sold and that was all a management person needed to know. What those things were was immaterial; managing was managing, whether it involved widgets, dohickeys or gizmos.

Now, with Polly looking at him expectantly, he felt foolish because he didn't know. He searched his memory for things he'd read about in his sister Flora's never-ending publicity packets. "Bolts, nuts, screws, rivets, pins, retaining rings, o-rings, hose clamps, grease fittings, and I think, maybe, ferrule crimpers. Or maybe not on that last one," he said. "I'm not sure about those." He knew he'd heard the term somewhere but couldn't remember what they were, or what relationship they had to industrial fasteners.

Polly's eyes glazed over and she decided not to probe any further. She couldn't make intelligent conversation about o-rings and ferrule crimpers; they sounded like something out of a Doctor Who television program. They'd certainly never been mentioned in *The New Yorker*. Best to change the subject. She said, "Are you absolutely sure you don't want to be an architect?"

"I don't know any more, I haven't thought about it in years." That was a lie; the idea haunted him in odd moments, like when he was sitting on a couch in Robert Bruce's office, listening to his brother wheel and deal on the phone, and pretending to read *The Economist*. It's hardly any of your business, his glance at her said. He took a miniature cream puff and bit into it. To change the subject, he said, "These are excellent."

"They're from the bakery in Ros Mór. All the pastries are from there."

"You didn't bake?" he said, a hint of disapproval in his voice.

"You should see my stove and you'd understand why not. It's probably the original from when the house was built."

"A one hundred and fifty year old stove? Surely not."

Polly said, exasperated, "You're very literal, William Wallace."

"Damn it, I wish you wouldn't call me that. I'm getting tired of that name. Dad uses it all the time, and people look at me funny." He selected a strawberry and frowned at it. "Sometimes I think they might even be laughing at me but it's hard to tell with these Scots; they're so tight-lipped. And close-mouthed, too."

"Well, it is a rather odd name. What would you prefer to be called?"

"Anything but Bill. Or Willie. Or Wallace. And especially not Wally."

"That doesn't leave much left. Wills, like Prince William?"

"No, I'm not the heir to anybody's throne." Or even to Dad's business, he thought; his older brother had that sewn up. Not that he minded; he just wanted to fit in where he could be useful.

Polly thought a minute, then offered, "How about Will?"

He said gruffly, "That's what they called me at Princeton. I liked it."

"Okay, I'll call you Will. My real name is Pauline but I've always been nicknamed Polly."

"My mother once had a maid by the name of Polly."

Irritated at his tone, she said, "There's nothing wrong with being a maid."

"Of course not. Mother's Polly was very good at her job and took pride in her work. She left Mother to marry our chauffeur and raise a family."

"How nice," she said sarcastically. Mother's Polly, indeed. And cooks, chauffeurs, mile long driveways and a family business. She was getting tired of the constant reminders that his people were wealthy. He might as well know the truth about her, and if he was too snooty to hang out with her after that, so be it.

She blurted, "My family never had a maid or a chauffeur. We come from a small town in Minnesota, and my mother had to work hard to support us both after my father died. He didn't have any life insurance and Mom had a hard time finding a job, so we were on welfare for a while until she got the job answering the phone in Mr. Johnson's insurance office."

Instead of commenting on her poverty-stricken childhood, he said wryly, "Insurance seems to run as a thread throughout your life. Perhaps your destiny *is* to be a claims adjuster."

"That's nonsense," she snapped, and glared at him.

"I was joking," he said and smiled suddenly. It lit up his face and made him quite handsome. Polly stared at him, dazzled by the smile and dumbfounded at the change in his attitude. He said abruptly, "Why didn't you want to dance the other night?"

"I told you, I don't know how."

"Would you like to learn?"

"Well . . . I don't know . . . I hadn't thought about it." That was a fib; she'd thought the dancing looked like so much fun that she was quite envious.

"Come on, I'll teach you." He drained his teacup, rose, picked up another cream puff and popped it whole into his mouth. With his other hand, he reached for Polly's hand. He pulled her outside and off the stoop before she could even feel the chill of the Frozen Zone, to which he seemed impervious. "Let's go around back," he mumbled through the cream puff. "There's more room there and it's private. No one can see us from the road."

When they got outside, he pulled off his sweater and threw it casually down on the ground. "Don't do that," protested Polly, alarmed at seeing the beautiful expensive sweater in the dirt. She scooped it up and ran to place it carefully on a large nearby rock.

He eyed her curiously. "You didn't have to do that."

"Yes, I did." He was probably used to the maid picking up after him, she thought.

He shrugged, and glanced around at the landscape. "This is pretty out here. You have a nice view. Now come and stand behind me and do as I do. Step down on your right foot, bring your left foot up against your arch, step down again on the right foot, and *jeté* – kick out – like this with your left foot. Transfer your weight to the left, and repeat."

He demonstrated. "Got it? Let me watch you. Good. Just remember to keep your movements low to the ground, rise on the balls of your feet, and point your toes. Keep your head up; don't watch your feet. That's called the pas de basque or setting step, used to greet another dancer. Let's try the skip change, a traveling step that gets you around the set. It begins with a hop, then step, close, step." He demonstrated that, then took her hand. "Dance it with me."

Polly stumbled, trying to keep up with him, but he didn't relinquish her hand. "You're doing fine. Now let's try a few formations."

In rapid succession he taught her how to lead down the middle, turn by the right and the left, and dance back to back. Then he made up a dance using those formations and talked her through it. And finally he seized her right hand in his right and they danced the skip change of step all around the top of the cliff. Polly caught dizzying glimpses of the sea below as they danced in a circle, exchanging delighted glances.

At last, winded, he drew them both to a stop. "Too bad we didn't have music to dance to. Did you enjoy that?"

"Oh, yes, it was fun." She'd been a little overwhelmed, trying to absorb so much information, but now she felt a wild rush of joy. "Thank you so much, William Wallace!"

"It's Will, remember. Except around my father." He glanced at his watch. "I must go; Dad is expecting me to have dinner with him at the Mac an Righs and I'll need to shave and change." He plucked the cashmere sweater off the rock and knotted it casually around his shoulders. "Thank you for the tea, Polly."

"Thank you for the dancing lesson."

"You're welcome. Remember to practice the steps, preferably in front of a mirror. You'll need more lessons, of course; we've just begun with the formations and we haven't worked on the strathspey at all. You'll like that; women always like the strathspey. Friday afternoon? Afterwards I'll take you to dinner at the Rose. No, Dad will be eating there and that will be awkward; we'd have to ask him to join us. I'd prefer it just be the two of us; we can talk more comfortably."

He was actually asking her for a date. No, he was telling her they were going to go out together. Stunned, Polly managed to say, "There's a pizza place in Airgead that I saw advertised in *The Island Star*."

"Right. I'll come by at four-thirty and we'll have Scottish country dance practice, then we'll go for pizza. Goodbye, Polly."

"Good bye, Will. It's been a lovely afternoon." He nodded his assent. And it had, she mused, watching him climb into the rental car and drive away. There'd been a few glitches and awkward moments, but on the whole it had gone quite well. She'd even managed to put on a proper Scottish tea without making any horrendous mistakes.

And he'd asked her for a date. She hugged that knowledge to herself as she went in to wash dishes in the huge old sink. Somehow the kitchen seemed much more comfortable and welcoming than it had before, and the doorstep hadn't been as chilly. She sang "Loch Lomond" – it was the only Scottish song she could remember all the words to – as she washed, rinsed and stacked dishes to dry on the board at the end of the sink.

She'd eat the leftovers from tea for her supper with a glass of wine and read a book until time to go to bed. Her meal had been a success and she was getting to know an attractive man. Yes, he was bossy and opinionated, but that just made him more fun to cross verbal swords with.

And wonder of wonders, he'd asked her for a date, a real one, for dinner. Whatever was she going to wear? Better get to work on that spot on the white blouse.

It was quite the nicest day she'd spent so far on Eilean Dubh.

Part III

Spirit Visitations

Eleven

Nay, every lone tenement, castle, or mansion-house which could boast of any antiquity had its bogle, its specter, or its knocker. The churches, churchyards, and crossroads were all haunted. Every green lane had its boulder-stone on which an apparition kept watch at night. Every common had its circle of fairies belonging to it. And there was scarcely a shepherd to be met with who had not seen a spirit!

D. L. Ashliman

Bam! Bam! Bam! Polly woke up that night to a heavy pounding on the door. Alarmed, she groped for her watch and studied the illuminated dial. It was midnight. Who on earth could be knocking at that hour? She slipped out of bed, shrugged on her slippers for protection against the cold stone floor, and crept to the window. She cracked the curtains a bit and tried to look through, but quickly realized that she could not see the front door; the three-foot sill was too deep and the angle was wrong.

Bam! Bam! Bam! The knocking came again.

She tiptoed cautiously to the door. Could she see anything through the keyhole? Carefully she removed the key and bent to look through the hole, and almost collapsed from shock when the knocking erupted a third time just above her head, even louder and more vigorous: BAM! BAM! BAM!

Her involuntary movement took her several feet from the door and she realized that she had not seen anything through the keyhole; it was too dark outside. She sneaked back to the door and placed her ear against it.

It was too thick; she could hear nothing. Shaking in her shoes, Polly made a decision. She was a woman all alone in the middle of nowhere, and she was not going to open the door to someone knocking fiercely in the middle of the night. The knocker might be a burglar, a rapist, a vampire, even a zombie. Or a werewolf. The idea of confronting a werewolf in this desolate house on this deserted road made the hair on the back of her neck prickle.

An even more horrible thought came to her. Would whoever it was try to get in the window? She shuddered. If only she had a telephone! She should arm herself for protection. She made her cautious way through the darkness to the fireplace and picked up the poker. Standing in the middle of the room, she brandished the poker bravely, then realized that the bedroom window was the most vulnerable; it was slightly bigger than the ones in the living room and conceivably could be breached. She hugged the wall for support and slipped back into the bedroom to crouch in a defensive posture next to the window.

She realized suddenly that there was no sign of light coming through the curtains, nor had she seen any when she peered through the keyhole. Wouldn't a midnight visitor have a flashlight? She'd marveled at times how black the Island night was, with no warm glow from cottage windows, street lamps or headlights. Who could be outside her door demanding entrance, with no friendly beam to show the way through the darkness?

As if in answer to her thought, a sudden light illuminated the area. Polly shrank back in alarm until she realized that the moon must have come out from behind a cloud. It was full tonight and it would illuminate brightly the land below. She leaned again into the window and pulled the curtains slightly open so she could peek out. Perhaps the person knocking had stepped away from the door and she could get a glimpse from the window.

She saw nothing.

She opened the curtains a little further and pressed her face up against the window, straining to see the front door. She was almost sure there was nobody there, and the last knock had come some minutes ago. Presumably the knocker had left.

Did she dare open the door?

The answer to that was easy: no, she did not dare.

She was suddenly very cold, so cold that she was shivering, and she could even see puffs of her breath in the air, like in Minnesota in winter. The upward draft from beneath the window frame was freezing her ankles and feet up through her flimsy slippers. She pulled the curtains back together and edged her way to the bed. She placed the poker on the floor beside her and got in, suddenly frozen all the way through. The chill made her pull up the covers over her nose, grateful for the summer blanket on the bed. She left her ears exposed so that she could hear any further scary disturbance.

In that position, she fell asleep.

She awoke the next morning with a crick in her neck and anxiety gnawing at the back of her mind, unexplained until she remembered the knocking on her door the night before. Thinking about it in broad daylight, she felt foolish for not having answered the knock. Probably it had been someone with car trouble who thought she'd have a telephone. Or a hiker who'd gotten lost and wanted permission to pitch a tent on her grass. Or perhaps it had been a medical emergency, and she'd callously ignored it.

Maybe it had been a bad dream. Yes, that's what it had been, a nightmare. That thought cheered her until she sat up and swung her legs to the floor, and her toes touched the poker. It had really happened.

She dressed and approached the front door, reluctant to open it. What if someone had collapsed and died on her front steps, all because of her cowardice?

She pulled the door open slowly in an agony of suspense.

All around her was the soft, warm atmosphere of Eilean Dubh in springtime. The blast of cold air from the step hovered in the background like distant fog.

There was no dead body on her steps. There was no broken-down car on the road in front. There was no lost hiker's tent pitched in her grass. There was not even a footprint in the dirt walk that led up to the cottage. There was, in fact, no sign that anyone had been at her door last night.

Except that there was a smeary patch of dried brown seaweed to the left of the door. Seaweed? Had that been there before?

Who had been at the door, and what had he, or she, or it wanted?

A truly unpleasant thought wormed its way into her mind. The cottage had been empty for a while before she arrived; Anna Wallace's husband had told her that when she'd called from Minneapolis so long ago. Did someone know that a woman alone had rented the place and come looking for her after midnight, someone who wanted to frighten her or worse?

The only person she knew of who fit that bill was William Wallace MacDonald.

No, it was impossible; he was much too straight-laced and sober for such a caper. Nor did he seem the kind of man to try to take advantage of a woman alone. Should she ask him and risk offense? The idea was ludicrous. She put it out of her mind.

She thought about calling Sally MacDonald for her opinion but something made her shy away from that idea. She didn't want people thinking she was eccentric or that she had bad dreams that she misinterpreted as reality. And what would be the first question someone would ask her? It had occurred to her in mid-morning. "Did you call the police?"

"Did you call the police?" asked William Wallace, when she related the incident to him while they waited for their pizza at MacShannock's in Airgead on Friday night, two days after her midnight visitor.

"No." She had not meant to tell him or anyone else about the visitation, but somehow it had slipped out.

"Why not?"

"It never occurred to me. Anyway, I don't have a phone. I would have had to go down the road to the telephone box, and I wasn't about to go outside the cottage in the middle of the night with a zombie or a werewolf on the loose in my front yard. Besides, the telephone box is full of spiders; I won't go near it unless I can see what's lurking where I'm about to put my hand."

"You don't have much of a gift for self-preservation, Polly. Someone hammers at your door in the middle of the night and all you do is crawl back into bed. Suppose that person had tried to get in through the window."

"I had my poker," said Polly defiantly.

He snorted. "Fat lot of good that would do you. Any criminal worth his salt would have gotten that off you in no time at all."

Chagrined, Polly said, "Anyway, nobody knocked last night, which is sort of a comfort." She played with her water glass, annoyed at the scolding.

"You should have called me the very next day to do something about it," he said, his concern so evident that she immediately dismissed the fantasy that he had been the midnight knocker. He opened his mouth to say something else and the pizza arrived, interrupting his train of thought. They ate for a bit, then he said, in his usual subject-hopping way, "This pizza is quite good; I understand the sausage is locally made. I think you should contact the constable. His name is MacRath."

"How do you know that?"

"Dad and I were introduced to him one day at the Rose. He's the only cop on the Island, which I suppose means that there isn't much crime here. Which makes your midnight of the full moon visitor even more puzzling."

"It's not a crime to knock on someone's door at night, and I'm not going to bother the constable about something that happened too long ago for him to do anything about," said Polly crossly as a man and a woman stopped by the table.

The woman said, "Hullo! How are you, Polly Gillespie? Remember me? I'm Anna Wallace. I met you at the dock in Airgead. This is my husband, Zach Trelawney, who set up your rental. Are you having a nice holiday? How are you finding the cottage?"

"Fine," began Polly, but William Wallace intervened, rising and extending his hand to Zach. "Hi, I'm Will MacDonald and Polly's cottage is not fine. In fact, she's had a bit of a fright. If you have a minute, sit down and she'll tell you about it."

"I'm sure you don't have time," Polly stammered, her innate shyness rising to the top like cream on fresh milk.

"We do, don't we, love?" Zach Trelawney, ever curious, glanced at his equally curious wife who nodded. The two of them pulled out chairs and sat down. "What's up?"

Polly told her story quickly and without embellishment. Spoken aloud for the second time, the incident seemed even more alarming, and her actions even more stupid. Anna and Zach looked at her, then at each other.

"Did you call the constable?" asked Anna, predictably.

"The knocking stopped and she thought whoever it was had gone, so there would be nothing the police could do," said William Wallace smoothly. Polly looked at him gratefully; put that way, her actions seemed perfectly logical.

"Nonetheless, I think the constable would like to know about it," said Zach. "I can't imagine any Islander would get up to something as nasty as trying to frighten a woman alone in a cottage, miles away from everyone."

Polly shuddered at the memory. She had, indeed, been very frightened. "Unless it was someone in trouble. That's what's worrying me that I should have helped an injured or distressed person." She had finally felt relaxed enough to confide her deepest fear.

"I haven't heard of any problems along that stretch of the road," said Anna, shaking her head, "and all information comes to me eventually, because I collect it for the newspaper. Though I really don't know why because every *Eilean Dubhannach* over the age of ten spreads gossip as efficiently as I spread butter on a scone. If something had happened, I would have had a dozen phone calls the next morning with callers dying to find out if I knew more than they did."

"Could it have been a previous owner?" said Polly suddenly.

"Why do you ask that?" said Anna.

"I only thought that perhaps someone who'd once lived in the cottage passed by, saw my bike, and thought there'd been a break-in or kids or vandals or something like that, and decided to investigate."

"That is highly unlikely, not to say impossible," said Anna. "The last owner was Cailean Ferguson, a fisherman, and he died many years ago in a storm at sea. His body was never found. His widow died of grief two days after Cailean's ship was reported lost. There was no heir so the Council finally took over the cottage because it was crumbling away. They've looked after it ever since but haven't done much with it because they could never establish clear title. No one wanted to spend Council money on a property they weren't sure they owned. It's been rented once in a while but tenants have never stayed very long. It's gotten a bad reputation and I'm afraid the condition of the place is not conducive to long stays," she added, with an apologetic glance at Polly.

"My student assistants Megan and Stephen were there for several weeks," said Zach. "They never reported anything out of the ordinary happening."

"Because there was a man on the property," said William Wallace. "That would deter a mischief-maker."

"You have a touching faith in the power of masculinity," said Polly.

Anna chuckled. "Like all men. Besides, how would a mischief-maker know the cottage was inhabited only by a woman?"

"Simple," said William Wallace. "There was one bike outside and it was a girl's bike." He folded his arms and looked smug.

"Excellent deduction, Sherlock," said Zach Trelawney. "Anna, love, we must go so our friends can finish their dinner. Their pizza is getting cold."

As she rose, Anna said, "I'll have a snoop around and see what I can find out about the cottage. I'll drop by and let you know if I do." It was a promise she had no intention of keeping. She'd heard certain stories about the Ferguson cottage that she did not want to share with Polly. She thought the American was already spooked enough by what had happened, and it wouldn't help her at all to hear gossip about other-worldly events, real or imaginary, anywhere on the Island.

"Thanks," said Polly to Anna's retreating back. She didn't care who suggested it; she wasn't going to bother the police with something that had happened two nights ago. Constable MacRath would laugh at her, and she hated being laughed at.

Besides, Will's easy deduction annoyed her. "Suppose there *was* a man here and he stored his bicycle round the back? Or walked everywhere?"

"In which case, he'd be in great shape to deal with an invader."

"In which case, the invader would have ignored my front door for fear of meeting a well-developed, fit man who could smash him to smithereens."

"You can't smash something that's living into smithereens. The term only applies to inanimate objects, like vases." Will, sure he'd gotten the last word, picked up a piece of pizza and took a bite.

Polly said defiantly, "It's my story, and I'll smash anything in it I want into smithereens." And she took the last piece of pizza.

Zach, on the way out, hissed in Anna's ear, "Are those two a couple?"

"Don't know. Why?"

"They bicker just like a couple does. Like we do."

Anna decided to snub him for that remark, and walked on with her nose in the air. She never bickered; that wasn't dignified. If she had a problem she discussed it with him calmly and quietly.

Twelve

*On looking at a Scottish Country dance, the first thing that should
be noticed is the expression of happy enjoyment on the faces and
in the movements of the dancers. After all, dancing is a joyous
thing . . .*

Jean C. Milligan

*W*ill arrived on the following Monday for more Scottish country
dance lessons to help Polly get ready for the *cèilidh* on Friday. He
was determined to make a good dancer out of her; he'd taken her on as a
personal project. "I've got a present for you," he said, with an air of suppressed excitement.

"You'd better come in," said Polly, wondering what he was up to.

Once inside with the two of them seated on the sofa, he handed her
a brown paper parcel. Inside was a pair of what looked like ballet slippers.
They were made of thin black leather and their long laces went all the way
up the front of the shoe from the toe to wrap around the ankle and up
the calf. Polly looked at them, then at Will, and said, "Thank you. What
are they?"

"Ghillies," he said in triumph. "I ordered them for you by phone from
James Senior's shop in St. Andrews on the Scottish mainland, and they
mailed them to me."

"But what *are* they?"

"They're Scottish country dance shoes."

Polly examined them carefully. "How did you know what size I
wear?"

He looked abashed. "The other day when you were in the kitchen I
sneaked into the bedroom and looked inside a pair of your shoes."

Polly was speechless with embarrassment for a minute, wondering
what might have been lying around in her bedroom that she would rather

a casual acquaintance, especially a male one, not see. Probably lots of stuff. She finally pulled herself together enough to say, "That's very thoughtful. How did you get them so quickly?"

"I ordered express shipping, so they've already flown once on the helicopter, breaking them in for you. Now you'll have to fly in them when you dance. I thought about asking Jean or Sally if either of them had a pair you could borrow, but then I decided you should have new ones to celebrate being a new dancer. You need ghillies because you can't dance properly in street shoes."

"I should pay you for them," she began.

"I told you they were a present," he said firmly. "For my best pupil. A reward for working hard and catching on so fast."

"I have a good teacher," she said with a smile.

"I enjoy it. I passed my preliminary exam as an SCD teacher a few years ago, but decided not to go on for the full certificate; I didn't have time because of school. Enough talk, let's get to work."

"Shall I put on the shoes . . . uh, ghillies?"

"Good Lord, no. Not to dance outside. That would ruin them. They're for dancing in a ballroom, or, in this case, in the Citizens Hall."

Properly admonished, Polly followed him meekly outside, and under his tutelage she added the strathspey setting and traveling steps to her repertoire, along with two more formations, the poussette and the allemande. "I can't teach you these properly without another couple to dance with us," Will fretted, "but at least you can learn the pattern."

Afterwards she fixed a spaghetti dinner, using a bottled sauce she'd bought at the Co-Op. It was well received by her guest but Polly felt that somehow she was cheating, serving bakery products she'd bought and using prepared mixes. I really must learn to cook, she told herself, and decided that might be fun as long as she had someone to cook for. Will wasn't the least bit uptight about food, she'd realized with relief; he was happy to eat whatever she put before him. It did not seem in keeping with the rest of his starchy personality, but perhaps she'd just been feeding him at times when he was really hungry. (And her simple meals were a welcome, relaxing change for Will from the elegant cuisine of the Rose Hotel, but Polly didn't know that.)

In addition to the shoes, that night she received another gift. Will asked her to be his date for dinner Wednesday night at Darroch and

Jean Mac an Rìgh's cottage, where his father would also be a guest. In her wildest dreams of Eilean Dubh she had never envisioned being seated at the Laird's table. Her eyes widened at the invitation, she stammered, and almost declined out of awe and shyness. She managed to say, "Are you sure they'd want me?"

Will said, "I asked if I could bring you and Jean said that would be grand; she'd been meaning to call round to your cottage and invite you over. So you have to come; I promised you would." And that is the end of that, his manner implied.

She fretted all the next day over what she should wear. She didn't have a big wardrobe back home in Minneapolis; she'd never been able to afford it, and she'd always been one to worry about whether or not she was properly dressed for an event. She usually wasn't; she was usually too fussy or too casual, whatever the occasion.

She'd not brought to Eilean Dubh the few pieces she considered her "best" clothes, because not even in her dreams did she think she'd have an occasion to wear them. But an invitation from the Laird and his wife demanded something other than jeans and tee shirts. Why had she brought those knit skirts instead of summery ones?

Fortunately, Wednesday turned out to be rainy with a stiff wind blowing off the ocean and unseasonably cold for June, so she wore a blue knit skirt, a matching cotton sweater and the short-sleeved white blouse she'd had to cover up the day of the tea party. She'd attacked the spot and removed it with dishwashing detergent and then pressed the blouse to within an inch of its life with the ancient iron she'd found in the cottage, an after-thought to its refurbishment contributed by Barabal Mac-a-Phi, who always paid heed to the niceties of homemaking.

But she didn't have a lick of jewelry to wear except for inexpensive earrings and a little gold ring set with a garnet that her mother had given her when she turned sixteen. She did not realize it, but her simple outfit fit in with the culture of Eilean Dubh, where money to splurge on clothing and jewelry was not readily available. Tidy, not gaudy, was the watchword when Islanders kitted themselves out for special events.

She was relieved to learn that Jean and Darroch's dinner party was informal and *en famille*, since it included Sally MacDonald, her husband Ian Mór, the doctor, and their twins, as well as the Mac an Rìgh children, ten-year-old Rosie and six-year-old Gaillean, neighbors Jamie and Màiri

MacDonald, and Robert Burns MacDonald. They were all to be seated around one table in the new sun room, a pleasant squeeze. To get to it, they had to go past a dog bed located on the floor just where the kitchen opened out into the sun room. It contained a small, shaggy dog with a tuft of cream-colored hair on top of its head and a pair of enormous round dark eyes that peered warily at the visitors. And with good reason for she was guarding two tiny puppies.

Polly loved dogs. It was one of the great regrets of her life that she'd never had one. She stopped, entranced, and forgetting her surroundings and her dignity, sank to her knees before the wee pups and their mother. She breathed out a long sign of pleasure, then looked up at Jean and asked, "May I touch them?"

"That depends on Cèilidh, the mamma. She's very careful about who comes near her babies."

Polly nodded, and extended her hand very slowly, palm upward, for Cèilidh to sniff. Which she did, and then gave it an approving flick from her pink tongue. Polly stroked the dog's head very gently and crooned to her, "What a lovely clever girl you are to have such darling twins."

"Twins must run in the family," observed Robert Burns MacDonald with a wink at Sally who grinned and looked possessively at her own pair propped up in baby seats at the table.

Polly asked, "Are the pups girls or boys or both? Have you named them?"

"One of each," said Rosie. "The girl, the mustard one, is Miss Petronella, Ella for short, and the boy, the pepper, is ET, which stands for Eye of the Tiger, named for their sire, Tiger. They're Dandie Dinmont terriers, a uniquely Scottish breed."

"Oh, how I wish I lived here and could buy one of the pups from you."

Rosie shook her head. "Sorry, they're both spoken for. They're a rare breed so puppies are reserved well in advance of whelping."

Polly sighed. "Oh, well, I couldn't take one home with me anyway. Why are the colors called mustard and pepper? Other than the fact that they're yellow and black."

Jean said, "It's from a book by Sir Walter Scott, and the breed is named for a character in it, Dandie Dinmont, a rough old farmer. They're the only dog in the world named for a literary character."

"Hmm, really Scottish," said Robert Burns MacDonald. "I'll have to get one of those. Maybe twins." He chuckled at his own joke.

William Wallace cleared his throat. "They're very cute, but enough puppy worship, Polly. I believe Mrs. Mac an Rìgh would like us all to sit down at the table."

"It's just Jean," said that individual, without much hope she'd be heeded. William Wallace was the starchiest character she'd ever met.

"Come along, just Jean," said Darroch, knowing what she was thinking, "It's time for dinner."

Polly, who normally loathed being bossed around, especially by William Wallace, accepted it this time without comment, but she took a moment to give each tiny pup a rub on the head before she rose to her feet. "See you later, darling puppies."

"Come and sit by me, Miss Polly," said Rosie. Anyone who liked dogs was automatically a friend of hers. "If that doesn't upset your table, Mama," she added.

"No, no, that's fine," said Jean, ushering everyone into the sun room ahead of her.

Polly thought the room was lovely; Rosie, Cèilidh and the pups were wonderful; and the Laird's wife was really nice, an outgoing, friendly American from Milwaukee, a Midwesterner like herself. And as she remembered, Robert Burns MacDonald was a pleasant down to earth sort of guy. She couldn't be afraid of him. Though she was too shy to address many remarks to him, she smiled at his jokes.

Most exciting of all, she had gotten to meet the Laird, Darroch Mac an Rìgh. Her hands were wet with perspiration and her voice quavered when she had to say, "How do you do?" to him. He had a warm smile that went a long way toward making her feel at ease, and was possibly the most interesting-looking person she'd ever met, with his jet-black hair, long elegant nose, and amazingly blue eyes. He wasn't handsome, but he certainly was sexy.

She'd read in *Celebration of a Small Island* that he was an actor, but there was nothing the least bit flamboyant about his lean six-foot-three frame, and he was quite ordinarily dressed in a green turtleneck and dark trousers.

The next door neighbors, the couple who made up the other half of *Tradisean* folk group were introduced as Jamie and Màiri MacDonald,

Ian Mór's parents. Màiri was voluptuously curved, short of stature and beautiful, with long red-gold hair that nearly reached her waist. Jamie was the best-looking man that Polly had ever seen, even more gorgeous than his Greek god offspring Ian Mór. He was golden-haired, well built and sweet natured; when he smiled it was like the sun coming out from behind a cloud. She would not have been surprised if she'd been told that he was known on the Island as Bonnie Prince Jamie, a nickname bestowed upon him years ago by Darroch.

She was even more flustered after being introduced to him, which surprised none of the women present; it was a common reaction in the female sex. At last she recovered enough to say to both MacDonalds, "I enjoyed your music so much at the *cèilidh*."

"Do you like Scottish music?" asked Jamie, nearly destroying Polly with his sunrise smile.

She stammered, "Oh, yes. I have recordings but I've never heard it live before. It was wonderful."

"Do you dance Scottish?" asked Màiri.

"I'm learning," she said, with a shy glance at William Wallace.

He said, "I'm teaching her. She's got the steps down and we're working on the formations. There's a few that are difficult to teach with only the two of us, though."

"Perhaps we could walk you through those after dinner," said Darroch kindly.

But they were all so busy talking that they ran out of time for dancing. Children and puppies had to be put to bed, Ian Mór had an early call at the surgery the next day, and Will liked to see his father retire at a reasonable hour for his health's sake. Polly was relieved; it gave her the shivers to think of dancing even in practice with tall, gorgeous Darroch, the famous actor, or his handsome friend Bonnie Prince Jamie. She'd be sure to trip over her own feet or step on her partner's and flub any instructions given her by Will. She felt faint, just thinking about everything that could and probably would go wrong.

But Darroch and Jamie weren't liable to ask her to dance at the *cèilidh*; they'd be busy with their own friends, so she didn't have to worry about that. And she had plenty to think about, after her introduction to all the interesting people at the dinner table, and the sweet pups and their mama. She'd stay out of sight, lay low, and no one would notice her.

Certainly, knowing that she was a beginner, no one but Will would ask her to partner him, and he'd pick out a dance that she could do with ease. She had nothing to worry about.

She hoped.

Thirteen

There are shortcuts to happiness, and dancing is one of them.

Vicki Baum

But Friday night at the *cèilidh* all her shyness came back in a rush and her misgivings took center stage, when Darroch presented himself in front of her and requested that she partner him in the next dance. Always the gentleman, he made it his responsibility to dance with new dancers and with ladies sitting alone on the sidelines. Seeing Polly hesitate – she'd successfully negotiated one dance with Will as her partner, and she thought it would take her a week to recuperate from the terror that had induced in her – he coaxed, "This one is quite easy. It's called 'Kendall's Hornpipe.'"

Drat, where was Will when she needed him? Each dance had its own set of formations, and his encyclopedia knowledge of Scottish country dances would tell him if she'd learned the formations necessary to successfully perform the dance. But he was standing in a just-forming set with Jean Mac an Rìgh as his partner. Newly knowledgeable about Scottish country dance etiquette that decreed a lady should never turn down a partner without good reason ("like a broken leg," Will had said), she gave her hand to Darroch and let him lead her into the set, her mouth dry, her heart pounding.

The set included Will and Jean, and judging by the look of horror Will gave her, it was one she should not be in. She looked at Darroch pleadingly. "I'm afraid I don't know this dance," she said.

Will shook his head, an indication to Polly to brazen it out. He'd taught her two basic Scottish country dance rules. "Never refuse an offer to dance, and then dance that same dance with someone else." And, "Never leave a set once you're in it, unless you're dying of some hideous contagious disease," he'd told her. Remembering the rules, she added hastily, "But I'm willing to try it," with a bright phony smile at her partner.

"You'll do fine," said Darroch cheerfully, with the supreme confidence of someone who'd been dancing for donkey's years and had unlimited faith in his ability to see himself and his partner through.

But the dance began with a two-couple formation Polly had never seen before: rights and lefts. She tried to watch with care what the couples above them in the set were doing, but got hopelessly confused. As a result, when it came their turn to dance as second couple, she looked in desperation at Darroch for cues, just as Will had instructed her. "You're not flying solo," he'd said. "Always pay attention to your partner."

"Cross by the right," Darroch said, thrusting out his hand, "and take Jean's left hand with your left." "Don't turn," whispered Jean, as Polly whirled outward away from her. She whipped back, changed places with Jean and started to twirl away into outer space again. Just in time she saw Darroch extending his hand to cross with her again. "Me now," said Jean quickly and turned Polly back into her place as second woman.

"That wasn't so bad, was it," called Jean, as she and Will joined right hands to lead down the set past the other couples. "And you did fine," she added as they swept by Polly.

Yes, she had done all right, Polly thought with pleasure. Maybe there wasn't a lot of style and grace in her dancing yet, but she hadn't completely messed up. She was so suddenly self-confident that when she was faced a few minutes later with another new formation, the ladies' chain, she let herself relax, followed the whispered cues and returned safely back to place with only one small bobble. Her face was lit with such a broad smile of happiness that the others in the set looked at her, then at each other, and then they chuckled.

"Another convert to Scottish country dancing," said Will, with pride in his pupil evident in his voice.

"No, just a survivor," said Polly chirpily. "It must be the effect of my new ghillies," and she put her left foot forward. The entire set laughed.

Fourteen

*. . . . feel assured, that there is no such thing as forgetting
possible to the mind; a thousand accidents may, and will,
interpose a veil between our present consciousness and the secret
inscriptions on the mind; accidents of the same sort will also
rend away this veil; but alike, whether veiled or unveiled, the
inscription remains forever . . .*

Thomas De Quincey

Shyness despite her successes so far still ruled Polly. As she grew more
confident about her dancing, she grew more self-conscious about her
clothes. Having the right thing to wear was always a preoccupation, as she
never had enough money to dress the way she would have liked, or that
she thought was in style. She could not wear the same skirt and blouse
to the next *cèilidh*; she'd convinced herself of that, despite the fact that
the other women attending were not conspicuously dressed up. Nor did
she realize that most of them had only one special outfit and wore it for
every *cèilidh*.

She would spend a bit of her hoarded money on a new top; that would
freshen up her look. The next week she shopped in both the Co-Op and
Deidre's Ladies Wear store in Ros Mór, and was confronted with old-
fashioned, vividly floral patterned blouses and tweed skirts more suitable
for women in their fifties than for her twenty-six-year-old self. Clearly
Ros Mór was not the fashion capital of the Hebrides. Desperate as she
was, she could not bring herself to dig into her precious stash of cash to
buy clothes that made her look dowdy and middle-aged.

So the pretty clothes that an attractive older woman was wearing at
the *cèilidh* two weeks later caught her eye: a soft blue short-sleeved shirt
with a delicate pattern of pink roses, and a denim skirt that flared becom-
ingly around her legs as she danced. Polly was sitting out a dance Will had
declared too hard for her to attempt, so she was able to study the other
woman with great interest. When the dance ended, she contrived to be
on the sidelines near her. A need for information overcame her shyness

and she stepped forward. "Hi," she said. "I just wanted to say what a pretty outfit you're wearing."

The other was a little taken aback, in her reserved Scottish way, by a compliment from a total stranger. But she recognized a newcomer to the Island and replied politely, "Thanks very much. I don't think we've met. My name is Barabal Mac-a-Phi."

"I'm Polly Gillespie."

"Oh, you're our new American," said Barabal. "I've been meaning to come by and introduce myself, and see how you are doing in the old Ferguson cottage. Are you enjoying your holiday on the Island?"

By now Polly recognized that as the standard conversational gambit of all Islanders to visitors, and she said, "Very much, thank you."

"How do you like the cottage? I'm afraid it's plain as a pikestaff and twice as ugly, but we tried to tart it up a wee bittie."

"Oh, it's fine. Very comfortable," Polly lied, and quickly got back to business before she was forced to confess her dissatisfaction with her little house's deficiencies. "I hope you don't mind my asking, but where do you buy your clothes? I can't find anything nearly as nice in the shops here."

"My mother makes them. She's a retired seamstress. Well, retired in practice but not in spirit. She came to live with us in our son Somhairle's room when he got married and moved out, and she's desperate to help out around the house, to earn her keep, she says. As if she needed to do that, for heaven's sake. She's my mother and more than welcome to share our home.

"But the arthritis in her knees is so bad she can't do housework and she can scarcely endure standing long enough to cook dinner. Her hands aren't affected, thank goodness, so she went back to sewing and makes clothes for my daughters and me. Mind you, I'm not sure the girls appreciate her work; they prefer jeans and tee shirts with peculiar sayings on them. But I certainly do. Appreciate her sewing, I mean." Barabal took a deep breath, wondering why she'd been so garrulous. Probably because the girl was hanging on her every word.

Polly clasped her hands together in entreaty. "Is there any chance . . . do you think . . . would she make something for me? I'd be glad to pay her."

Barabal cocked her head to one side and surveyed the young woman before making her decision. After all, sewing kept her mother happy and busy and she would love to have a new customer to sew for, especially a pretty young woman like this one and a new American to boot, someone to chat with and tell stories. Her last order had been for the Mac an Rìghs' drapes, and although she'd loved working with the fabric and the pattern, she'd said that sewing curtains bored her silly and she much preferred making clothes, where she could use a bit of creativity and imagination. Barabal said, "Why don't you come over one day and ask her?"

"I'd love to! Would tomorrow be okay?"

The other woman smiled at her eagerness. "Of course. Around three? After you and Mama have talked, we'll have a nice cup of tea and get better acquainted."

"Where do you live?"

"We're the second croft north of you, towards Airgead."

"I'll be there," promised Polly, the eagerly anticipated new clothes quite overriding her customary dread of meeting new people and her caution about dipping into her horde of money.

She presented herself promptly at three at Barabal's cottage the next day and was ushered into the presence of Elspeth Mac-a-Phi, an elderly woman with white hair, bright eyes and a lively expression. "*Tha mi toili-cht' d'fhaicinn,*" she said, extending her hand.

"Miss Gillespie's an American, Mama; she won't have the Gaelic," said Barabal.

"Oh, aye, I was forgetting that. I was just saying that it's pleased I am to see you, Miss Gillespie."

"Please call me Polly," she said, clasping the other woman's small, strong hand.

"Such a pretty name and there is no Gaelic equivalent. You may be calling me Elspeth." With the formalities dispensed with, Elspeth said, "How am I to help you?"

"I hope you'll do some sewing for me. I'd love to have a couple of pretty skirts and tops like those you made for Barabal."

"Aye, I can chust be doing that. Will we take your measurements then? Barabal, measure the young lady's length; I can't get down on my knees anymore for that. How long do you wear your skirts, Polly, *m'eudail*? And will I be putting elastic in the waistbands in case you gain weight on our good Island cooking? Which you need to do because you're spare as a wild hare, as we say here."

Polly laughed. "I'm doing my own cooking and it's not something I'm liable to gain weight on, because I'm pretty hopeless in the kitchen." She submitted to being measured. Then she and Elspeth settled down to discuss patterns, fabrics and prices while Barabal went to the kitchen to make tea.

Sharing a cup later, Polly said to Barabal, "I appreciate all you did in getting the cottage ready for me to rent. Anna Wallace told me how hard you all worked on it."

"Do you truly like the place?"

"It's . . . ah . . . cozy."

Barabal laughed. "You needn't fear I'll mind if you criticize it, *m'eudail*, for I know well its failings, having worked with little success to minimize them before you moved in. I'm afraid it's not what you are used to, being from America."

"What, is she not staying at the Rose, then, like the other Americans?" asked Elspeth.

"No, Mama, she's renting the old Ferguson cottage."

"That place!" She clicked her tongue in surprise. "Is it still standing? I would have thought it had crumbled away years ago, from sheer ugliness." Turning to Polly, she demanded, "Have you seen any sign of the ghostie?"

"What ghostie?" gasped Polly.

"Now, Mama, don't be telling your stories and alarming the girl."

"No," said Polly hastily. "Don't stop, because I've encountered something strange and if you can explain it, I'd be very grateful." She told the women about the three knocks on the door in the middle of the night.

"*Dè seòrsa rud a th'ann? Dè 'n coltas a tha'air?*" said Elspeth, forgetting her English in her excitement, then hastily translating, "I mean, what sort of thing is it? What does it look like?"

"I don't know, I haven't seen it," said Polly, "but it certainly has a loud knock."

Elspeth nodded her head and settled into what Barabal recognized, with a sigh, as her storytelling mode. She picked up the pot and went into the kitchen to make fresh tea; her mother's stories tended to be both fascinating and lengthy. When she came back into the lounge, Elspeth was saying, "And as the story goes, Cailean Ferguson came back from the deep cold sea to look for his Peigi, who died of grief two days after she heard of his drowning. But no one's ever seen him, at least that they'll admit to." She leaned forward. "So you didn't open the door to him when he knocked."

Polly shuddered. Had she been only a door away from a real live ghost, no, a ghostie? She was bluntly, abruptly confronted with the idea she'd been resisting for days. "I was much too frightened."

"That's a sensible girl to be frightened of a spirit for they are unpredictable. They do say . . ." She paused, uncertain as to whether to continue.

"What do they say?" demanded Polly. "I really need to know."

"They say that there's no way of being sure what a ghostie will be doing if it is meeting a human being. It might vanish or it might hold its ground or it might grow angry and attack."

"Nonsense," said Barabal, observing that Polly was looking a little white, and determined to reassure her. There was no point in scaring her so badly she wouldn't want to return to the Ferguson cottage. "A ghostie can't attack a human. There's no substance to them, they're made of air, or something like that."

"How many ghosties have you seen, *a Bharabal*?" demanded the old lady tartly.

"None, and I'd like to keep it that way, for I don't believe in them and would hate to be forced to change my mind."

"I don't believe in ghosties, either," said Polly, hoping that she meant what she was saying. "Not that I doubt your word, Elspeth. But I'm sure there's a rational explanation for what people think of as haunted houses and spooky visitations."

"I am hoping that you are right, *m'eudail*," said Elspeth with a shake of her head that signified she believed just the opposite.

"If it was a real ghostie," said Barabal skeptically, "why didn't it just walk through the door? Why did it knock?"

Elspeth said, "Ah, there will be a reason for that. The story is that Cailean and Peigi had a terrible argument one evening and she threw him out and locked the door against him. Folks saw him pounding away all night, bam! bam! bam! And never an inch would Peigi give in and never would she open up to him no matter how loudly he yelled or how hard he knocked. So in a rare old fury he marched away the next morning down to the dock at Airgead and signed onto a fishing boat so decrepit it never should have been on the water, let alone out in a gale. When the storm blew up, the crew had no chance of surviving it."

Elspeth drew herself up, looked around at both her listeners, and nodded her head wisely. "And that's the reason he knocks, to get his Peigi to be opening the door because it's locked to him, even in the afterlife. But she was dead of heartsickness, and probably also a touch of the consumption, for her family was always chesty."

"So the idea is that he won't rest till he finds her," Barabal said, nodding her head solemnly. Privately she considered it all nonsense, but was unwilling to say so to her mother; that would be disrespectful.

Polly looked stricken, so pale that Barabal thought she might faint. She poured a fresh cup of tea, added extra milk and sugar for medicinal reasons and urged it and the plate of cookies on her guest. She put her qualms about offending her mother aside and said, "Now that's just a silly old story, Polly, an old wives' tale. And yes, Mama, you are an old wife, and it is only a tale. You mustn't tell it as true."

"You weren't there when he came knocking," Polly muttered, taking a calming sip of her tea.

Biking the short distance home, recovered enough from her fright to think logically, Polly turned over in her mind what she'd learned. A drowned fisherman had come seeking his wife, who'd died of grief (and tuberculosis) because she hadn't forgiven her man and so had caused the impetuous act that resulted in his death. Sounded like a recipe for a very unhappy, cranky ghostie, one that might howl and moan and clank the chains of an anchor since he'd been a seafaring man. Not one who'd knock on a door and then saunter away casually. And leave a blast of frigid air behind him.

And seaweed.

The whole idea was preposterous. There must be another explanation, if she could only think of it.

Fifteen

A house is never still in darkness to those who listen intently; there is a whispering in distant chambers, an unearthly hand presses the snib of the window, the latch rises.

J.M. Barrie

*B*ut she couldn't come up with an alternative explanation a couple of weeks later when the terrifying knocking on the door came again at midnight on the evening of the full moon. Bam! Bam! Bam! She bolted out of bed, forgetting her slippers and leaping in shock at her first contact with the frigid stone floor. She crept close to the door and waited until the knocking came for the second time.

Bam! Bam! Bam!

Did she dare open the door? She couldn't decide. She took the big old-fashioned key off its hook and stood in front of the door, debating what to do. Could there really be something unearthly outside? If it were a ghostie, would it disappear or would it attack? Would it speak to her? Could her heart stand the sight of it, whatever it was and whatever it did and whatever it said?

She dithered, shaking with fear.

Abruptly she heard a scraping noise in the vicinity of the keyhole. She bent down to listen, then straightened up in shock. Apparently whatever it was had lost patience, for a key was being inserted into the lock. The hair rose on her scalp; she could feel it going straight up. Babbling aloud "No, no, no," in terror, she grabbed her own key, inserted it into the lock, and knocked the intruding one out. She heard, faintly, a clink as it hit the doorstep. She jammed her key in as far as it would go.

The knocking came for the third time just above her head, much, much louder: BAM! BAM! BAM! She gathered enough courage to press her ear against the door, straining to hear any hints of ghostly moaning or chains rattling. There was no further sound, just the knocking and the clink of the key against the stone doorstep. How amazing had it been that she'd heard *that* through the thickness of the door?

A ferociously frigid draft poured from under the door. She was cold now, very cold, as she'd been the first time she'd heard the knocking, and her bare feet were icy slivers. She went on tiptoes into the bedroom and found her slippers, then sneaked to the window to peer out through the crack in the curtains. The moon was even brighter than the last time, and it shone down on a landscape completely empty of anything animate.

What had it been, that thing at her door, and where had it gone?

Absolutely freezing, she got into bed, crawled down under the covers, and curled up as small as she could make herself, but it was ages before she thawed out and even longer before she fell asleep. And even after she slept her feet throbbed with cold and she dreamed about being lost, barefoot, in a howling Minnesota blizzard, pursued by a creature that was like something out of a horror movie.

The next morning the layer of cold air that enveloped the front door was so thick and heavy she could almost touch it. Shivering, she found outside by the step an overturned rock, and on the rock was a large, old-fashioned brass key, its luster dulled by a thick coating of what looked like a combination of rust, dirt and salt.

It was a perfect duplicate of hers, and it was icy cold in her hands.

It made her teeth chatter and not from the cold.

Part IV

Kindred Spirits

Sixteen

Gravity is a contributing factor in nearly 73 percent of all accidents involving falling objects.

Dave Barry

Polly was on her way to the shops in Ros Mór two days later when, distracted by ghostly worries, she hit the dreaded curve in the road too fast. She braked, skidded and ended in a heap in the ditch, the bicycle on its side above her, spinning its wheels, her frightened yelp still ringing in her ears. She lay dazed, trying to decide whether or not she was hurt, hoping no one had seen her fall, and cursing her clumsiness.

A car braked behind her. A door opened. She heard, "Hullo, Polly, are you all right?"

She looked up into the concerned face of Darroch Mac an Rìgh. Oh, hell and damnation. Not only had she made a fool of herself by crashing her bike, she'd done it in front of the Laird, the most important person on the Island. What could be more embarrassing than that? Was he laughing at her, concealing his chuckles behind a concerned face? "I'm fine," she mumbled, and started to struggle to her feet.

Darroch put a hand on her shoulder and said comfortingly, "Steady on, take it easy. Give yourself a wee bit of time to recover. That was quite a tumble. Took the corner too fast, did you? Happened to me once when I was a youngster and I ended up in the ditch not far from where you're lying. Totaled the bike, too. My Da had a few choice words to say about that."

An elderly pickup truck headed their way pulled over and a man got out, this one with a crown of brilliant golden hair. Polly closed her eyes in chagrin. Not only the Laird had witnessed her disaster, Bonnie Prince Jamie, the most gorgeous man on the Island, had seen it, too. She wished fervently to disappear into the chilly depths of the ditch, which was as cold as her front doorstep, a fact she accepted with an odd foreboding.

"What's amiss?" said Jamie, hurrying to the scene of the accident.

"Polly crashed her bike on the curve."

"Oh, bad luck, did that myself years ago. Sprained something; I forget what, but I was damned uncomfortable sitting down for a couple of weeks. Are you hurt, love?"

Bonnie Prince Jamie had called her "love." She could die right now happy even though she was desperately embarrassed. "I think I'm okay," she said, and started to get up, hoping she hadn't torn any revealing holes in her clothing. "Careful now," said a deep voice, and two strong hands reached out, one from Darroch and one from Jamie, and slid under her arms, hoisting her up. The contact with two Eilean Dubh icons made her knees so weak she almost fell over. She righted herself with dignity, and tried to smile at her rescuers.

"Looks like you've done your knee," observed Jamie, and the attention of all three went to Polly's left leg, down which a stream of blood was trickling, heading for her sock.

"Do you think you've broken or strained anything? If that's the case, we should head for the surgery," Darroch said. "Best check that cut to start with."

There was no help for it, she had to lift her skirt and inspect the wounded area. Both men looked away discreetly. Polly was happy to report that the knee was only skinned. "It just needs to be cleaned and a Band Aid slapped on. No need for a doctor."

"Let's get you home, then. Jamie, you'll fetch the bike?"

"Aye." Before she knew what was happening, she found herself being escorted to Darroch's elegant old Bentley and tucked carefully inside, while Jamie picked up the bike and stowed it in the back of his pickup truck. Darroch turned the Bentley around and headed for the cottage.

Jamie followed him, frowning. There was something not quite right about that bend in the road, something cold that he'd never noticed before, and that gave him the heebie-jeebies. His son Ian Mór, the doctor, had mentioned a strange occurrence here late one evening a month or so ago, something about nearly falling asleep at the wheel and being saved from crashing over the cliff by an unearthly figure.

Jamie had shrugged it off as one of those unexplainable events he was only too familiar with on Eilean Dubh, but now he wondered. Whatever could be going on here? Had some new spook been set loose among the hapless *Eilean Dubhannaich*? Since it had presumably saved his son's life, it must not be malignantly inclined. He certainly hoped not. A malignant spirit was something to be both feared and dreaded.

Polly limped in through the door of the cottage on Darroch's arm, noticing in the back of her mind the absence of cold. In deference to the Laird? Did the Laird outrank the spirit? Was she crazy to be so preoccupied with the supernatural?

Darroch asked, "Have you got an Elastoplast for your cut?" Polly shook her head, baffled at the word. "The fixer-upper crew probably didn't think of that. I'll get the first aid kit from the car." He was back quickly, carrying a metal container with a large red cross on it. She twitched with nerves at the thought he might perform the Band Aid ritual himself, but he only said, "Use what you need and drop the kit off at *Taigh a' Mhorair* when it's convenient. Anything else we can do? Cup of tea, plate of toast, comforting words, bit of a singsong? I'd suggest a knees-up, but it wouldn't do your cut any good."

Polly giggled. "I don't think it would. Thank you for your help. I'd still be struggling up the hill all blood and dirt if you two hadn't come to my rescue."

Jamie, outside, stowed the bike against the cottage wall, having inspected it and pronounced it none the worse for its tumble. "Well made, these old contraptions," he said to himself then turned to go inside the cottage. He recoiled abruptly from the icy blast of Polly's doorstep. His bones got all prickly, an extension of the way he'd felt at the road's curve, the way they always did when there was major weirdness lurking about. *A Dhia beannaich mi*, something was up for sure. He stepped through the door, and said, just to have something to say to disguise his apprehension, "A bit chilly, isn't it."

"It's always cold around the door, sometimes so much that it gives me the shudders. I call it the Frozen Zone. It's not that bad inside," said Polly, having noted with interest his reaction. Since he'd noticed it, she was on the verge of telling him about her unknown visitor and asking for his opinion and advice when Darroch spoke in his matter-of-fact way.

"It's these old stone walls. They hold the cold even in the midst of a heat wave which we've never had on Eilean Dubh in living memory. Or legend, come to think of it. I'll build you a fire; that'll take the chill off of the cottage innards." He knelt by the fireplace and quickly had a brisk flame going.

Distracted, Polly said, "Oh, thank you. I have such a hard time getting a fire started, and then it usually goes out within ten minutes."

"No wonder, the fixer-uppers forgot to leave you any coal. Best stop by the petrol station or the Co-Op and buy a bag. The secret is to light a bit of peat, build a wall of peats around it, and when that gets going pop some coal on top. Makes a longer-lasting fire." He smiled at Polly. "I'll be on my way," he said and headed to the door. "Mind how you go on that road next time. Brake early and often on that curve."

"I will, for sure. Thanks again."

Jamie said, "I'm awa', too," and went out after Darroch, moving quickly through the doorway. He had a hunch Polly knew something odd was up and he didn't want to get involved in a wee chat about it. But it was worrying, just the same, and once off the doorstep he paused and took a quick look around, then departed, shaking his head.

Polly applied herself to cleaning her knee and applying a couple of large Band Aids, no, Elastoplasts, to her cut. She was still chagrined about the crash, but at least she had another tip on how to build a fire in her fireplace. What was that? Three, now?

But Jamie's reaction to her door stuck in her mind. Might he have an idea about her spectral visitor? If she'd had her wits about her, she could have asked him. Could she finagle a meeting with him? She didn't realize it, but she was not the first woman to have that thought about Bonnie Prince Jamie.

Seventeen

Whoever wishes to keep a secret must hide the fact that he possesses one.

Johann Wolfgang Von Goethe

Polly didn't want the entire Island to know about the spooky happenings at her cottage; the idea would get around that the new American was a complete nut case, freaking out over an imaginary visitor. Nobody believed in spirits; at least they wouldn't admit it if they did, and they'd laugh at her. She'd kept quiet up till now; she'd only told William Wallace, Anna and Zach, and Elspeth the seamstress and her daughter Barabal. Would it matter if she told one more person, Jamie? Surely no one she'd already confided in would have spread the story around.

Given the Island's well-developed gossip network, that was the opposite of unlikely, but Polly didn't know that. Neither Anna nor Barabal gossiped, William Wallace didn't know anyone local to talk to, and Zach didn't care, but Elspeth was concerned about someone disturbing a young woman in the middle of the night. She never thought twice about sharing her concern with her friends at the Seniors' Residence. So the story had already gotten around via the seniors that something odd was going on, and that it involved the Island's newest visitor. Tongues wagged busily. The *Eilean Dubhannaich* loved a new nugget to chew on; it was better than anything on the telly.

The talk reached the ears of Jamie MacDonald, who immediately linked the tale with the strange cold atmosphere that surrounded the Ferguson doorstep, and the experience of Ian *Mòr* with the lifesaving specter. He groaned, and awaited stoically the call for help that would inevitably come, given his unwanted reputation as a spook specialist. He'd already promised himself he'd not get enmeshed this time. He'd done

125

more than his share of time with the Other World, he had the scars to prove it, and he was sick to death – if that was the right word – of all of it.

The expected call came from an unexpected source, one he couldn't deny: Sally, his daughter-in-law. Polly had gone to her to inquire about Eilean Dubh supernatural happenings, and not to her surprise Jamie's name turned up right away.

"He has the Sight," said Sally, "which means that he can sometimes see the future. But he also senses things. I don't know exactly how he did it, but he sensed something was wrong at the archaeological site, and stopped the condo project from being built on it. And it turned out there was the ruins of a Mesolithic village on the site and he'd saved it from being destroyed. I saw it all and it freaked me out to watch him deal with it. He heard voices, no doubt about that, and he was terrified."

Polly understood immediately. "He knew something was wrong with my front door. He felt the same blast of cold air around it I've felt ever since I've moved in. I saw him react to it and wanted to ask him about it then, but he left in too much of a hurry."

"He doesn't like to talk about the supernatural, especially about anything he's been involved in. But you need to get his input because he's the resident expert. His daughter Eilidh has the Sight, too, but she's not as experienced as Jamie. She told me he'd been involved in all kinds of weird happenings, but I had to promise not to tell anyone about them."

"How am I going to get him to talk to me? He hardly knows me." And he saw me fall off my bike, so he already knows I'm a complete klutz, she thought, her usual lack of self-confidence bubbling to the surface.

"One way to find out. Let's go talk to him."

"Now?"

"Yep. I can see him through the kitchen window. He's in his shed. Wagons roll!"

Jamie saw them coming and his heart sank. It didn't take the Sight to know what they wanted. "Right then, inside for a chat. I'll make a pot of tea." He held the door.

"I'll do it, pa-in-law. You listen to Polly." Sally headed for the stove.

Jamie turned his brilliant smile on the girl, and watched as she collapsed into a gibbering puddle. He sighed. He didn't mean to reduce women to jelly, he just couldn't help it. He said kindly, "Polly, take a seat and tell me what I can do for you."

"You know about my front doorstep. The Frozen Zone, I call it. Am I right? You felt it?"

"Aye," said Jamie reluctantly.

"What is it?"

"Why do you want to know? Why don't you just ignore it?" He already knew the answer to that one; he'd tried ignoring haunts with unpleasant results. Once a spook got its hooks into you, it was damned near impossible to get rid of it until it got what it wanted. The problem was to find out *what* it wanted, and Polly would have to figure that out for herself. It was, after all, her spook. It had chosen her. And her doorstep.

Polly said, "It came knocking on my door twice on the nights of the last two full moons. I've never seen it; I've just heard the knocks. I don't know why it shows up, I don't know how to talk to it, I'm afraid to open the door, and it scares me to death. I'm afraid it might attack."

"Unlikely. They really don't have the weapons to harm humans."

"Who don't?"

"Ghosties, of course."

She stared at him in alarm. So Jamie, the supernatural specialist, thought there was indeed a ghostie hanging around her cottage. On one hand she felt vindicated; she wasn't out of her head. On the other hand, the idea she'd been afraid for days to put into words was confirmed. A ghostie. A real live ghostie. Or should that be a real dead ghostie? Were they dead or alive? She pondered that idea and silence fell between them, broken by Sally bringing the tea tray to the table.

"Okay," said Sally, as she passed out mugs. "All sorted?"

"Not in the least," said Polly. "I haven't the slightest idea what to do next."

"Neither have I," said Jamie, and both women looked at him in shock.

"But pa-in-law, you must know what to do. You've met hundreds of these critters." Sally had been certain that he would suggest a solution, something quick and easy and efficient that would banish the knocker forever – problem solved.

"A slight exaggeration, dozens maybe. Besides, each one is different."

"Don't you have any advice?" Polly pleaded.

Jamie said promptly, "Don't annoy it, don't confuse it, and give it what it wants. But you don't need my advice, love. It's not me he's chosen to appear to, it's you. You're the one he's asking to help him."

"Help him! How can I help him? I have no idea what he wants."

Jamie nodded in understanding. "Ah, that's the dilemma, isn't it. Spooks always want something."

"How the hell do I find out what it wants?" Polly shouted, and immediately shrank back in embarrassment, hearing how loud and pushy-American her voice sounded. She wanted Jamie to help her; she didn't want to annoy him.

Jamie smiled, not the least bit annoyed. "It'll tell you, love. It'll tell you."

He rose. "Now if you ladies will excuse me, I've got to remove a thorn from my dog's foot before it festers. Nice to have had this little chat with you both. Cheerio, and good luck, Polly love."

Despairing, Polly watched his beautiful broad-shouldered back as he went out the door. He hadn't even invited her to check again with him if her troubles continued. She'd hoped so much that he'd take charge and solve her problem. Now she'd have to solve it by herself.

She was on her own again, just like after she'd lost the baby. Damn. She was getting tired of being a loner. Loners are losers, she thought, and that was certainly true in her case.

Eighteen

It would be mortifying to the feelings of many ladies, could they be made to understand how little the heart of man is affected by what is costly or new in their attire.

Jane Austen

In addition to the stress imposed by the ghostie, Polly was becoming uneasily aware that she had feelings about William Wallace MacDonald that were growing more intense. It worried her. She'd never felt this way about a man before, not even Duane. Especially not Duane. At first she thought it was only a crush growing from her admiration of his handsome exterior and her gratitude for his friendship and dance lessons, and because he had a good sense of humor even if he was a bit starchy at times.

We're only friends, she reassured herself. Strangers together in a strange land, Americans in a world of unfamiliar Scottish customs and traditions. We get together to chat and dance and eat pizza. It's nothing more than that, and it's fine. No problem.

Lately, however, she worried that her emotions might go deeper than a crush or friendship. Will occupied most of her thoughts when they were apart and she missed him when he wasn't around. She'd even dreamed of him one night, a circumstance that both thrilled and alarmed her. She couldn't remember the details of the dream but it had been immensely pleasant; she remembered that much. She repressed the fact that it had also been delightfully erotic.

And she'd been thrilled witless to see his eyes light up with appreciation when she appeared in her new Elspeth-created top and skirt at last Friday's *cèilidh*. His compliment had turned her pink with pleasure and tangled her tongue so badly she had a hard time thanking him for it. It might be only a crush, but it was certainly making her behave foolishly.

Love. The word danced menacingly in her mind.

She dared not let herself slip into the mistake of caring about him. That would be dangerous, even more dangerous than if she'd been able to convince herself when she was pregnant that she was in love with Duane the weasel. She and Will were so different. Friendship was the most she could hope for from a man of his background and wealth and that would have to be enough for her. She had to suppress the unruly emotion that was beginning to take over her brain and consume her heart.

But it was hard, because the feeling grew stronger every time they met, and they saw each other now several times a week. Of necessity he spent a lot of time with his father, but his free hours were increasingly devoted to Polly. They explored Eilean Dubh together, by car and on foot, when it seemed perfectly normal to link their fingers as they strolled the Island roads, chatting and laughing.

Their excursions took them hunting for wildflower preserves (map provided by Anna Wallace), to the archaeological dig (tour given by Zach Trelawney), and all the way to the southernmost part of the Island to the Glen Logan distillery, where A Drop of Eilean Dubh whisky slept quietly in oaken casks.

It would be five more years before the initial batch of single malt was mature enough to bottle, but already a skeleton staff worked at the distillery preparing for the launch of what everyone involved confidently expected would be the finest whisky in the world. There were golf visors and tee shirts available already, bearing the name of the whisky, its slogan "A gentleman's dram," and a likeness in silhouette of Darroch Mac an Rìgh dressed in kilt, velvet jacket and shirt with lace frills at collar and cuffs. Will and Polly bought each other tee shirts, and Will bought one for Robert Burns MacDonald, in size XXL.

He bought the largest size because he thought uneasily that his father was putting on extra pounds; his face and his hands seemed puffy from weight gain. Will had been postponing the chat he knew they should have, because the older man was having such a grand time on Eilean Dubh that it seemed a shame to spoil his fun by nagging him about his weight and what he ate. The odd thing was that he did not seem to be overeating, at least at the meals he and Will had together, and he was getting more exercise than he'd gotten at home. They took an hour's walk every morning around the town and a shorter one in the afternoon before Will went off to visit Polly while his father took a nap.

Unwilling to rock the boat, Will persuaded himself that it was pointless to look for trouble and tried not to worry. But he looked forward eagerly to the day when his mother would arrive on the Island to help him keep an eye on his lively father. That day was drawing nearer, but there was still over a month to wait.

In the meantime, he was enjoying very much his association with Polly with never a thought in his head as to where it was leading. He only knew that he was happy to see her on every visit and reluctant to leave her. She was pretty, smart, and easy to talk to, all around good company. He found it a relief to be with an American after being engulfed by Scots whom he found usually reserved, often terse and frequently unpredictable. And they talked funny, and drove on the wrong side of the road. He could not quite forgive them for that last quirk, after he'd had a couple of embarrassing incidents with the car.

His father didn't really count as American anymore; he fit in so snugly on Eilean Dubh that it was as if he'd been born there. Any complaints Will might have about the Scottish way of doing things (like serving one cup of coffee in a restaurant after dinner instead of unlimited refills throughout the meal) were brushed off by Robert Burns MacDonald. *When in Scotland do as the Scots do* was a favorite saying of his that his son found particularly irritating.

One day it occurred to Will to invite Polly to have dinner with him and Robert Burns at the Rose Hotel, following an obscure, unarticulated and unrecognized impulse that made him want to show off his girl to his father. He was taken so strongly by the impulse that he wondered why he hadn't thought of it sooner. He would ask her the next time he saw her.

Nineteen

. . . always, always, always believe in yourself, because if you don't,
then who will, sweetie? So keep your head high, keep your chin up,
and most importantly, keep smiling, because life's a beautiful thing
and there's so much to smile about.

Marilyn Monroe

*P*olly ran into Sally and the twins in the Co-Op one morning and was
invited over to the younger MacDonalds' house that afternoon for
what Sally described as, "A bit of a chinwag and a nice cuppa." That translated to talk and tea. Sally loved British slang, which she delivered with a
broad American accent, just for fun.

Polly arrived to a noisy house, both twins crying, and she immediately pitched in, snatching up the one that seemed most amenable to
comfort. That was Fiona. "Is your butt sore again, precious?" she crooned.
She cleaned the baby's messy bottom with a wet wipe from a handy box,
anointed it with the white ointment she'd seen Sally use the other day,
and put her into a clean diaper.

That seemed to do the trick and, when Sally came out of the bedroom
carrying Hamish, she exclaimed with pleasure at the sight of the placid
baby cradled in Polly's arms. "You've got a real knack with kids. Can I hire
you as a babysitter? Like, full time, starting now? No wages, no benefits,
just a mother's heartfelt gratitude."

Polly smiled at the compliment. It made her feel that she would have
been a good mother to Walter, had he survived.

Little by little, the women from the lane gathered for an afternoon
coze. Jean Mac an Rìgh turned up with a plate of cookies hot from the
oven while Sally was making the tea. Màiri MacDonald was close behind
her with fresh warm scones and her homemade lemon curd, and soon the
two grandmothers were sitting on the floor, playing with the twins, while
Polly helped carry in the cups and plates and handed them around.

Talk turned, somehow, to self-improvement, as it usually does with women, and Polly found herself confessing her latest experiment. She'd gotten tired of looking at her mousy locks in the mirror, and had remembered one of her frugal mother's tricks for brightening hair: a vinegar rinse. So she got a bottle of vinegar at the Co-Op and, after she'd washed her hair in the bathroom sink, poured a cupful over her head.

"Did it work?" asked Sally.

"Well, I think my hair looks a little brighter, but it smells like salad dressing, and I should have kept my eyes more tightly closed. That vinegar sure does sting."

"I remember using that," said Màiri, and "So do I," chimed in Jean.

"Your hair is a pretty color," said Sally. "Why do you want to fool with it?"

Polly ran her hands through the errant locks. "Ugh, dishwater blonde. I hate it."

"Needs a bit of styling," said Màiri. "That's all."

"Should I go to that hairdresser up in Airgead that advertises in the paper?"

"Ha, Frizzy Fiona," said Jean. "Only go to her if you want to look like Margaret Thatcher."

"Oh, she's updated her style," said Màiri. "Now she gives all her customers hairdos like the Queen's."

"I don't want to look like the Queen, no disrespect intended and she does have that lovely white hair," said Polly. "What should I do?"

"I think . . . ," began Sally, "all you need, really, is to have your ends trimmed and bangs cut. You'd look good with bangs."

"A do-over, what fun. Eilidh," said Jean and Màiri at the same time, and Màiri headed for the phone. As she hung up, she said, "She's on her way with her scissors kit and wee Joey." To Polly she explained, "My daughter Eilidh is a concert violinist, plays with the Edinburgh Chamber Orchestra, but she's at home now because early summer is the orchestra's resting season. She's married to Joe Munro, one of our Island veterinarians, and they have a wee bairn named Joe Junior." She added, "She's a dab hand with a fringe."

Polly stared at her, puzzled. "A what with a what?"

Jean said, "That means she cuts bangs very well. She does mine and Màiri's, too."

Eilidh was tall and slender, blonde and beautiful like her twin Ian *Mòr*, and she arrived with little Joey on her hip, toting two bags, one of baby gear and one of make-over equipment. Màiri gathered up her grandson and gave him a cuddle, then put him down on the floor with the twins, and the babies stared and cooed and kicked at each other. Joey was old enough to sit up, which gave him a tactical advantage.

Eilidh pronounced herself delighted to meet Polly and quite willing to cut her fringe for her. She cocked her head and studied the other woman. "Maybe not quite eyebrow length, parted on the left, a little slanted in shape."

Soon Polly was seated in a chair, towel around her neck, submitting herself to Eilidh's ministrations. She not only cut the desired fringe, she trimmed Polly's split ends, cutting them so cleverly that they turned under in a natural pageboy. She was pronounced "Done," Sally offered a hand mirror with a flourish, and Polly gazed at herself as at a picture of a different, unknown woman.

"Quite nice," said Màiri, and "Isn't it amazing how much difference a little change can make," said Jean.

"You're so pale, you want your eyes done for a bit of color," said Sally suddenly, and disappeared into the bedroom, returning with a box full of make-up. "A friend in Milwaukee sent me all this because she was convinced I wouldn't be able to find a decent eyebrow pencil in the wilds of Scotland. But I'm too busy with the kiddies to fuss with my face and they don't care if Mama wears war paint or not. So I took out what I'd use when I get dressed up, and here's all the rest of it going to waste. Help yourself, Polly."

"Oh . . . I don't wear make-up." Her comment was ignored as the three other women pawed through the box. Jean surfaced with a brown eyebrow pencil and Sally came up with a little case of blue, green and white eye shadow and a round container of face powder. Màiri offered a turquoise eye liner pencil. "I don't know what this is for," she said, "but it's a pretty color."

"Let me," said Eilidh. "I'm used to helping the other women make up for concert performances." Swiftly she applied eye makeup and the women all nodded approval as a color-enhanced Polly emerged. "Your lipstick, madam," said Sally, proffering a silver tube on her outstretched hand.

Polly took it and the mirror, and stared at herself in astonishment.

In a daze, she applied the soft rosy shade of lipstick to a face only subtly changed, but one that just as subtly didn't look like her. "Wow," she said softly. "I look glamorous. I've never been glamorous before." She glanced away from the other women, as to her chagrin tears came to her eyes, threatening her new look. She wiped them away carefully with the tip of a finger. "I don't know how to thank you," she said.

"No thanks needed; we've enjoyed ourselves," said Jean, and meant it. It wasn't often the four had an opportunity to coax a flower bud into opening, and Polly had been a very promising and very needy blossom.

They were used to get-togethers where they all fooled around with different looks. Only Sally and Eilidh tried on each other's clothes and experimented with make-up, but Jean and Màiri enjoyed critiquing and commenting on the results. Occasionally they allowed themselves to be made up, just to give Darroch and Jamie something to think about when they got home, and for Jean, a memory of back home in Milwaukee where she painted her face every day, because her first husband Russ had liked it.

It slowly dawned on all four that the do-over session was a new experience for Polly. Sally remembered that she'd said she didn't have any close women friends. What a shame, she thought, nobody to play dress-up with. What a lonely life she must lead.

Polly said, "I won't want to wash my face for a week."

"That's not necessary and besides it would give you spots. Take the gear along and experiment, now you know how it's done. Enjoy playing with it." Sally got a bag and packed up a selection of pencils and packets, including a bottle of perfume she'd never even sniffed. Polly needed it more, she figured. She had a hunch Polly was sweet on Will, and thought it'd take more than perfume to land that starchy character. But perfume couldn't hurt and it might even help.

Polly pushed Bouncing Betsy the bike up the steepest part of the hill so she didn't sweat off her new face. A car passed, pulled in ahead of her and stopped. Will got out.

"Polly, hi, I was just on my way to your cottage." He stepped closer. "You look different. You seem to glow. What have you done to yourself?"

Polly concealed a grin of triumph, and said only, "I probably got some sun on my face while I was biking."

"Hmmm." He peered at her intently. "Whatever the cause, you look very nice today. Especially your hair." In one of his lightning change of subjects he added, "I was on my way to your place to invite you to have dinner with Dad and me at the Rose."

"Oh, my. When?"

"How about the day after tomorrow?"

"That would be umm, fun." Already the butterflies were starting to flutter in her brain.

"I'll pick you up at seven. Do you want a ride to your cottage now?"

"No, I'm almost home."

"Okay. I have to go; I'm on my way to Airgead on an errand for Dad. See you tomorrow afternoon for tea and dancing."

She waved goodbye, then pulled herself together enough to bike the rest of the way home, so she could worry about the dinner invitation in the privacy and minimal comfort of her cottage. But she refused to let her new fear dim the pleasure of the afternoon she'd spent in the company of four kind Eilean Dubh women, new friendships well worth cherishing, that made her feel a part of Eilean Dubh. It was a very warm feeling.

Twenty

*Just around the corner in every woman's mind – is a lovely dress,
a wonderful suit, or entire costume which will make an
enchanting new creature of her.*

Wilhela Cushman

*P*olly, true to form, was terrified about the dinner invitation. She didn't
know what frightened her most, the idea of having to make conversation with Will's father or the idea of dining at the Rose which she'd
heard was the poshest restaurant on Eilean Dubh. She knew she'd be
too nervous to enjoy the meal, she'd say something stupid that would
make both men disdain her, and she'd be sure to spill something on her
clothes or on the tablecloth, or worst of all, on one of her fellow diners.
Would she know what fork or spoon to use? Her association with Will
had been going really well, she fretted; why did he have to introduce a
new element?

And she didn't have a thing to wear. She had a new face and a new
hairdo, but nothing to wear with them.

She fled to Elspeth Mac-a-Phi, so nervous that she didn't even call
first; she just showed up. Barabal was out, but Elspeth was always home,
thanks to the arthritis which limited her ability to walk. "What a lovely
surprise!" she exclaimed, seeing Polly on the doorstep. "I was just wishing for cheerful company." Then, taking a closer look at her unexpected
caller, she said doubtfully, "You don't look very cheerful. What's amiss?"

"I need help, Elspeth," Polly said, her voice full of desperation.

"*Ceart math, m'eudail.* Is it that *spiorad* again, hammering on your
door in the middle of the night? And do you want me to come over and
shake my walking canes at him? Or maybe give him a belt in the middle
of his ectoplasmy?"

"No, it's not that, it's something real. I need clothes."

"What's happened to the ones I made for you?" asked Elspeth, astonished.

"They're great. I wore them at the *cèilidh* and got lots of compliments, but now I need something fancy to wear to dinner at the Rose Hotel."

Elspeth nodded in understanding. "Oh, aye, always a body will be having to dress up for the Rose. And when would you be needing this frock?"

"Wednesday night."

"But it's Monday today!" exclaimed the older woman.

"I know, but Will just asked me this morning."

"That's your laddie, is it? That MacDonald from *Ameireaga*?"

"Yes, and we're going to have dinner with his father."

"Oh, *mo ghaoil*, that sounds as though he's thinking seriously about you."

"Does it?" said Polly in surprise. "That didn't occur to me. I thought he was just tired of pizza." She was suddenly very quiet, thinking deep female thoughts.

Elspeth was quick to sense an interesting change in the young woman's relationship, and she was eager to help out young lovers and even more eager to get all the details. "Well, whatever the reason, you need a lovely new outfit and we're going to have to hustle, as you Americans say, to get it ready by Wednesday. Let's be having a look at the fabrics in my collection; there'll not be time to buy special. *Dè seorsa rud a tha thu 'lorg*? I mean, what sort of frock are you wanting?"

They worked through the afternoon after they'd selected a dress pattern and fabric. Elspeth did the bulk of the work but she enlisted Polly in simple tasks that the young woman could handle. Polly hadn't had anything to do with sewing since junior high school, and found it so fascinating that she resolved to ask Elspeth for lessons once this crisis was over. In the meantime she helped where she could and kept the teapot filled, something she now knew how to do, thanks to Sally.

Barabal came home to find them so deeply engrossed in the dress project that they did not hear her enter the house. "I might have been a burglar, Mama, and you never would have noticed," she said.

"There's no burglars on Eilean Dubh," said Elspeth briskly around a mouthful of pins. She said something else that Barabal couldn't understand at first but that she eventually deciphered to be something about Polly staying to eat with them. "Otherwise," she said, removing the pins one by one and sticking them into the dress Polly was modeling, "we'll never get this *dreasa* finished in time."

"Oh, you don't have to bother with anything for me, Barabal," began Polly, covered with guilt at the idea of imposing on someone's kindness.

"No bother at all, young Polly," said Barabal, looking at her mother's animated face and feeling a surge of gratitude to the American for Elspeth's new lease on life.

A while later Barabal's two youngest daughters came home and popped their heads into their granny's room. as usual, to be polite. "*Feasgar math, a Sheanmhar*," they chorused and prepared to pop back out, as usual. Then, noticing the stranger, they grew quiet but seethed with interest.

"*Feasgar math*, and will you not come in and meet my friend," said Elspeth.

Shyly they entered. "Polly, these are my granddaughters, Siùsaidh and Seonag. Girls, this is an American visitor, Miss Polly Gillespie."

"*Bana-Ameireaganach*," whispered one of the girls in awe. The new American woman, visiting their granny!

"She doesn't have the Gaelic," reminded their grandmother. "It's a good chance for you to be trying out the English that you are learning in school."

"Me first," said Siùsaidh pertly. "Why are you for leaving wonderful *Ameireaga* and coming to this poky little Island, Miss Polly? And aren't you bored to death?"

"I love it here," said Polly, surprised at the comment, but realizing that teenagers disparaged everything familiar. "Everyone's so friendly and it's lovely and quiet."

"Too quiet," Seonag said disdainfully. "It's like *an tòrr*, I mean a tomb. Nothing exciting ever happens here."

"Except a spectral appearance," said Polly, disliking their criticism of Eilean Dubh and blurting out the first exciting thing she could remember that had happened to her on the Island. "A ghostie."

"A ghostie! A real ghostie? Have you seen one?" chorused the girls.

"Well, I haven't seen it yet but it's been knocking on my door. Ask your grandmother; she knows all about it."

And nothing would satisfy them until Elspeth told the story which the younger girls, out of the Island gossip chain, had not heard. Quite without realizing it, the girls began to help with the sewing, picking up pins and sticking them in pincushions, retrieving scraps of fabric from the floor, and folding patterns to return to their jackets. As they worked, they listened and "oo-ed" and "ah-ed" while their grandmother talked.

"So that's the story of Cailean Ferguson, Miss Polly's ghostie," she concluded.

Siùsaidh and Seonag twittered with excitement. "May we come over some night and help you watch for it? Please, Miss Polly, may we?"

Polly, taken by surprise by their interest, was spared having to answer when Barabal stuck her head in the door. "Mama, you're going to need a bigger room if you keep filling it with girls," she said.

"We're all cozy in here," said Elspeth in satisfaction. It had been a while since her granddaughters had taken the time to come in and visit with her after school; these days they seemed so busy with their own affairs. She was enjoying herself immensely.

Barabal, recognizing that, withdrew without enlisting the girls to help prepare dinner. If they were having a good time with their grandmother, that was more important than setting the table, and she would manage without help.

Distracted from the spirit world, the younger girls now took turns plying Polly with questions about America. What sort of house did she live in? What kind of job did she have? Did she own video games and a huge flat screen television set and pocket-sized music players, and a digital camera and a cell phone that took pictures and videos? And a Wii? They weren't sure what that was but thought the name was cool.

Polly, not wanting to disappoint them, tried to make her poky little apartment and her boring job sound as glamorous as possible. But she had to confess that the only electronic gadgets she owned were an ordinary cell phone, a CD player, and a digital camera. Plus her television set was modestly sized and its screen was not flat in the least; the whole thing was as fat as a Thanksgiving turkey. She attempted with little success to switch the conversation to Eilean Dubh which she thought was much more marvelous than Minneapolis. But she supposed it was normal that the girls would feel the opposite. What you didn't have always sounded better than what you had.

But then they started to quiz her about the nightlife in her hometown, and Polly had to confess that she didn't go out to clubs or shows and very seldom went to movies. "I don't have a boy friend back home or gal pals, and I don't like to go out in the evening by myself. I think being out alone at night is asking for trouble. The last time I did that a really scary guy stopped me and asked for money. I was afraid he was going to snatch my purse but luckily several other people came up along the sidewalk and he ran away."

Their eyes grew wide. It was not safe to go out at night in America? They thought about their Island, where it would never occur to anyone that it was dangerous to venture forth after dark. What difference would it make if there were tons of things to do in a place but a person was afraid to do them? They became quiet and thoughtful.

Polly added, "Of course, there's dangerous people everywhere. I suppose that's true of every city, including Edinburgh and Glasgow."

"Maybe even Inverness," said Elspeth, "but I wouldn't be knowing about that, never having been there."

The girls glanced at each other, thinking about their pact to run away to Edinburgh in search of excitement when they were eighteen and nineteen and had saved enough money for tickets on the Cal-Mac ferry. For the first time it occurred to them both that there might be disadvantages to that idea.

It also occurred to them that if the clothes their grandmother made for them were stylish enough for an American woman, perhaps they shouldn't be scorned. Siùsaidh picked up a piece of fabric and considered it. "A Sheanmhar, would you make me a dress after you've finished with Miss Polly's?"

"Of course, mo fhlur. You can look through my patterns and fabrics and choose something pretty," said Elspeth, immensely pleased.

"I'd like the same pattern as you're using for Miss Polly," the girl said, with a shy glance of admiration at the American woman. Polly looked back at her, surprised and flattered. "Ni sin a' chùis." That'll do fine. "You won't mind, will you, Miss Polly, if I have a dress like yours?"

"But you won't be having the exact same dress," said Elspeth. "I've got a few tricks that will make it look different and the fabric, too."

"I want a dreasa, too, a Sheanmhar," said Seonag, determined not to be left out. "Like Miss Polly's, only a little bit different."

Barabal, noting at dinner the increased respect her daughters showed to their grandmother and how they hung on her every word, correctly attributed it to Polly's influence. Nothing counted more than a little outside admiration, she thought, and her heart warmed to the American.

Twenty-one

We are indeed much more than what we eat, but what we eat can nevertheless help us to be much more than what we are.

Adelle Davis

Elspeth's dress, a modestly scoop-necked, long-sleeved style made of a soft green fabric, made Polly's eyes shine like emeralds and flattered her vinegar-brightened hair. She carefully applied eye shadow and lipstick as Eilidh had taught her, and when Will came by to pick her up, she had the satisfaction of receiving his impressed attention.

He was suddenly aware that Polly was not just a person to talk to and laugh with and dance with, she was also an attractive woman. "You look lovely," he said, a slight note of surprise in his voice. "That's a very pretty dress. And I like your hair that way."

"Thanks," said Polly. Thanks to Eilidh's skilled cut, her hair had fallen naturally into place after she'd washed it. But it had been a tussle getting the dress finished in time; even now the hem was only basted in. She would finish it tomorrow but it would do for tonight, Elspeth had said, as long as she didn't attempt any acrobatics in it. Polly promised to avoid cartwheels and high kicks, and to sit quietly and demurely at the table.

Dinner at the Rose Hotel was every bit as terrifying as Polly had feared, but it was also surprisingly pleasant. Robert Burns MacDonald was one of those people who could talk easily to anybody – even a shy person – about anything, and Polly had ready her usual list of conversational subjects, overachieving this time with eight. She could only remember six of them, but as it turned out, she didn't need even that many; Robert Burns kept the conversation moving right along, and Will contributed his share of chat.

The Rose was charming, with a relaxed atmosphere created by Sheilah Morrison, the owner's wife, a gourmet chef. She came round to each table to talk about the three special dishes she'd created for the evening. Polly didn't have to worry about not understanding obscure French culinary terms, because Sheilah, a no-nonsense ex-Londoner, described them in loving detail in clear English for her guests. To Sheilah, *Poulet aux Noix* was chicken with walnuts, *Escalope de Veau Normande* was a veal cutlet cooked in a sauce of mushrooms, cream and brandy, *Soufflé au Fromage* was cheese soufflé, and she had no hesitation in saying so.

Polly's fears slipped away and she found herself enjoying the evening. The Rose was like everything else on Eilean Dubh, she thought; it was cozy and friendly, not scary at all. She was beginning to feel quite at home on the Dark Island. This feeling was amplified when Sally and Ian Mòr came in for dinner. Sally greeted them with a cheery, "Hi, guys!" as if they were old friends, and Ian Mòr offered a winning smile reminiscent of his father Jamie's and a friendly wave of his large hand.

Sally stopped by Polly's chair and looked her over, and said, "Hey, nice dress. Bet you didn't buy it anywhere on this Island."

"Elspeth Mac-a-Phi made it for me."

"I didn't know she made clothes! Wonder if she'd do something for me?"

"Ask her. She seems very willing. Where's the twins?"

Sally gave her a conspiratorial grin. "Stashed them with Ma so we could have a romantic dinner, just the two of us. Ma's a sucker for romantic dinners. It's Darroch's influence; must be because he's an actor and loves big dramatic moments. So they baby-sit the twinnies for us and we baby-sit Rosie and Gaileann for them on alternating weeks. Works out great."

Polly smiled and nodded, thinking how pleasant it must be to be part of a large loving family who enjoyed helping each other out. She sighed, thinking of her mother and their lonely life together, a loneliness that had led her after Polly's departure for Minneapolis to join a strict religious cult that disapproved of practically everything Polly had done since she left home: premarital sex, unwed pregnancy, and, perhaps worst of all, dancing.

And now, through no fault of her own, she was dabbling in the supernatural. Her mother would disown her for sure.

She could never go home again, she thought sadly. She couldn't live with her mother's strictures, she could never confess to her the forbidden adventures, and she couldn't bear the idea of deceiving her into thinking that she was still an innocent church-going virgin. And she really didn't want to be lectured any more on proper behavior. She wanted to decide for herself what was right and chart her own course of action.

For a moment she sobered, remembering she had no idea about what she was going to do after she left Eilean Dubh. Her money was holding out, but it wouldn't last forever. She needed a plan and she didn't have one. She'd come to the Dark Island to find answers, but instead she'd found more questions.

Then Robert Burns woke her from her musings with a joke of the gentle kind he favored. "What do you get when you cross poison ivy with a four leaf clover? A rash of good luck."

She replied, without stopping to think, "What do you get when you cross a snowman with a shark? Frostbite."

Robert Burns let out a whoop of laughter. Will, not to be outdone, said, "What do you get when you cross William the Conqueror with a power station? An electricity Bill."

The three of them fell about laughing. Heads turned in the dining room, and the *Eilean Dubhannaich* smiled at the three Americans enjoying themselves so much. They themselves would never laugh so heartily in a public place, but everyone knew that Americans were different, sometimes annoying, sometimes endearing. Rather like their own children.

When Will took her home, he hesitated at her door, and, untouched by the Frozen Zone and warmed by the evening's companionship, bent to kiss her on her cheek. Polly moved nervously, their lips met quite by accident and clung together for a tender moment. Then he straightened up, they moved apart and stared at each other in surprise.

"Good night," he murmured, thinking that it was a shame they had to part.

"Good night," Polly said, wishing she had the courage to invite him inside.

But she didn't. Not yet, anyway.

Twenty-two

I was happy and contented. I knew nothing better and made the best out of what life offered. And life is what we make it, always has been, always will be.

Anna Mary Robertson (Grandma) Moses

With that kiss, the ice was broken on physical intimacy. At the cinema in Airgead the following Tuesday, Will tried putting his arm around Polly's shoulders. Finding that quite uncomfortable, he changed his mind, took her hand and held it throughout the main feature, squeezing it every now and then. They both enjoyed this, and found themselves concentrating more on each other than on the movie. When they bought ice cream afterwards at the stand on the square, they escalated contact to licks of each other's cones, and Will stole a kiss from Polly's chocolate ice cream-coated mouth. "Tastes sweeter that way," he said, and she blushed.

When they reached the cottage door later, she took her courage by the scruff of its neck and said, "Do you want to come in for a cup of coffee?"

He shook his head. "Too late for coffee; it would keep me awake the rest of the night."

She sighed. "It's not very good coffee, anyway. It's instant. You probably wouldn't like it."

"Could I have a cup of tea instead?"

"It's made with a tea bag," she warned.

"Of course. Why make a full pot at this time of night?" He took her key from her hand and unlocked the door. "This is a really old-fashioned key."

"Look at this one." She showed him Cailean Ferguson's duplicate. She'd been keeping it on the fireplace mantelpiece, carefully isolated from any of her possessions. If the ghostie decided to come back for the

145

key, she didn't want him to rummage through her stuff looking for it, scattering ectoplasmy and seaweed all over.

"They're just the same, except that that one is dirty and yours is clean."

"The ghostie left it on my doorstep. It's not just dirt, it's salt from the sea."

"There's no such thing as ghosts, Polly," he said with his usual superior air.

"Believe what you like, but something got this key out from under a rock, tried to open the door with it, and then left it on my step when it couldn't get in. Have a seat."

Instead of sitting down, he followed her into the kitchen when she went to make the tea. Looking around, he said, "I can see why you don't do much cooking. This place wouldn't inspire flights of culinary imagination. How do you endure it?"

"It's not so bad." Over the last few weeks she'd gotten used to the kitchen and had come to relish her small triumphs in overcoming its inadequacies. She'd figured out how to regulate the burners so that she could scramble eggs and not burn them to a crispy black mass, and she'd even learned to light the oven using just one match and without singeing the hair on the back of her hand.

She hadn't yet come to the point of hanging decorative cookware from the rafters and hand-stenciling the cupboards, but she felt more at home now with the kitchen's quaint atmosphere. She supposed "quaint" was the right word to use to describe the place, although "dump" had come to mind once or twice in moments of frustration.

She added, "I'm not very good about cooking. My mother didn't want me to help in the kitchen. I think it was because her mother died very young and Mom and her older sister had to do all the housework, so she wanted to spare me what she regarded as drudgery." She removed the spent tea bags from their mugs. "It's too bad because I wish I knew how to cook. Maybe someday I'll be able to afford to take classes."

"How did you manage for something to eat when you lived by yourself in an apartment?" He'd lived in a dorm at the university and taken all his meals in the Bus Admin cafeteria, so he'd never had to face the problem of cooking.

She shrugged. "Oh, you know, I microwaved stuff or opened a can of soup or bought take-out when I could afford it, which wasn't real often."

"Your job didn't pay enough?"

"Jobs never pay enough," she said. Probably he didn't know that, with his wealthy background. "Let's go into the living room, which Sally told me Scots call the lounge." She picked up her mug and a plate of cookies she'd bought at Beathag the Bread'sbakery and led the way.

Following her, he said, "How did you have enough money to come to Scotland?"

This was the night for awkward questions, she decided; he would have to ask that one. She could ignore it or laugh it off. But then she thought, why not tell him? If he thinks less of me after hearing about my out-of-wedlock pregnancy, I should find out before we get any more involved. If he's going to break my heart, better get it over and done with. The possibility for heartbreak suddenly loomed large in her mind.

Sensing her hesitation, he was tactful, for once, and said, "I'm sorry. That's none of my business."

She regarded him steadily. "Do you really want to know?"

"If you want to tell me." That was a neutral enough response, he thought. From her behavior, he guessed that she had a deep, dark secret. Would he regret hearing it? Would he like her any the less for hearing it? He thought about that and then decided that, no, there was nothing that she could admit to that would make him dislike her. He might disapprove but he would still like her. She was, after all, his girl.

That insight shocked him and he quite forgot to get ready to listen to her confession. Was it possible that he was falling in love with her? Had he already fallen in love with her? He sat, glassy-eyed and unmoving, pondering the state of his heart. It was beating quite normally, but something had waked up in his brain.

Polly stared at him, aware of his inattention. "Will," she said gently. "I'm about to tell you something very personal and your mind is wandering. Do you want to listen?"

"No," he said. "I want to do this." He took the mug from her hand, set it down and gathered her into his arms. He kissed her and a surprised Polly kissed him back. After several long, passionate minutes, Will surfaced. "What were you saying?" he asked, dazed. "Were you about to tell me something?"

"Oh, dear," said Polly. "I don't want to tell you now, you might not want to kiss me anymore and I was enjoying it so much." She burst into tears.

Her tears required a lot of cuddling and reassurance, which Will was happy to provide. Finally she said, "All right, I'm ready to talk." She told him the story of Duane, the miscarriage and the money. She told it bare and unvarnished, not glossing over her own mistakes, not making excuses for her behavior.

Will was indignant, and at first Polly didn't understand that the indignation was directed at Duane, not at the woman in his arms, until he said, "What a rat! Abandon his girl friend and his baby? How could you be in love with someone that rotten?"

"I wasn't in love with him," murmured Polly. "We were friends. Although I didn't like him very much, come to think of it. He was someone to do things with and I was lonely. Sex was sort of an accident and so was the baby and so was losing it. The story of my life . . . a series of accidents." A tear of self-pity trickled from her eye and she sniffled.

"Nothing happens by accident," said Will sagely, and he gathered her close for more kisses. It mattered a lot that she hadn't been in love with Duane; he didn't want her in love with anyone except himself. It was a surprisingly primitive reaction for someone who considered himself highly evolved. And he couldn't tell her that, not yet. Suppose she didn't feel the same way? Cautious by nature, he decided to ascertain her feelings first, and it was too soon to pry that deeply.

Kissing and cuddling were so pleasant that he realized that he wanted to make love with her. He couldn't suggest that, after hearing what had happened the last time she went to bed with a guy; that would be tactless. So when desire threatened to overtake him, he detached himself. "I've got to go now; it's getting late. I don't want Dad to worry. It's bad for his health." He gave her a final kiss, then rose.

"Good night, Will. Thanks for listening and for being such a comfort."

Did she think he was comforting her instead of being half out of his mind with lust? Apparently she didn't know how a man's mind worked after a few kisses. She was clueless about sex, but somehow he didn't mind. He wasn't all that experienced himself. "Good night, Polly. I hope you won't agonize any more about, umm, losing the baby and umm, what's his name, the rat."

"No, I think I'm over it." And she was; she felt free of worry and regrets and shame for the first time since she'd found out she was pregnant and unmarried. Will's acceptance of her story had helped to ease her guilty feelings. She'd been worried about his reaction, and he had been wonderfully understanding. Sally and Catrìona had been, too; maybe she hadn't done such a bad thing after all. Maybe it was all right to make a serious mistake if you learned from it. It was a whole new idea to her.

"I'll see you tomorrow. Good night, honey." The endearment tasted good on his lips.

As he went out the door she murmured, "Good night, honey, yourself," and giggled when she shut the door behind him. It had been a giggly sort of evening and she felt as light as a feather tossing in the wind.

Twenty-three

*Courage is the most important of all the virtues, because
without courage you can't practice any other virtue consistently.
You can practice any virtue erratically, but nothing
consistently without courage.*

Maya Angelou

The next morning Will remembered that he had forgotten to inform Polly that he was going to stay with her until the so-called ghost showed up, the next time it was expected. That time was coming up soon, he reckoned; the full moon must be due any day or so. After breakfast he confirmed that with Sheilah Morrison, who he'd learned tracked such things as the phases of the moon and, as a hotel keeper and amateur psychologist, the effect on behavior, especially of their guests.

"The full moon is tomorrow night," said Sheilah, confirming it with her calendar and her recollection that room number 16, normally a very reserved woman, had brought down into the kitchen today's morning tea tray and had stayed to chat in a hyperactive sort of way. Sheilah was forced to work around her and smile and nod all the while she was making breakfast for her other guests. It reminded her once again that she should post a "Private" sign over the entrance to the kitchen. Not that a sign would deter someone as antsy and talkative as this guest, especially not on the eve of the full moon.

Will wandered outside, thinking that tomorrow was going to be the big day. What should he do to prepare for a ghost watch and, hopefully, for a bit of a cuddle with his girl? Perhaps they would make love for the first time. They'd start with a good dinner, since it was their weekly pizza night at MacShannock's. Extra-special toppings, like shrimp or barbecue chicken and artichoke hearts, if the café could run to that. Perhaps a bottle of wine to share at the cottage while they waited for the knocking on the door, or one of those liqueurs that women liked, such as Drambuie.

And maybe a fancy dessert from Beathag the Bread's bakery to have with proper coffee, to help them stay awake. Tea wouldn't do it and he hated instant coffee. He had a great idea; he'd buy her a coffee maker if one were to be found on the Island.

He spent a good bit of time rummaging around the Co-Op the next day. At last he and Flòraidh Ross, who was on duty as cashier/clerk that morning, unearthed a small electric coffeepot and a package of filters on a corner shelf, proving once again that the Co-Op did, as it boasted, stock a little bit of everything anyone needed. Flòraidh blew dust off the cellophane-wrapped filters. "Not much call for something like this around here," she said. "Do you know how to make the wee machine work?"

"Of course, we use them at home. It's just what I want," said Will. "It's a present for a friend."

"Ooooh," said Flòraidh, thrilled. "Will I be wrapping it pretty then?"

"That's not necessary," he began, but then thought, why not? "Sure, if you want to. Go ahead and wrap it."

While Flòraidh bustled around with fancy paper and ribbons, Will occupied himself looking for ground coffee or whole beans, without success. "*Tha mi duilich*," said the cashier when he inquired. "Sorry, we don't stock that because we don't get much call for it around here. Mrs. Jean and Sally MacDonald are our only Island coffee drinkers, and of course Sheilah makes it for her customers at the Rose, but they all order theirs from an Edinburgh shop. I have some lovely instant, though."

"Instant won't work in a coffeemaker," said Will in frustrated tones. He would have to borrow some from Jean Mac an Rìgh, he thought. He was determined to have proper coffee for the evening. Otherwise what a fool he'd look, bringing Polly a coffee maker with nothing to brew in it.

Luckily the Mac an Rìghs had recently gotten a shipment of beans, and Jean was happy to grind some for him, especially when he confided that it was for Polly and himself and their ghost watch. She'd heard about the spirit of Cailean Ferguson from Elspeth Mac-a-Phi and was very curious. "Have you seen it?" she asked.

"No, and I don't expect to see it. Ghosts don't exist except in stories. Someone's playing tricks on Polly, and I'm going to find out who it is and fix their little red wagon."

"I don't know anyone here who'd do a thing like that," said Jean dubiously, and remembered that she did know someone who *saw* ghosts:

Bonnie Prince Jamie. She didn't know that Polly and Sally had already spoken to Jamie, and she didn't volunteer any information to Will; it would be just like him to knock on Jamie's door and demand that he join the ghost watch. Which Jamie would refuse to do, of course, preferring to keep his psychic gifts personal and private unless someone was in danger of life or limb. That didn't seem to be the case now; at least, not as far as Jean knew.

Will, however, had no intention of asking anyone for assistance. He could protect Polly from prank-players and from spooks, too, and he didn't need spectators for his proposed cuddling. It was lucky that he didn't know that Polly had consulted Jamie for he would have been indignant: she was his girl, it was his responsibility to look after her, and she should know that and not going around asking almost total strangers for help.

"I'll be late tonight, Dad," he explained to Robert Burns, whom he hadn't told about the knockings because he didn't want to alarm him. "Polly and I are doing something special. So don't wait up for me."

His father had an idea of which way the wind was blowing as far as William Wallace's and Polly's relationship was concerned; he'd suspected a romantic involvement even before his son himself had. The boy was long overdue; even in high school he hadn't been much for the ladies, being so involved with his studies. And at Princeton he had had only a mild interest in the Seven Sisters women to whom Flora, a student at Bryn Mawr College, had introduced him. Hip, self-assured and intellectual, they weren't his type. Too much work to keep up with them.

Robert Burns thought Polly was definitely William Wallace's type; a smart, down to earth type of gal, the kind a fellow could marry, and it was about time that one of his children committed himself to a life partner. His older son Robert Bruce was too busy at work to settle down with one woman and frequently changed girlfriends, and though daughter Flora had a steady beau, there was no sign of an engagement ring and no ding-a-ling of wedding bells. They both worked too hard, he thought; the firm took too much of their time.

William Wallace hadn't yet gotten entangled with his father's business and Robert Burns thought that was a fine thing. Two out of three of his children involved was darn good, and he could spare his youngest to some other occupation. But the boy didn't seem to have a career in mind which worried Robert Burns a wee bittie. The boy was just floating.

Marriage to a sensible woman like Polly would help him settle down and plan the rest of his life, especially if children came along – and he devoutly hoped that they would. He and Louise were looking forward to having grandchildren, eager young minds that Robert Burns could teach to be proper Scottish-Americans, Highland dance lessons, bagpipes and fiddles, haggis, and all that jazz, he thought.

When Robert Burns MacDonald made his mind up about someone, he thought about it hard, then made it up once and for all, and he'd made it up about Polly: she was the young woman for William Wallace. He wasn't going to tell the boy that, though; he knew kids always did the opposite of whatever their parents approved of.

So he was happy that William Wallace had moved along to spending an entire evening with his girl, not rushing home to hold his old dad's hand as he usually did. Maybe they'd come to an arrangement if the night turned romantic, which it probably would. "Go along and have a good time with your nice young lady and don't you worry about me. I've been feeling a little tired lately, so I'll appreciate an evening off from the social whirl. Besides which, Gordon Morrison lent me his copy of Jean Mac an Rìgh's collection of Eilean Dubh fairy tales. I'm looking forward to a pleasant evening of reading until I fall asleep with the book over my face and pixies dancing on my tummy."

Good, thought Will. He wouldn't have to worry about his dad; he could concentrate on Polly and her visitor, the nefarious trickster who enjoyed frightening helpless young women. This time he'd be prepared and he'd catch the culprit red-handed.

Twenty-four

*.... tall, strong, heavy, nut-brown man; his tarry pig-tail falling
over the shoulders of his soiled blue coat; his hands ragged and
scarred, with black, broken nails ...*

Robert Louis Stevenson

*W*ill loaded up his equipment for the evening, coffee, coffeemaker, pastries, and Drambuie, the Co-Op's last and very dusty bottle, and took it to the Ferguson cottage. While Polly exclaimed over the gift of the coffee pot and said how much she'd missed a real cup of coffee, Will took a sly look around and made sure that he knew the location of the poker in case he needed a weapon. He hoped it wouldn't come to that, of course. Shaming the perpetrator of the knocking might well do the job. If not, he'd collar him and turn him over to Constable MacRath for appropriate detention and punishment.

They went out for shrimp pizza, garlic bread and wine at MacShannock's and returned to the cottage after nine. Will insisted on making the coffee himself, to check out the new percolator for her, he said, but really because he enjoyed performing the occasional domestic chore.

"Aren't you afraid coffee at this time of night will disturb your slumbers?" teased Polly.

"Not at all. I plan on being awake for your visitor."

"Oh ... are you going to stay here till it comes?"

"That's why I brought all this," he said, indicating the coffee, the pastries and the liqueur with a wave of his hand. "I'm going to find out once and for all who's been knocking on your door, and then I'll deal with him."

Polly was tempted to giggle at his self-assurance; it was so like William Wallace to be a bit smug. What would he be like if that façade of control ever slipped, she wondered. She was pleased to find out that he planned to stay with her till Cailean Ferguson came. It was nice to have someone around to help her deal with the ghostie in case it turned fractious. And if she were honest, she was scared of the ghastly knocker; fractious or friendly, it creeped her out. "What are you going to do?"

"I'll know when the time comes," he said with assurance.

Polly shook her head dubiously. With three hours to wait for the spectral visitor, searching for a way to entertain her guest and not knowing about the intended cuddling, she unearthed a pile of board games from a bookcase. They played Draughts (it was like Checkers), Chinese Checkers, and finally the children's game Snakes and Ladders. Will won most of the time; his powers of concentration were awesome, Polly thought.

Next they drank another cup of coffee and a thimbleful of Drambuie and ate their dessert. Afterwards, Will coaxed, "Come sit beside me on the sofa." He had decided that it was time to begin the cuddling. Polly complied and soon found herself the recipient of delightful kisses that she was happy to return in full measure. Will was quite gentle, slow and serious in his lovemaking, not at all like hasty, aggressive Duane, and he murmured to her sweetly as he caressed her. The ghostie receded to the back of her mind, and Will, carried away by his pleasure in Polly's lips, nearly forgot why he was in the cottage in the first place.

Bam! Bam! Bam! Startled, Polly glanced at her watch. Twelve midnight, right on time. Carried away by kisses, she had not realized it was that late. She pulled away from Will and stood up, buttoning her blouse and straightening her skirt. She needed to be tidy for what she had in mind.

She approached the door and waited, holding herself as still as a statue.

Will, left alone on the sofa, found himself frozen with horror, quite unable to move. So this was what she had heard twice before, he thought in wonder, such an aggressive knock. It really had happened just the way she'd said; there was nothing exaggerated or imaginary about her story. How brave she had been not to make a fuss about it because the knocking was really quite alarming, even to a rational person like himself who didn't believe in ghosts. Or ghosties. He would get up in a minute and do something about it, as soon as he had recovered from the shock.

Bam! Bam! Bam! The knocking shook the door. Polly stepped closer, gathering courage for the course of action she'd been contemplating since the ghostie's last visit.

With an enormous effort, Will pulled himself together, rose from the sofa and headed for the fireplace, seeking the poker. He would set Polly aside, throw the door open, and brandish his weapon at whoever or whatever was out there. But he dropped the poker, just missing his toes, when the knocking came for the third time, so loud that it seemed the thick cottage walls trembled. He staggered backwards and fell into a chair.

BAM! BAM! BAM!

This is it, thought Polly. Face what you fear now, or be doomed to be a scaredy cat forever. She took a deep breath, held it for a minute, exhaled, and opened the door.

She saw nothing, and no one.

No one? There's no one here? she thought in surprise, blinking in the full glare of moonlight. She'd expected some sort of weird wispy thing or a flickering light or a drift of oozing ectoplasm.

Then, well above her eye level, the air began to glimmer. It quivered and jumped and swelled till her eyes burned from the brightness. The outline of a hulking figure slowly materialized. It raised a transparent arm trailing tattered remnants of clothing and flesh, and lifted a slouchy broad-brimmed hat with a bony-fingered hand. Beneath the hat was a bare skull with a mouth that gaped open, showing the ruins of teeth. A whisper on the wind sighed, "*A Pheigi?*"

Before her brain could register what her eyes saw and her ears heard, a wave of cold air flowed out to envelop her. It chilled her down to her toes and froze her in her tracks. It was as frigid as if she'd opened the door on a full-scale Minnesota blizzard. She was so cold that she couldn't move a muscle. And she was utterly terrified.

The whisper came again, louder, raising to a ghastly, angry moan that raised the hair on Polly's head like the fur of a frightened cat. It howled, "*O mo Pheigi! Tha mi 'g iarraidh Peigi agam!*"

"I want my Peigi!" She could understand the Gaelic, she had no idea how or why. Jamie had said to find out what the ghostie wanted. Now she knew what it wanted, and had to answer. She had to tell the specter Peigi was gone, and hope it would be satisfied and leave; she couldn't face it much longer and remain upright. But her throat was dry and her lips were frozen; she could not force them to say the words aloud. If all you can do is whisper, get closer so it can hear you, she told herself. And pray it understands English.

She forced herself, one foot at a time, to take two steps forward, closer to the skeletal figure. She opened her mouth and pushed the words from her icicle of a larynx through her chattering teeth. As she spoke, her voice grew stronger and her fear abated. "Cailean Ferguson! The one you seek is not here on Eilean Dubh. Your Peigi died of grieving for you two days after you drowned. You must look for her in the dimension you inhabit. I wish you the best of luck in finding her, and I ask you not to come back here again to frighten us poor mortals." That was all she could think of to say and closed her mouth so firmly that her teeth met with a sharp, audible click.

The air glimmered again, pulsating vividly like a computer processing information. Then the flickering waves slowly began to disappear. She thought – *was she imagining this?* – that she saw the nod of a head and the tip of a hat before the awful creature turned away and a final frigid gasp enveloped her.

Will, blinded by the glare and lost in a blizzard of cold back by the fireplace, had been frozen to the chair, numb to the eyeballs and power-less, once again, to move. At last with a tremendous effort he rose, and pushing his way through the frigid air as though walking through knee-deep mud, forced his way across the cottage to Polly's rigid figure.

He couldn't believe what he'd just seen. He gasped, "What the hell was that?"

"Something that doesn't exist," gasped Polly, and fell backwards into his arms.

He sagged under her weight and it took several minutes for him to right them both. "My God, you're even colder than I am," he said and gathered her close. She was shivering so violently that he could think of nothing but getting her warm again. He tried to grab the blanket from the sofa to wrap around her but her legs buckled when he let her go and he had to abandon that idea. At last he thought of the bed. He steered her gently into the bedroom and stripped the sheets and blanket back. "Get in," he said.

She complied and cried out, "It's freezing! The cold will kill me!"

The lightweight summer blanket was of no use. She'd never warm up without his help, she'd die of hypothermia if he didn't do something. Already she was wheezing for air and shivering convulsively. Will kicked off his shoes and climbed in with her. The sheets, like the air above them, were very cold, so cold that it seemed as though they'd never be normal again. He clasped her to his body and wrapped his arms tightly around her. In a last desperate attempt to generate warmth, he kissed her.

Polly yanked him closer and kissed him back with enthusiasm. The bed grew warm, warmer, so warm that they wiggled out of their clothes as though emerging from cocoons. Will's kisses grew less frantic and more passionate and his mouth moved from her lips to her throat, then at last to her breast. She sighed in pleasure and relief. "Darling Polly," he murmured. "What did you see, my brave little love? What was out there?"

"Cailean Ferguson, I saw Cailean the sailor boy, but he's gone, gone, and I hope, gone for good," she whispered in tones of deep conviction. "And I think . . . I think he thanked me. He tipped his hat to me." She wrapped her arms around him as tightly as she could. "Let's make love, Will. Let the dead go and let's celebrate being alive!"

That was something he could do, even if he hadn't been able to get rid of the ghost. No, the ghostie. He hadn't believed, but now he knew it had been a ghostie, a true Eilean Dubh spook; only something dead could have projected those terrible waves of cold, produced that bright-hot glare and fueled the dread that had enveloped him. And she had stood up to it, she'd faced it with raw courage when he'd been paralyzed and useless. Now she wanted life and it was up to him to provide it. That, at least, he could do.

He made love to her with all the skill at his command and at last came into her and made her his own. He whispered, "I love you, Polly," and heard her respond, "I love you, Will." Then, warmed to their bones, they fell asleep.

Will woke when the light of morning came through the bedroom curtains. He whispered in her ear, "I've got to go, Polly, my dearest; my father will worry himself to death if I'm not there when he wakes up. He'll think I've been in a car accident or fallen off a cliff or been bitten by a rabid dog or something like that. Go back to sleep and I'll come to you later."

She mumbled her understanding and Will got up, dressed and left. She listened to the car leave, then snuggled back down into the warm place he'd left, happy with what she remembered of the night before. She had confronted the ghostie, vanquished her own fears, and she had taken Will as her lover. And he'd said he loved her, and called her "dearest" when he woke.

A good evening's work, she thought, and fell back into a deep, dreamless sleep.

Part V

Family Spirit

Twenty-five

*Right from the moment of our birth, we are under the care and
kindness of our parents, and then later on in our life when we are
oppressed by sickness and become old, we are again dependent on
the kindness of others.*

The Dalai Lama

Will arrived back at the Rose Hotel just after Gordon had unlocked the front door for the day and had headed into the kitchen to start the first pot of coffee. Will climbed the stairs to his room, where he undressed, showered and dressed again in fresh clothes. Then he opened the door to his father's room. "Good morning, Dad," he said, peeking in.

There was no response.

"Still asleep," he said under his breath and went to the window to open the curtains. Then he turned and looked at his father in the bright morning sunshine.

He was drowsing, eyes closed, and he looked dreadful, his face puffy and gray.

Alarmed, Will moved swiftly to the bedside, found his wrist and took his pulse. It was weak and it fluttered erratically. "Dad," he said frantically. "Dad, can you hear me?"

The older man's eyes opened and he whispered, "I don't feel so well, son." Robert Burns had wakened during the night gasping for breath and had had to prop himself up on two pillows to go back to sleep. Even then he waked frequently, feeling as though he were suffocating. And his abdomen had hurt; it hurt now, in fact. Couldn't be appendicitis, he'd thought; he'd been through that years ago and his appendix was long gone, stored in a bottle in some lab somewhere. Maybe it was indigestion; maybe he'd eaten too many from that tempting plate of Sheilah's cookies while he was reading.

The shortness of breath, though, was a strange symptom for which he had no explanation. He felt as though he'd run a mile in four minutes. He tried hard not to gasp, not wanting to alarm Will, but he couldn't stop himself; he was desperate for air.

"I'm going to get a doctor, Dad," said Will. "Hang in there, I'll be right back." He bolted from the room and down the stairs, shouting for Gordon when he got to the lobby.

"I'm here," said the hotel keeper, coming from the kitchen. "What's amiss?"

"My father is ill. We need a doctor right away."

Gordon seized the phone and called Ros MacPherson at home, and within minutes the Island doctor was in Robert Burns' bedroom, examining him. Ros did not believe in keeping information from his patients, but the name of this condition was alarming and he thought it best to tell Will first. He beckoned him out into the hall and said bluntly, "It's congestive heart failure."

"My God, is he going to die?"

"We need to get him to hospital in Edinburgh at once. The Royal Margaret there specializes in heart cases and they've got the equipment for a proper diagnosis and treatment."

"Edinburgh! How can we do that?"

"By helicopter. If you agree, I'll have our secretary call the hospital and Murdoch the Chopper to arrange the flight. The Royal Margaret has a helipad so he can fly your father directly there."

"All right," said Will grimly. "I'll get Dad ready."

Robert Burns, predictably, wanted to call his Eilean Dubh friends and tell them where he was going. He had a dinner date with Darroch and Jean that should be canceled, he insisted weakly, and he would not relax until Will had called and left a brief garbled message proffering his regrets without explanation on the Mac an Righs' ansaphone. After that he supervised the packing of a small case for the trip, forcing out instructions from his tortured throat. At last Will said, "I know what you need, Dad. Relax, take it easy and let me do it for you."

By then Robert Burns was glad to rest. Talking took so much effort, he thought, and wondered what was wrong with him. But he was strangely reluctant to ask. It did not seem like another heart attack to him but it must be something serious if he was being flown by helicopter to an Edinburgh hospital. Was he dying? He lay still, tried not to worry, and longed for his dear wife Louise.

It took less than an hour to arrange the flight. Robert Burns was moved to the helicopter pad by Eilean Dubh's trusty old ambulance, and strapped on a stretcher in the back of the chopper, Will by his side holding his hand for the entire flight. The chopper swept over sea and the Highlands and down the length of the country to Edinburgh and the Royal Margaret Hospital, where the older man was transferred to intensive care and surrounded by a team of doctors, nurses and orderlies, who began treatment and further evaluation.

Will paced and worried during the electrocardiogram, the echocardiogram, and the x-rays, and worried even more after his father's primary surgeon confirmed Ros MacPherson's diagnosis of congestive heart failure. He was only slightly reassured when he was told that it was treatable with a combination of drugs, rest and a sodium- and fluid-restricted diet. The physician did not think that surgical procedures would be necessary, but he would monitor Robert Burns for several days before making a decision.

By the time this verdict was rendered, it was afternoon and Will was at last able to search for a phone to call his mother and siblings. He woke Flora, who roused the rest of the family, and the house erupted into a flurry of plane reservations and packing. Relieved to have other family members involved and rushing to his rescue, Will slumped against the wall by the phone. It had been in the back of his mind off and on all day to call Polly and explain what had happened, and why he hadn't come to see her as he'd promised. She'd probably be worrying about him, he thought.

Then he realized that he did not have her phone number and that two other people were waiting impatiently to use the telephone. "Sorry," he mumbled and wandered off down the hall, wondering how he could get Polly's number. It would be too new to be listed anywhere. Should he call Darroch? Or Sally? He realized that he did not have their numbers, either, and wanted to gnash his teeth in frustration.

It came to him that he was hungry and if he ate something perhaps he could think more clearly. He hurried off in the direction of the hospital cafeteria. He was just putting the last bite of something vaguely resembling meatloaf into his mouth when he heard himself being paged. Frantic with fear – had his father taken a turn for the worse? –he ran for the stairs and quickly presented himself, breathing hard, in Robert Burns' room.

His father was sleeping peacefully and looked to be much improved. Wondering why he'd been paged, Will hurried to the nursing station and was hailed by the ward secretary. "A call came in for you from the United States, Mr. MacDonald. Here's the number for you to ring them back," and she presented him with a slip of paper on which his mother's home number was written.

He ran to the second floor phone, called, got Flora and heard the details of the trip she'd booked for herself, her mother and brother, arriving early the next morning. "Can you make us a hotel reservation? I've got to have a few minutes to help Mother pack and I'm running out of time. We need to be at the airport in two hours to check in," she said.

Will asked the ward secretary for assistance in finding a nearby hotel, and acted on her suggestion. He had already booked a visitor's room in the hospital for himself. Once his mother arrived, she could move into it and he would go to the hotel. After he'd made these arrangements, he went to work again on the problem of calling Polly.

But every idea he came up with for obtaining her number was a dead end. He had no phone numbers for anyone on Eilean Dubh and precious little chance to obtain them; every time he went to the public phone on the second floor where his father was, it was suddenly busy and there was a line waiting to use it. The ward secretary politely declined when he asked if he could use her phone; it was reserved for medical personnel, she explained, and she could not break the rule. But there were public phones on every floor of the hospital, she assured him.

There were, but the first floor was in an exceptionally noisy space near the entrance, the third floor was out of order, the fourth floor always had a line waiting, and the phone on the fifth floor had been commandeered by a large family, all of whom were impatiently waiting for their turn. And the sixth floor phone was also out of order.

Will cursed, and longed desperately for the cell phone he'd left home in America because it wouldn't work abroad. Why hadn't he rented a Scottish cell phone, if such a thing existed? He should have anticipated a situation like this, knowing his father's health.

That evening he spent an hour wandering the streets near the hospital looking for some place decent to eat, finally locating a small pub down an unsavory side street that provided him with a disgusting microwaved lasagna, a side of soggy chips and a mug of tepid beer. The hospital cafeteria had been closed by the time he'd finally gone down, after helping his father with his meal. "It doesn't have any taste," Robert Burns had complained about the salt-free food, and had gotten uncharacteristically cross about his supper. It had taken a lot of coaxing to get him to eat and Will was worn out from the effort afterwards.

He gave up the idea of calling Polly that evening, tucked his father in with the aid of a nurse and two orderlies, and staggered off to the closet-sized space that was the hospital's visitors' accommodations. He fell asleep and woke at three, then at four, worrying about his father, even though he knew the staff would let him know if there were any problems during the night. No one disturbed him, but he still felt when he woke the next day as though he hadn't slept a wink.

Twenty-six

*To me the ideal doctor would be a man endowed with
profound knowledge of life and of the soul, intuitively divining
any suffering or disorder of whatever kind, and restoring
peace by his mere presence.*

Henri Amiel

The morning was taken up with breakfast, his father's and his own, and a long wait for the doctor on duty to make her rounds, during which time Will didn't dare to leave Robert Burns's room for fear of missing her. She was quiet, soft-spoken, and terse in what Will recognized from his time on Eilean Dubh as a peculiarly Scottish way of communicating, but she gave him full, frank information without equivocation. She said that his father was improving, but the danger was not yet over.

When it was nearly time to head for the airport to meet his family, he realized he had no means of transportation; the rental car was left on Eilean Dubh. The flight was arriving at Prestwick Airport between Edinburgh and Glasgow. He'd have to take a train to the airport and pick up a rental car there to drive everyone to the hospital. The complexity of these arrangements had him tearing his hair, and at last the ward secretary took pity, and got someone from the hospital's volunteers' association to help him.

By the time he was in a taxi and on the way to Edinburgh's Waverly train station, Will was exhausted; and by the time he got to Glasgow Prestwick Airport, he was frustrated beyond belief. But seeing his mother and siblings deplane made his struggles worthwhile. He'd finally have others involved in making decisions about his father's care, a responsibility which had weighed heavily upon him; he was, after all, the younger brother and not used to being in charge.

But first his family needed help and they all depended on him to provide it. All three were exhibiting signs of frayed nerves. "Helluva long flight," Robert Bruce had snapped at him as though it were Will's fault. The other two said little, but Flora was pale and the older woman was trembling with fatigue and nerves.

There was a scare that Louise's luggage had been lost, until it finally tumbled onto the carousel fifteen minutes after the rest of the baggage had been spewed out. Then there was a hassle at the rental car counter; Robert Bruce and Flora both wanted to sign on as drivers but only Flora had thought to bring her driver's license with her. And when that was straightened out, Will had to negotiate the complex tangle of the M8 Motorway after dark to get back to Edinburgh. His shoulders and lower back were aching with tension by the time they arrived at the Royal Margaret Hospital.

He led his party into Robert Burns's room to be greeted with a querulous, "Will, can't you do anything about this food? It's awful." And then, "Why, Louise! And you kids! Where the heck did you all spring from?"

Free of responsibility for the first time since he'd left California, Will sank down on a chair, slipped back into a subsidiary role and let the rest of the family take over. He was able to relax only until Robert Burns's chief surgeon, extremely distinguished and very crisp, came in for his final evening check on his patient. Will stood up respectfully. "Good evening, Mr. MacKenzie," he said. "Allow me to present the rest of our family," and he introduced each one.

They immediately surrounded the surgeon and began to interrogate him, led by Robert Bruce in his authoritative businessman's manner. Flora produced an electronic notepad and began to write down everything that was said. Louise, used by her hospital work to dealing with medical personnel, stood quietly and put in a word now and then in her soft, gentle, insistent voice.

Will wanted to slink out of the room in embarrassment. He realized suddenly that he had gotten used to the reserved manner of the Scots who'd surrounded him for the last few weeks, and he felt sorry for the surgeon, besieged by this pack of Yankees who seemed surprisingly loud and aggressive in contrast, though they were just normal Americans. He caught his father's eye and realized he was sharing the same experience, and they smiled at each other ruefully.

Taking charge, Robert Burns raised his voice. "Here now! It's me that Mr. MacKenzie has come to see, not you folks. Step back and let him have a gander at me so he can get himself home to the wife and weans for his supper."

"Of course, Dad." "Sorry, Daddy." "I beg your pardon, Mr. MacKenzie." The family parted as if by magic and the surgeon was able to advance to his patient's bedside.

"Your family is concerned about you, of course, Mr. MacDonald. Not surprising at all," said the Scot, smiling his frosty smile. "How are you feeling this evening?"

"I'm a lot perkier, but I can tell you I'm longing for some food that has a wee bit of taste to it," grumbled Robert Burns.

"You'll get used to the natural taste of food in time, and you won't want anything different." The surgeon completed his examination and left, and the family began to pour its comments and worries once again into Will's increasingly less sympathetic ears.

"Are you sure that man is qualified?" asked Robert Bruce.

"You called him 'Mister,' William Wallace," said Flora. "Can't we get a real doctor for Daddy?"

"He is a real doctor," said Will in exasperation. "He's one of Edinburgh's most eminent surgeons and supremely well qualified and we're lucky he could take us on. Everyone in the hospital calls him mister, not doctor. Don't ask me why but that's how it's done here."

They pondered that for a while, then turned to Robert Burns, who forestalled their remarks by saying firmly, "I'm very well satisfied with Mr. MacKenzie and the care I'm getting here, so let's not rock the boat. Settle down, all of you, and fill me in on how things are at home. How's the expansion into France going, Robert Bruce? Are we getting new orders from your marketing campaign, Flora? Is your fund raising campaign for the hospital under way, Louise? Come on, you guys, I've been out of touch for weeks and I'm dying for news." An unfortunate turn of phrase, Will thought, since he had, indeed, been close to death.

They all began to talk at once and Will slipped away, his ears ringing. He had never realized it before, but his family *en masse* was a bit overwhelming. He had other things to think about, though; he had come up with a great idea while sitting in a traffic jam on the M-80, Polly as always in the back of his mind. He'd call Anna Wallace, the newspaper editor who Polly said had arranged her cottage rental. She'd certainly have the phone number of the place.

Earlier in the day, before leaving for the airport, he'd tried to get a phone number for Sally and Ian *Mòr* MacDonald. The two women were friends and might have exchanged numbers, he'd thought. But he had had a run-in with an exasperated Directory Assistance operator, who had asked him in a snappish Scottish way if he had any idea how many Ian MacDonalds there were in the Highlands and Islands area of Scotland. (There were millions of them or so it appeared.) She had informed him tartly that he'd have to have the address of the man he was seeking for her to be able to help him further.

As deflated as a pricked balloon, Will had surrendered the phone to the person waiting and had gone off to ponder another option: if he could figure out how to spell Darroch Mac an Rìgh's name, which he'd never seen written down, he could get that number and call Jean.

But his new idea, Anna Wallace, was a much better possibility. Hers was an easy name to spell; it was his, after all. And he even knew the name of her newspaper: *The Island Star*. He could ask for both numbers. He was raring at the bit, now, to tackle Directory Assistance again. He twitched impatiently as he waited in line until it was his turn again, at last.

The Island Star's number was produced with no trouble whatsoever and so quickly that Will had to scramble to get his paper and pen into his left hand to write it down. Mercifully there was no one else waiting for the phone and he was able to dial her right away. His hopes rose, only to plummet to the bottom of his soul when Anna said, "Sorry, Will, the Ferguson cottage doesn't have a phone."

Damn, he knew that. Polly had told him about the lack of a phone after the first haunting; how stupid he was not to have remembered it. He thanked Anna and hung up, too numb with shock and disappointment to even think of asking if she had any idea of how he could contact his love. Anna was left staring at the phone, wondering why she hadn't thought to volunteer Zach to deliver a message to Polly; he went right by her cottage on his way to his archaeological dig.

"Now I wonder what that's all about. He sounded quite agitated," she said aloud, her newswoman's instincts and Island gossip genes both aroused. But she had no way of calling him back; she had no idea where to reach him. She dialed 1471, the Call Return number, but got a message that the number was in service for outgoing calls only. She grimaced in frustration, but could think of nothing else to do.

Will leaned dispiritedly against the wall by the phone. He was out of ideas, he hadn't the slightest clue, he was terminally baffled about how to reach Polly, and he was seriously freaked out about the whole situation. Reluctantly he decided that he'd have to wait until he could talk to her in person. Hopefully that would be soon, as his father was getting better every day, and at the point of being in a stable situation. He would slip back to Eilean Dubh once the rest of the family was firmly installed around Robert Burns' hospital bed.

He glanced at his watch. It was past ten o'clock, too late to try anything or anyone else. He pulled himself together and went off to say goodnight to his father, to get his mother tucked into the Royal Margaret's tiny visitor's room, and to cart the rest of his family off to the Hotel Holyrood. Once there, and with everyone checked in and settled at last, he collapsed into bed and fell instantly asleep.

Twenty-seven

Air an doras air an tig amharas a-steach, thèid gràdh a-mach.
When doubt comes in, love goes out.

Gaelic proverb

Two days earlier Polly had waked to find herself alone in the cottage. Will was gone from her side. She vaguely remembered him kissing her goodbye, and whispering that he was returning to the Rose Hotel so his father wouldn't worry about him.

That seemed very thoughtful to her. What a nice guy he was and how sweet he was to his father, she'd thought, and gone back to sleep.

Now she was up, dressed, and ready to celebrate life with her new lover. He'd promised he'd come, and she looked forward to his arrival eagerly, but it was getting on toward lunch and there was no sign of him. Full of joyous energy, she occupied herself with housekeeping chores, sweeping the living room and kitchen briskly, and rinsing out laundry in the kitchen sink and hanging it on the line in the back of the cottage where Will had taught her to dance. She danced around that area twice using the skip change of step, singing about the bonnie banks and braes of Loch Lomond to express her happiness.

She kept her hands busy but her mind scarcely knew what she was doing, filled as it was by thoughts of the evening past. The encounter with the ghostie had left her awe-struck and trembling. Where had she found the courage to open the door, she wondered. And had she seen what she'd thought she'd seen? Was it really Cailean Ferguson, and if it was, would he do as she asked and look elsewhere for his Peigi? Was she finally free of his awful presence?

There was one thing of which she had no doubts and no qualms: Will had made delightful love to her. He'd told her he loved her and called her "dearest." Every time she thought about that her heart swelled with pleasure and picked up its rhythm to jig time, because she was no longer afraid to face the truth. She knew that she loved him, too.

And when he came to her today, she'd tell him that over and over, and between kisses and cuddles they could discuss their future, a future that loomed as golden in her eyes as California sunshine. They would plot out a wonderful life together. She could hardly wait for him to arrive so they could start making plans.

But he didn't come.

By tea time, she was seriously worried.

He couldn't have had an accident in the short drive to the Rose; she would have heard sirens and seen signs of activity on the road in front of the cottage. But the day had been unusually quiet and still with no signs of disturbance of the Island's tranquility.

Something must have happened, though, to Will or his father. At seven in the evening she decided to assert control over her worries. She would call Will at the Rose Hotel to ask him bluntly why he hadn't shown up as he'd promised. She gathered a fistful of coins of varying denominations, marched out in the early evening light to the spider-infested red telephone box and found the Rose's number in the dog-eared phone book hanging from a hook. She filled the slot with coins, dialed and got Gordon Morrison on the other end of the line.

It was the height of the evening rush in the dining room and Gordon was beside himself with frustration. Someone – it must have been that scatty new girl they were training in – had taken a reservation for six people without checking to ensure that there was a table available. There wasn't, and he had to figure out where he was going to put the excess guests; he couldn't very well send them away without dinner. Word would get around. It would ruin the Hotel's reputation and people would never again trust a reservation there. The *Eilean Dubhannaich* had long memories, and they were slow to forgive mistakes, especially ones that deprived them of a much-anticipated posh dinner in a suitably posh atmosphere. And that did not include dining in a corner of the kitchen.

Such things never happened at the Rose, which Gordon ran with military precision at all times, and he hadn't a clue about what he was going to do. Normally the soul of patience, he couldn't keep himself from snapping at the inconvenient caller.

"Can you please connect me to the room of William Wallace MacDonald?" said Polly timidly.

"No, I can't. He's gone."

"Will's gone?" she said in a trembling, astonished voice.

"Aye, he and his father. They left this morning." Gordon wanted only to get back to his dining dilemma. He didn't know who the caller was and it was his policy not to give out information about his guests, especially information about a medical emergency. He'd already said too much. Into the yawning silence, he said curtly, "Is there anything else I can help you with?"

"No," Polly whispered, and hung up.

She was never quite sure afterwards how she got back to the cottage. She stumbled in, dropped the handful of coins on the floor and made her way across the room, using the chair for support for her shaking legs, aware only that she had to sit down before she fell down. She collapsed onto the sofa, breathless with effort.

Will was gone. It was a classic betrayal, the stuff of old time novels and movies, so predictable she felt like the most foolish kind of fool. He had made love to her, made promises – at least, implied promises – and he had left her. They would have no golden future together, and she could not believe it. Her dreams were smashed to tiny, nay, miniscule bits.

It was just like what had happened with Duane except that she wasn't with child. Or was she? She couldn't remember Will using any sort of protection during their impulsive lovemaking, and given the ease with which she'd become pregnant the last time, it could have happened again.

Her life could be ruined, all over again.

It was *déjà vu*, all over again.

Polly burst into tears and wept until her eyes were swollen shut and she was nearly unconscious from dehydration. She fell asleep on the sofa and woke in the middle of the night. For a moment she thought she heard the seafaring ghostie hammering on the door, then realized it was the sad, solemn beat of her broken heart echoing in her ears.

The ghostie would have been preferable, she thought crossly; at least he'd been polite and tipped his hat to her before he left. That was more than William Wallace MacDonald had done. For a moment she almost missed her spectral companion. That dilemma had been easy to solve, compared with what she now faced.

Why did Will leave her? She pondered that as she hauled herself up into a sitting position, massaging neck and shoulders made stiff and sore from her awkward position while she'd slept. Was it something she'd said? Or done? Wrack her brain as she might, she couldn't think of any misstep she'd made.

It must be her basic inadequacy, she thought. He'd thought it over and decided she wasn't good enough for him, not pretty enough, not smart enough. Not good enough for his family (though Robert Burns had seemed to like her), not special enough for his ranch home with its mile-long driveway and its cook and chauffeur. Not good enough for his love and his lovemaking.

All her old doubts about herself came to full flower. She wasn't up to snuff, she couldn't toe the mark, she had nothing to offer, she wasn't attractive, she wasn't smartly dressed, and she had no scintillating conversation except what she read in *The New Yorker*. She was a cold and lonely loser once again.

She was useless.

There was one thing she could do well and that was to cry.

So she did.

Twenty-eight

There are a terrible lot of lies going about the world,
and the worst of it is that half of them are true.

Winston Churchill

The *Eilean Dubhannaich* were consumed with curiosity about what had happened to Robert Burns MacDonald. They had heard through the Island gossip hotline about his emergency airlift to the Royal Margaret hospital in Edinburgh, but no one knew what was wrong with him. Speculation was rampant. Some thought he'd had a fall and broken a limb, some thought he'd gotten sick, and one person even dared to whisper that she had it on good authority that it was food poisoning.

Had she heard it, the latter speculation would have made the Rose Hotel's gourmet chef Sheilah Morrison glow red-hot at the insult to her cooking, and fear of her temper caused the story to die a quick and harmless death before it got to the Rose's kitchen. Sheilah didn't get mad often, but when she did, gale warnings were hoisted and small craft were advised to return to port at once. "She's an East Londoner, and you know how short their fuses are," was the Island saying about Sheilah, although only Gordon knew if it was true or not. No one else had dared test it.

The airlift *dramatis personae* weren't talking either. Ros MacPherson and his medical staff regarded patients' privacy as sacrosanct. Gordon Morrison felt the same way about his hotel guests. And Murdoch the Chopper's other nickname was Murdoch the Clam, for his taciturnity was a legend on the Island. He was so close-mouthed that no Islanders bothered any more trying to worm information out of him; they knew all they'd get was an insult. "How's that a matter of concern to you?" he'd snort, before he turned away, his rumpled old face assuming an expression of disgust.

174

On the other hand, Deirdre MacQuirter, the helicopter firm's secretary, was a babbling, burbling, free-flowing fountain of information about everything that happened or didn't happen on the helipad. But she'd been sick at home at the time of the emergency flight, and not even she could get Murdoch the Chopper to tell her what had happened to Robert Burns. She was as much in the dark as the rest of the *Eilean Dubhannaich,* and her frustration was intense. She was one of Eilean Dubh's most dedicated gossip mongers and she had a reputation to maintain of always being first with the news.

Most Islanders knew that William Wallace and Polly had been walking out together, but since Polly was playing least-in-sight, no one could ask her about her boyfriend's father, as they certainly would have found a way to do had the girl been available for interrogation. They'd ask delicately out of genuine concern, of course, and they'd get the information or choke in the trying. But the American was nowhere to be seen. She'd vanished like the ghostie that everyone knew was haunting her cottage. Had she gone off with Murdoch the Chopper and his two important passengers?

No one, not even Deirdre, had quite enough *chutzpah* to knock on Polly's door, and if she was home, demand that she tell them everything they wanted to know.

The one person on the Island who could get information out of the tight-lipped Murdoch, Ros, Gordon and their ilk was Darroch Mac an Rìgh, the Laird, and he was tied up by influenza and utterly unavailable for chit-chat of any kind. Both Hamish and Fiona had particularly nasty cases of the flu, and both cottages were engulfed by mounds of dirty diapers, despairing wails, and soaring temperatures. All four grandparents worked in shifts to relieve Sally, and Ian Mòr stopped by on his rounds as often as he could. The twins' misery left no one in the combined Mac an Rìgh/MacDonald households time to worry about their American visitors, although Darroch had been meaning to call Robert Burns to check on his welfare. But he never got the chance, there was always another load of diapers to wash.

Only Elspeth knew how serious Will and Polly's relationship had become, and she was so worried about her young friend and the man who was Polly's prospective papa-in-law that she wanted very much to hobble down to the cottage to commiserate with her. But the arthritis in her back was particularly troublesome this week. She'd not even been able to visit the Seniors' Residence for tea with her friends, an outing always eagerly anticipated, because it was too painful for her to get in and out of a car, let alone sit up in a straight, hard chair for a couple of hours of chat and Oighrig MacShannock's homemade scones.

So she stayed at home, supplied with hot water bottles and cups of Earl Grey by her concerned daughter and painkillers from an equally concerned doctor, Ros MacPherson, and fretted about Polly. No use asking Barabal for news; she was a charter member of the Island anti-gossip battalion. She would have done anything for her mother except snoop.

"Really, Mama, it's none of my business, or yours either," would have been her firm reply.

Elspeth sometimes wished she hadn't brought her daughter up to be so correct in her behavior. It was a nuisance at times, and this was one of them.

Twenty-nine

Only when we are no longer afraid do we begin to live.

Dorothy Thompson

Will thoughtfully contemplated his father's hospital room, once so quiet, now seething with activity. It was filled with his mother Louise and her knitting (a comfort to her in times of stress), his brother Robert Bruce and his smartphone (constantly texting his office in California), and his sister Flora and her ever-present tablet (what was she always scribbling notes about?). Flora always had with her a china mug of gourmet coffee; she must have stashed a gallon of it somewhere, held at perfect drinking temperature, and purchased from the ultra-hip coffee shop she'd located within two blocks of the hospital, to Will's bemusement. All he'd been able to find in the area were the slovenly pub with the soggy chips and a row of sinister boarded-up shops plastered with advertising placards for defunct rock groups' latest concerts.

In the midst of the hubbub Robert Burns reigned supreme. Drugs and the severely-restricted diet had eased the fluid build-up in his body so the puffiness and shortness of breath were nearly gone, and the enforced bed rest had eased his fatigue so much that the staff were talking about getting him up for a longer walk about the ward that afternoon.

Bright-eyed and bushy-tailed, as he would have called himself, and clear-headed, he was in his element, ruling the family and the family firm as usual.

Will felt himself unneeded, and that was all right with him. With the help of the *Eilean Dubhannaich*, he had gotten his father the medical help he required, and now Robert Burns was on the road to recovery. Better than that, he was on the road to correcting the bad habits that had led to his sudden illness, habits that no one had dared nag him about. Under the stern guiding hand of his physician, he was even beginning to accept his salt-free and fat-depleted diet, though he still grumbled about it.

My work here is finished, and I've done a good job, Will thought proudly, and came to a decision. He missed Polly very much and was desperate to get back to her; surely there'd be no problem if he left the hospital now. He made his way to his father's bed, sat down by him, and waited until the rest of the family was distracted and he had Robert Burns' complete attention. "Dad, may I talk to you for a minute?" he said quietly.

Robert Burns scrutinized his son. Then he raised his voice and said, "William Wallace and I need a private confab. Can the rest of you find something to do in the hall? Maybe somebody could get me a decent cup of coffee instead of this hospital slop."

"Of course, darling." "Sure thing, Dad." "I'll fetch the coffee, Daddy; I know just where to get it." And in twinkling they had all bustled out. Will marveled anew at his father's firm grasp on the family reins. He was always jovial and good-natured but he ruled unconditionally. That knowledge made Will even more nervous about what he was going to say, but he was determined to speak his piece. He gathered his courage and said, "Dad, I need to go back to Eilean Dubh."

"Back to your little lady friend?" asked Robert Burns, smiling.

Will, who had been prepared to babble excuses about settling the Rose Hotel bill or packing up changes of clothes and underwear for them both, breathed a sigh of relief. No need to be a coward; he could be straight with his father. "Yes. I haven't been able to reach her by phone and she'll be wondering if I've deserted her." He said the last bit with a chuckle, never dreaming that Polly was thinking exactly that.

"Well, you'd better be on your way; we don't want her to worry. Let's get that Murdoch the Whathisname fellow back here to pick you up."

Will protested, "Oh, that's an unnecessary expense. I can take the train to Inverness and catch the helicopter there."

"And waste all that time with your girl worrying her head off about you? Nonsense. It's not an unnecessary expense; it's what money is for, to grease the wheels and make life easier. We'll have Murdoch collect you here at the hospital helicopter pad."

"Yes, Dad," said Will gratefully. "Thanks, Dad."

"Now let's talk about that young lady waiting back on the Island. Time to level with me, son. Are the two of you going to make a match of it?"

"If she'll have me," said Will. In the few spare moments he'd had since he'd left Eilean Dubh, he'd come to a decision. He was going to ask Polly to marry him and he'd thought deeply about how to word his proposal. He was still working out the details, in his methodical way. He'd never proposed before, and he intended this time to be the only time, so it had to be good. He'd like it to be elegant and graceful and so romantic that she'd have to say yes. Not that he doubted she would, of course, but a little window dressing would grease the wheels, as his father said. It seemed an inelegant figure of speech to describe a proposal, but that was how Robert Burns talked.

"I'll bet she'll have you in a New York minute. She seemed mighty fond of you."

"I hope you're right." He hesitated, then he decided he may as well come out with the rest of his deep thoughts. He'd never been afraid of his father, but he was desperately afraid of hurting his feelings and seeming to reject him. He thought briefly of Polly and her bravery when confronting the ghost and her example gave him the courage to forge ahead with what had to be said. "I've got something else to tell you, Dad."

His father gave him an appraising look. "Out with it, William Wallace."

"I'm going back to school and I'm not going to take more business courses. I'm going to study architecture."

Robert Burns leaned back against his pillow, his brow furrowed. "Are you? That's going to be hard to work into the business unless we decide to build a new headquarters and have you design it. And that would be only a one-off, not a career."

Will took a deep breath and said, "I'm not going to join the family business, Dad. I'm sorry, but I can't see any way I can fit in. And I don't think you or Robert Bruce or Flora need me."

His father stared at him consideringly for an interminable period of time. Will fidgeted, but held his head high and met his father's gaze bravely. Then Robert Burns grinned. "I've been wondering when you'd come to realize that," he said.

Astonished, Will gasped, "You're not surprised?"

"Nope. You never seemed to have the passion for the industrial fastener business that Robert Bruce and Flora have," said his father. "Frankly,

I consider myself lucky to have inveigled the pair of them into my clutches. So I lose one, but two out of three ain't bad, is it?" He chuckled.

"You're not disappointed? You don't mind?"

"No, son, I don't mind. You go off and become an architect if that's what you want. I'll be glad to foot the bill for whatever education you need and I'll be proud to have an architect in the family; it's a noble profession. But here's the tradeoff: you marry that little Polly gal pronto, so that Louise and I can look forward to grandchildren before we get too old to chase around to Scottish festivals with them."

He smiled and extended his hand to Will, who shook it solemnly. "I don't blame you at all for striking off on your own. To tell you the truth, I haven't especially enjoyed being the boss of the company all these years. It was something I had to do when we were getting started, because there was no one else with the guts and the drive to do it. Designing, now that's another story. That's my real love; there's nothing like working out a simple design to solve a complicated problem. Maybe that's where you get your interest in architecture. Part of that is about designing to solve problems.

"I'm looking forward to the day when I can spend all my time on the design side of the biz and let Robert Bruce run the whole shebang. He took to being in charge right away; he's a bright boy and a natural-born leader. Now let's call him back in here and get him busy arranging your helicopter flight. He loves to arrange things, you know, and we may as well take advantage of that. Find people's talents and use them; that's my motto. Open the door and let in the mob, William Wallace."

Will hesitated at the door, his hand on the knob. "There's one more thing, Dad. Would you mind calling me Will instead of William Wallace?"

Astonished, Robert Burns said, "But you're named after Scotland's greatest hero. Don't you like that?"

"Of course I do, Dad, and when I become an architect I'll let everyone know that my name is William Wallace MacDonald. Famous architects always have three names, like Frank Lloyd Wright or Charles Rennie Mackintosh. But William Wallace is a lot to live up to and right now I feel more comfortable being just Will."

His father snorted. "Okay, just Will. Got any more surprises for me?"

Will grinned. "No, sir. Three is enough for one day."

The other three MacDonalds flooded back in when he opened the door. Robert Bruce and Louise looked at him with questions on their faces, and Flora said, "What was that all about, William Wallace?"

He said, "I'm going to be married, I'm going to be an architect, and you can call me Will from now on." He grinned at the three astonished faces.

And the next morning, courtesy of his brother's meticulous arrangements, William Wallace MacDonald found himself in Murdoch the Chopper's chopper on his way back to Eilean Dubh.

Thirty

*The past isn't **dead**. It isn't even past.*

William Faulkner

*P*olly surfaced slowly from a sleep filled with bad dreams and ominous portents. Four days, she thought, coming awake to unhappiness. This was the beginning of the fourth day since she'd been abandoned by her lover. Would she feel this terrible every morning for the rest of her life? How could she bear it if she did?

She went into the kitchen and made herself a cup of tea and a piece of toast. She'd been living on tea and toast the last three days, and had barely been able to keep that down, so sick had she felt. This morning's toast took her last piece of stale bread, she noted; she was going to have to get a new loaf if she weren't to starve to death. And she certainly wasn't going to starve over a man so cruel he could walk out on her without a word, she thought with a fierce flash of anger.

She'd stayed in the cottage the three previous days, avoiding all contact with anyone on Eilean Dubh. She reasoned that since somehow they'd all known about the haunting of the cottage, she was sure that they also knew about her involvement with Will, and they'd know he had left her. They might even know why.

She couldn't bear the thought of their pity. But she'd pull herself together and make a trip down to the village as surreptitiously as she could manage, and hope she could slip in and out of town without having to talk to anyone. That was highly unlikely, since the *Eilean Dubhannaich* were on the lookout for her, but Polly didn't know that.

She'd skip riding her bike; that made her too easy to spot. She'd walk into Ros Mór and go to the second bakery on the square, the one she'd never patronized before. No one knew her in that one. She'd grab a loaf of bread and slink away without a word to or from anyone. That might be cowardly, but she was tired of being brave. A person could only endure so much.

She felt a sudden wave of fatigue. She'd go into town later. Right now she felt like doing nothing more than staring at the walls of her kitchen, which had lost all semblance of coziness and had returned to dismal reality. What a desolate place this cottage is, she thought, forgetting the fun she'd had mastering the house's quirks and deficiencies, and the plans she'd made for her future there. She'd even looked forward to baking muffins now that she could light the oven without causing a major conflagration; and if that project was successful, maybe she'd try baking a cake to surprise Will.

Staring and remembering and thinking, that was all she could do. Her last worrying thought the previous night, before she put her head down on the table and dozed off, was that she was running out of money.

A hard truth had dawned upon her: she would have to leave Eilean Dubh. She could not stay here until she was completely broke; that would be a disaster. She needed to return to Minneapolis with enough money to pay for a couple of months' rental on an apartment, the security deposit, and food to last until she got a job. And she had spent herself down to almost that amount. She had her open-ended return flight and ferry tickets and three thousand dollars, and that was all that was left of her stash.

After she'd gotten involved with Will, she'd forgotten about money. She was having such a good time and her daily life was so bright and rosy that money receded to the background of her thoughts. Something would turn up, she'd thought, and refused to worry about it. And now the time of leaving fantasy land and facing the reckoning was upon her. What was it called? Oh, yes, "paying the piper." She'd danced – oh, how she'd danced! – and now she had to pay.

She had a week left on this month's rental and enough cash to scrape by on food if she shopped carefully. After that, it was farewell, Eilean Dubh.

She lifted her head from the table; she couldn't waste time sleeping. As soon as she got up the energy, she thought dully, she'd find her airplane ticket and the phone number to call to book a return flight. Maybe she'd even leave tomorrow on the ferry if there were a seat available on the plane the day after; she could pack and be out of here in no time. But right now she was too tired to move.

She slumped in the hard kitchen chair and contemplated the rickety old stove and the washtub-like sink. She was going to miss it all, strange as that seemed. The cottage had certainly posed challenges, and she couldn't help but realize that she'd grown in independence and maturity in her time on the Island. Her future might be lonely and desolate but she knew now that she had the courage to face whatever life threw at her. She'd hit bottom, but she knew that somewhere there was a way up.

Right now the way up was slippery with her tears.

She rose, trudged into the living room, picked up her purse and counted her money. "Plenty of cash if all I eat is toast for the next week," she said bitterly and wondered when she'd started talking aloud to herself.

She slung her purse over her shoulder and reached for the door.

Bam! Bam! Bam!

Polly recoiled with a yelp, stumbling back a full five steps. A wave of indignation swept her. Weren't her romantic troubles enough to bear? Was the ghostie back, too?

Bam! Bam! Bam! She was suddenly furious. *If it were the ghostie, she'd give him an earful,* she thought. She had enough to fret about without being haunted by some salty old spirit. Forgetting that Cailean had never come in daylight or when the moon was not full or when not preceded by a wave of cold, and without waiting for another, even louder knock, Polly seized the doorknob and flung the door open. "Damn it all to hell, I thought I told you where to go!" she shouted.

"What? Why?" gasped Will, staring at Polly in astonishment. He'd picked up the rental car from where he'd left it at the helipad four days ago and had driven straight to her cottage. And though he was worn out and a little groggy from the week's exertions, he was awake enough to look forward to a happy reunion, expecting hugs and kisses that would end in glorious lovemaking. He had not expected his love to react to his reappearance with screams and curses.

"What are you doing here?" demanded Polly, recovering from her shock at seeing him, and absolutely seething, furious that he'd turned up without warning after an interminable, inexplicable absence. The weasel. Had he come back to be sure her heart was completely broken?

"I'm here to see you. Why else would I be here?"

"A likely story. Go away," and she started to shut the door in his face.

"Polly, stop that at once," he said, taking the door from her grasp and inserting himself into the cottage. "What's the matter with you? What kind of a welcome is this?"

"What kind of a welcome did you expect, after disappearing for three, no, four days?" She grabbed the edge of the door and tried to push him out.

"I didn't disappear. I went to Edinburgh with my father," he snapped.

"Oh, that makes it all right? You make love to me and the next day you desert me and go gallivanting off to the big city without a word of whatever. You leave me all alone after professing your undying affection, and I'm supposed to smile sweetly and say, 'hello, darling' when you deign to return?" she snarled.

He said in high dudgeon, "I wasn't gallivanting. My father was suddenly taken ill and I had to get him to a hospital in Edinburgh by helicopter to save his life."

Taken aback, Polly said, her voice quivering, "Did you? Save his life, that is?"

"Yes. And once he was stabilized and my family arrived to take over, I came straight back to you. Although I wonder why, given the welcome I've received." He lifted his chin and stuck his nose in the air, his feelings seriously wounded.

Polly sniffled, the precursor of tears. "You could have called, at least."

That was the last straw for Will. "I tried! I tried so hard! God knows I tried, but you don't have a telephone, you silly woman!" Will shouted, remembering his struggles with pay phones, cranky telephone operators, and the endless queue of people waiting impatiently to snatch the receiver out of his clenched fist.

"Oh, that's right, I forgot," Polly said, and, feeling like a complete fool, burst into tears of humiliation.

"Darling Polly, don't cry," said Will in alarm. "Or I'll start bawling myself. These last four days have been awful. I thought my father was going to die before I got him to the hospital, I thought that wobbly old helicopter was going to crash into the sea, I thought my family was going to drive me mad, and I almost ripped a telephone off a wall in frustration. I missed you so much and needed you so much and I need you right now. And I'm truly sorry you were worried about me." He stepped forward and pulled her into his arms. He hugged her tightly against him and stroked her hair, enjoying its softness and the faint, odd whiff of vinegar that clung to it.

Polly sobbed against his sweater front and he had trouble deciphering what she was saying. Finally he understood. "You thought I'd left you for good? Why would I do that?" he said in astonishment.

"Duane," he heard her gasp, and remembered that was the name of the villain who'd left her pregnant and alone. He said firmly, "I'm not Duane, dearest. I love you and I'm never going to leave you."

"Really?"

"Yes, really. In fact . . ." He held her at arm's length so that he could gaze into her eyes. "We might as well get this settled once and for all. I don't have flowers and I don't have a ring and it's not how I planned to ask you, but will you marry me, Polly?"

"Marry you?" she gasped.

"Marry me, live with me, have fun with me."

"Fun?"

"Is there an echo in here? Yes, fun. I've been staid and serious and goal-oriented all my life and I've always done what was expected of me. Now I've declared my independence, and I want to have fun and I want to have it with you. I've been thinking hard about our future together and I've got some great ideas, Polly. Let's sit down and I'll tell you all about them." He put an arm around her waist and steered her to the sofa.

"First of all, we're going back to school, like you said you wanted to do. I'm going to learn to be an architect, and you can take classes in anything you fancy. What'll it be? French literature? Russian history? Chinese art? Mexican pottery? What would you prefer?"

"I'd like to learn how to cook," she whispered, dropping her head against his shoulder. William Wallace's enthusiasm was wonderful but a little overwhelming to her frazzled brain, and she had to concentrate to keep up with him.

"Super. You can study gourmet cooking."

Gourmet cooking? Like Julia Child, whom she'd always admired? Why not? "Then I'd like to learn how to sew and design clothes," she said, thinking of Elspeth Mac-a-Phi and her beautiful creations. Carried along with Will's ideas, anything seemed possible.

"You can major in home ec, or whatever they call it these days. Super. We'll rent a cute little apartment on campus and do all the fun things graduate students do. We'll go to arty movies and have deep conversations about the meaning of life and give dinner parties with strange food that you've learned how to prepare in your cooking classes in our apartment that you've learned how to decorate. And when we're finished with school, we'll have babies, grand kids for my parents to love and play with.

It's going to be wonderful, Polly. We are going to have such a good time together.

"Here's my next great idea. I'm going to buy this cottage and we'll spend our summers here on Eilean Dubh. I'll fix it up using what I learn in architecture school and I'll get the local carpenters and plumbers and roofers in to teach me about authentic remodeling of traditional Eilean Dubh properties. I'm going to speak to Darroch and that Mrs. Barabal about using the cottage as a demo to show people what they can do with their old houses. And – wait for it – here's a third great idea: I'll bet I can get Dad to set up a special grant to help fund anyone on the Island who wants to remodel. What do you think of all that?" Will finished triumphantly.

Polly stared at him, her own great idea dawning in her brain. "Could you put a thatched roof on this cottage?"

"Why not?" He had no idea at all of the trouble and expense involved in thatching a roof, but it would be traditional, and excitement and optimism led him to assent. He'd build her a deck, a sun porch, a sauna and a spa, anything she wanted. The cottage would become cozy and comfortable, the closest thing on Eilean Dubh to the ranch back home in California, he thought, forgetting all about the authentic remodeling he'd planned.

"Oh, that would make all my dreams come true! Fifteen minutes ago I was deserted, a loner once again, and now . . ."

"You've got me," he said, beaming, and kissed her. "Except that you haven't said 'yes' yet."

"Yes," said Polly, with a sigh of happiness. Bossy as usual, he was in charge of all the planning but she didn't care; they'd sort it out when it came to the actual doing and she knew he'd be reasonable. Just now she was enjoying riding the crest of his wave. She didn't have to manage her life all alone. She had a loving companion for the road ahead, an affectionate presence across the table from her morning, noon and night.

She felt like Cinderella. And that was all right; every woman deserved to feel like Cinderella at least once in her life.

Thirty-one

Call it a clan, call it a network, call it a tribe, call it a family.
Whatever you call it, whoever you are, you need one.

Jane Howard

Robert Burns MacDonald was discharged from the Edinburgh hospital and given a clean bill of health as far as going home was concerned, with stern instructions from Mr. MacKenzie to put himself under a doctor's care as soon as he returned to California. He agreed with a meekness that surprised his family, but reasserted himself when it came to his destination. "I'm heading back to Eilean Dubh," he said.

"But Dad . . . ," said both Robert Bruce and Flora, and Louise looked alarmed.

"I've got friends there I want to say goodbye to and I promised your mother I'd show her the Island. So that's where we're going, all of us. I've told William Wallace, uh, Will, to arrange accommodations for everyone at the Rose Hotel. You'll like it. It's very comfortable and Sheilah, the proprietor's wife, is a great cook. Best food I ever ate. I'll bet she can even make salt-free food taste wonderful."

"But the business . . . ," protested Robert Bruce.

"Can take care of itself for another week or two. Surely you've trained someone to take over in an emergency? It's time for them to prove themselves. Remember, you've always got to give your subordinates a chance to show they can cope; it's good for their morale. You can stay in touch with that electronic thingamajig you're always fiddling with." He said, staring imperiously at his son, "It's just industrial fasteners, boy. It's not world peace and the future of the universe."

"Daddy!" said Flora, shocked.

"You kids are too wrapped up in the business. You need to take some time off to smell the heather and listen to the music and do a little dancing. That's what I did and look at all the good it did me."

"Hmmmph," snorted Robert Bruce. "It got you congestive heart failure, if you call that good."

"Is that what I had?" said his father, shocked.

"Yes, but you're fine now. Dr., er, Mr. MacKenzie said so," said Louise, throwing a cross look at her oldest son. They'd all agreed not to mention Robert Burns's ailment in his presence. Now the curtain of secrecy had been lifted and he might start to fret about his health, and worrying would be unhealthy. She hurried to smooth over the *faux pas*. "And if he says you can go to Eilean Dubh, that's where we're going. All of us," she said, giving Robert Bruce her firmest mother's stare. Privately she welcomed the chance for a shorter journey to test her husband's endurance before they had to brave the long plane ride home.

That young man shrugged his shoulders. "Okay, whatever you say goes, Dad, as usual. But if William Wallace can be Will, I've decided that I want to be called R.B. from now on. It's more dignified, more in keeping with my position as an executive. And besides, I've had enough of Robert Bruce, Scottish hero or no Scottish hero."

His sister bent to kiss Robert Burns's forehead. "I'll always be Flora, Daddy."

"That's my girl," he said. "Now let's get packed and skedaddle off to my Island."

Robert Burns MacDonald returned in triumph to Eilean Dubh by helicopter, accompanied by his family. He was welcomed back by Will, by Darroch and Jean, and by Jamie and Màiri MacDonald, and driven in state to Ros Mór in the Bentley, which impressed Flora and R.B. very much. The fact that the Bentley was old made it even more valuable in their eyes; they knew that made it a classic.

The MacDonalds settled happily into the Rose. They'd expected that they'd be roughing it in a dingy, old-fashioned, small town fleabag with hard beds, dirt-smeared windows, and hideous carpets, and were surprised and delighted by the hotel's cheerful, tidy appearance. Their first bites of Sheilah's cuisine confirmed their initial impressions, and won them over once and for all.

Polly did not attend the MacDonald reunion with the *Eilean Dubhannaich*. Will had not allowed it; he was saving her for a formal presentation to his mother and siblings at the Rose that afternoon, after they'd all gotten settled into their rooms and had time to relax and eat lunch. "Get dressed up and we'll wow them," he'd told her.

Oh, dear, clothes worries again, and this time it was really important because she was meeting Will's family. She didn't have time to have Elspeth make her something new, of course, and the green dress would do fine, but how much better she would look if she had dressy shoes, not just her plain walking ones. And did she remember how to put on her new make-up? And what should she do about her hair? Would more vinegar help?

Would they like her? Would she be able to talk to them? Nerves brought her near tears again until she remembered the specter of Cailean Ferguson. Will's family couldn't be as scary as the ghostie of a long-dead seafaring man. And Will liked her just as she was, so that was how the others would have to take her. Why was she worrying about all these inconsequential matters? She didn't have to be shy any more. After all, she had talked to a ghostie. Live people shouldn't scare her; she'd communicated with the dead.

What was important was making sure she had interesting subjects to talk about, so she'd have to make a new list. But a lot had to be ruled out when talking to strangers! No politics, no religion, not the weather (boring), or ghosties (they'd think she was mad). She finally decided on the subjects of her cottage and its history, Sheilah's cooking, Island wildflowers, the archaeological dig, and the quaint roads and byways of Eilean Dubh that she and Will had explored. That ought to get her through the evening, if others did their conversational duty.

Will arrived at the cottage later that day to sweep her off to the family gathering for tea. "You look great, honey. Are you ready to knock 'em dead?"

Polly said dubiously, "I'm not very good at knocking people dead, but I'll try."

The California MacDonalds were convened in their private parlor, a spare room on the second floor that Sheilah had converted for their use. Since they'd hired the rest of the floor for their accommodations, she thought they might as well have the small bedroom, too. It would make a cosy sitting area for the whole family.

Anyway, she couldn't put anyone Scottish on that floor in the midst of a bunch of hearty Americans; they'd go bonkers from the cultural shock. So she whisked around finding chairs and a couple of end tables, moved the single bed against a wall and covered it with a pretty spread and pillows to transform it into a couch, and set out two vases full of flowers. And for this afternoon's gathering she'd prepared an elegant tea with her prized silver service and best china, heaping plates of dainty sandwiches, cakes and fruit and her own private blend of tea crafted for her in Edinburgh, which she called Afternoon Rose.

All the MacDonalds' eyes were focused on the door when Will and Polly appeared. Will took a deep breath and announced, "I'd like you all to meet my fiancée, Ms Polly Gillespie. Polly, this is my family."

A storm of excited surprise broke out. Robert Burns and R. B. were already politely on their feet and the ladies rose, too. Everyone rushed the pair, all talking at once. "Will, you sly devil!" "Where did you find such a pretty girl to marry on this funny little Island?" "What part of Scotland are you from, Polly?" "Will, darling, you might have warned us."

And Robert Burns, always wanting the last word, said, "Took my advice, did you, and popped the question. Good lad."

Polly looked at Will. "Your father told you to marry me?"

Will said, "No! Well, yes. But I was going to ask you anyway; that darn ghost . . . ghostie . . . just interrupted my train of thought."

"Ghost?" "What ghost?" Predictably, everyone's attention was caught.

Polly sighed. The cat was out of the bag, the beans had been spilled, and now her family-to-be would think she was a nut case. It was Will's fault it had been mentioned, so she'd let him talk his way out of this one while she sat and tried to look innocent.

Undeterred by her expression, Will took over and made the story his own. "It's three months worth of happenings, so everybody sit down and we'll fill you in on the details in chronological order." He took his time in the telling, realizing that his audience was hanging on every word. It was a pretty good tale, he thought, especially the bit about the ghostie and Polly's heroism. He swept into that part without a minute of hesitation, forgetting that he didn't believe in spooks and that his listeners probably didn't, either.

After he'd finished, Flora was the first to voice her doubts. "How can you be sure it was a ghost?"

"Unless there was an unseasonable blizzard, what made us so cold?" said Will.

"Could you have imagined it all?" asked R. B.

Polly spoke up to defend herself. "I'm not given to wild flights of fancy; I'm a prosaic kind of person. Anyway, if I did imagine it, I'd imagine something a lot pleasanter than a dead seaman hammering on my door in the middle of the night and scaring me half out of my tiny little wits. I mean, I could see through his raggedy clothes to his bones, and he dripped horrible wet seaweed. It was major league scariness."

R. B. nodded in his businesslike way. "That makes sense to me."

His father said, "Strange things happen on remote little Scottish islands."

Louise said, "You were very brave, Polly, to speak up to the ghost that way."

"It's a great story," said Flora, wondering if she could weave a ghostly thread into her marketing plans. The paranormal always made good copy and the media loved a spook and spirit angle. Hard to make the concept work with industrial fasteners, though.

Whether they thought it was her imagination or not, the story broke the ice between Polly and the American MacDonalds. They went down to dinner chatting happily and only three of her prepared subjects were needed to keep conversation going.

After dinner, when everyone was enjoying a post-meal whisky upstairs in their private sitting room, Robert Burns looked around at them all. "Well, folks," he said, "I've made a decision. It's partly based on my most recent health scare, and partly on the fact that Will has found himself a fine lassie to marry and has a new direction for his life. I can't be outdone by some young whippersnapper, so I'm going to head in a new direction, too. I'm giving control of the business to Robert Bruce, R. B., I mean, who will be our new chief executive. And Flora, honey, you'll be co-chief executive, in charge of marketing. The pair of you will keep things running just fine."

The family burst into cries of surprise and the loudest was from R. B. "Dad! Are you sure? What am I going to do without your guiding hand?"

"You'll do just fine. I'm not leaving the business; I'm going to start and head up a new division and get back to doing what I enjoy most, finding answers to industrial fastener problems. And I'm only going to work half-days so that I can spend more time with my lovely Louise. Is there a place for me in that hospital volunteer mob of yours, Lou, my bonnie dearie?"

"Oh, yes," cried his wife in excitement. "I can think of at least half a dozen places where your business skills and connections would come in handy."

"Who knows," said Robert Burns. "I might even consider retiring in a couple of years, if I can't find enough challenges in the firm to keep myself busy. Maybe buy a sailboat, or take up woodworking, or coin collecting." He chuckled. "And it'll give me more time to be active in Scottish activities back home. Chair a festival or two, run a Burns' Night dinner, raise dough for Eilean Dubh, that sort of thing." He was already doing all that, had done for years, but no one pointed it out to him.

The MacDonalds looked at each other. They couldn't imagine the family firm without Robert Burns in the driver's seat, but if that was what he wanted, they would have to adjust. He was, and always would be, the boss.

Talk turned, inevitably, back to Will and Polly's engagement, and a long involved discussion began about wedding plans that everyone, especially the women, enjoyed. "Do you want to be married in Minneapolis among your relatives and friends, dear?" said Louise anxiously. A born and bred Californian, all she knew about Minnesota was its reputation for frigid weather, and she could imagine her family bundled in thick coats, ugly hats and galoshes, mushing by dogsled to a cold church through a howling snowstorm. But if that was what the bride wanted, they would have to comply.

"Oh, I haven't had time to think about it. Anyway, the only relative I have in Minnesota is my mother." She ignored the friends part, since she really didn't have any.

"Perhaps you could be married in California and we could fly your mother to the service. She'd stay with us, of course."

Polly looked dubious, but postponed discussing her mother's self-imposed isolation until another time. It wasn't that she was ashamed of her mother; it was that her mother would be ashamed of her. She would weep and wail over everything connected with the wedding that the MacDonalds would expect and Polly and Will would want: dancing, music, laughter, joy, and a minister who would not preach eternal damnation.

To avoid tears and pointless recrimination, she thought it a much better plan to get married in the midst of the MacDonalds in California, and visit her mother with Will on their wedding trip. Yes, that was exactly what she'd do. Present Mom with a *fait accompli*, and there'd be less stress all around.

How to explain that to the family-obsessed MacDonalds? Perhaps she could hint that her mother had taken the veil and become a nun. It was almost true, except that she wasn't Catholic. Something else to explain.

Thirty-two

They . . . threw themselves into the interests of the rest, but each plowed his or her own furrow. Their thoughts, their little passions and hopes and desires, all ran along separate lines. Family life is like this — animated, but collateral.

Rose Macaulay

There was really not enough room for Will in the MacDonald encampment at the Rose, and the hustle and bustle, wheeling and dealing, twisting and turning that went on constantly with R. B., Flora, and their smartphones and digital whats-its got on his nerves. He'd never realized the world of industrial fasteners was so complicated, nor had he realized that the firm had expanded so far into Europe. Some of the phone calls were made to France and Germany, and he had to listen to Flora working her wiles in French and German. She was a natural linguist, and her command of both languages was already very good and getting better with each conversation.

He sighed, thinking of his siblings' many talents; he only hoped he could measure up to them one day. At least he wouldn't be competing with them in the family business. He'd be on his own as an architect. The thought gave him enormous pleasure, and he realized he'd made the right decision.

That the MacDonalds were all important members of their respective circles was shown by the fact that even gentle, quiet Louise took time out from knitting and reading to her husband to call California and her hospital committee. This involved long soothing murmurs and reassurances on her end, as no one wanted to do anything without her approval. She had modestly declined to be the committee chairperson, but had rapidly become its mother figure.

Partly to find some peace and quiet, but mostly because he wanted to be with her, Will began to spend the nights with Polly. He made a good roommate, despite his occasional bouts of bossiness, which she was learning to ignore. Besides being an enthusiastic lover, he was also tidy and helpful, and he never left the toilet seat up or strewed dirty clothes on the floor. He fixed breakfast every other day, too, once Polly had shown him how to coax along the elderly toaster so that it did not scorch the bread, and how to regulate the burners on the stove so he did not frizzle the eggs.

Their union came to fruition when she cleared out a bureau drawer and a corner of the little bedroom cupboard for his clothes. Both realized what an important step that was. He had moved in with her, into the funny old haunted stone cottage.

It was almost like being married, except that they'd probably get a better toaster as a wedding gift, Polly thought, and decided she could get used to the married idea very easily. She was still pondering the bliss of going back to college, changing her mind daily about what she wanted to study. Right now she was thinking about creative writing, as she had a ready-made plot for a novel in Cailean Ferguson's ghostie story. With a little practice and a good editor, she could take on Stephen King. She was ever the optimist.

Happily playing house with Will, she never once thought about tonight being the night of the full moon; she'd lost track of that after what she assumed had been Cailean's last visit. So what happened next came as a complete surprise.

Bam! Bam! Bam! The knocking woke her out of a sound sleep. She looked at her wristwatch on the bedside table. It was twelve midnight.

"What the hell?" Muttering, she dragged herself out of bed and into her slippers and robe. "What has this cottage become, Spook Central? If it's a ghostie I've never met before, I'm going to boot him off to Elspeth or the Laird or Jamie," she mumbled crossly as she inserted her feet in her slippers. "They can deal with the local haunts; it's their territory. I'm just a visitor."

Bam! Bam! Bam! The noise reverberated through the cottage, and Will stirred.

"All right, keep your hair on," grumped Polly, stomping through the lounge.

She staggered back in surprise at the wave of cold emitting from the door. Good heavens, it really was another ghostie visitation, and not one to be taken lightly if the hyper-activity of the Frozen Zone around the door was any indication. She hesitated, her hand on the knob. What if it wasn't Cailean? What if it was somebody dead she hadn't met before?

There were probably lots of other ghosties on Eilean Dubh, all with an ax to grind, frustrations to vent, complaints to register, and all looking for a captive listener. Why did it have to be her?

BAM! BAM! BAM!

"Damn it, here we go again," she growled, braced herself, and threw the door open to the blazing light of the full moon.

There on the doorstep stood Cailean Ferguson, misty and wavering, but undeniably her previous visitor. He was smiling, a ghastly caricature of a live person's grin. Polly shuddered, looking at the exposed bones of his skull, and grasped the door so she didn't collapse from fright.

"*Mo Pheigi*," he whispered, and flourished a bony arm dripping sea-weed at the insubstantial female figure beside him that glimmered in and out of focus. She was very pretty, in a transparent sort of way. Dark hair spilled over her shoulders and bright eyes gleamed through the mist that surrounded the couple. She bowed her head and curtsied deeply.

"Umm, hi," mumbled Polly, and curtsied awkwardly in return. She was seriously freaked now, her mind blank with shock; she'd been so sure Cailean was gone for good, and now he'd come back and brought yet another ghostie, his wee wifie, yet. Did they want to come in for tea and crumpets? Did they want their cottage back? Did they want her to arrange a welcome home party? Or did they just want to scare her to death? If so, they were doing a hell of a job of it. "So you found her. Super," she managed at last.

"*Sann dhutsa a tha e. Mòran taing*," said Cailean, extending something to her on his see-through hand. *This is for you, with many thanks*, Polly mentally translated from Gaelic to English.

The object was pale white, shaped like a knife, and about six inches by two inches in measurements. Polly took it cautiously, putting her hand under the opposite tip so as not to touch Cailean. The air around the object was so frigid that she almost dropped it.

"Thank you," she said, hearing with no surprise that her words came out in the Gaelic as "*Tapadh leat*."

There was a tip of the hat, and a second curtsey bobbed by Peigi. Then the pair vanished, no slow fade-out, no trailing bits of ectoplasm left behind. They were gone, abruptly, as though a television set had been switched off. And the Frozen Zone had thawed; the temperature on the doorstep was evening-cool and pleasant.

Polly was left framed in the moonlight, staring at the object in her hand.

"Was there a knock on the door? What's that you're holding?" Will, coming up behind her, jolted her out of her abstraction and almost out of her senses.

"Cailean was here with Peigi and he gave me this," she said, when her accelerated heart rate had returned to normal and her voice had reappeared. "It's some sort of carving. Isn't it beautiful!" It was shaped like a horn or a tusk, and its tip had been fashioned into a long, slightly hooked beak, connected to a beautifully rounded head with deep small indentations on each side for eyes. The rest of the piece was delicately carved to represent wings, highlighted by a sooty substance rubbed into the edges of the feathers to darken them. They stared at it in silence.

"It's an albatross," said Polly, and with perfect certainty. She'd never seen an albatross, she had no idea how she knew what it was, she just did. "It's made of ivory."

"An ivory carving is the soul of a lost sailor," whispered Will, and he had no idea how he knew that. It was as though someone else's words were coming out of his mouth.

"Albatrosses dance," said Polly. "They dance with their chosen mate when they're courting. And they mate for life." How had that idea gotten into her head?

"We'll follow their example," said Will. "We've already got a good start on the dancing part."

Polly moved to the mantelpiece with the carving, turning on the light as she went, and set it between the two keys. She and Will stood looking at its beauty in awe.

"That's proof, Polly, that this really happened," Will said.

She smiled at him. "I never felt any need to prove that. I know it all happened." Just as she knew why the Frozen Zone outside her door had disappeared. She patted the carving to welcome it, then took Will by the hand and led him back to bed. Time for her to get warmed up again, in the nicest possible way, with the nicest possible person.

Thirty-three

The distance that the dead have gone
Does not at first appear—Their coming back seems possible
For many an ardent year.

Emily Dickinson

Of course she couldn't keep the carving, she knew that; she'd never be able to get it through the American customs inspectors between Eilean Dubh and California. Only antique ivory could be imported to America and she had no documents proving the age of Cailean's gift, though she suspected it was very old.

Besides, she had an overpowering feeling that the object should not leave Eilean Dubh. She knew there was an Island museum up in Airgead but she'd never been there, and had no idea whom to contact for a possible donation. Someone who didn't know her might think she'd stolen the carving; she had no good explanation of how she'd come by it. She wasn't going to try to tell a stranger the real story and be laughed out of the joint.

She decided to ask the Laird for advice, had she but known, a normal *Eilean Dubhannach* idea; she was becoming acclimated to Island ways. She went to the red telephone box to arrange a convenient time for a visit and chat about a new spectral happening. At the appointed hour, she and Will presented themselves at *Taigh a Mhorair*, the Laird's house.

"Given the subject of this meeting, I hope you don't mind that I asked Jamie to sit in, Polly," said Darroch, ushering them in. "He's our resident expert on unearthly matters."

"Not at all," said Polly, dipping her head in salute to an extremely uncomfortable-looking Jamie, who was morosely sipping a dram of Darroch's whisky. He'd had to come because the Laird had asked him, but he hated being involved with other people's supernatural events. He had enough of that sort of thing going on in his own life. Why just the other day, up in the pasture, he'd seen . . . . He dragged himself back to the present with difficulty.

Jean brought in tea and cookies and asked permission to stay. It was granted.

"Stand in the middle of the room, Polly, and let's hear what you have to say," said Darroch, who as an actor always liked to block a scene properly.

She stood as directed, looked around at them, and began. "Some of you may know that I've had an unusual visitation at my cottage several times." She prepared to explain, but they all nodded their heads, leaving Polly wondering how many people had heard the story.

"Everyone knows," said Darroch, guessing her question from the look on her face. "It's a good story, very typical of Eilean Dubh, and so, of course, it would spread like wildfire once one person found out. It's all right; nobody thinks you're mad. Hauntings are not uncommon on this Island. It's a Scottish thing, I suppose. Ghosties and ghoulies and long-legged beasties, all that sort of mixty-maxty."

She caught a sympathetic nod from Jamie, who'd been in her place before, trying to explain the inexplicable. "Okay," she started again. "So you know about what's been going on; that makes it easier. The visitation came three times, and I thought it was over. But last night it returned . . . he returned, I should say . . . and he brought a friend."

There was a hum of excitement. "A female friend, if I am remembering the story aright?" said Jamie.

"Yes, her name is Peigi and she's vaguely pretty. He introduced us, talking in the Gaelic like he always does and me understanding him like I always do, and she didn't say a word, she just curtsied to me. And then he gave me this as a thank-you gift." She took the ivory carving out of her pocket.

Her audience stared, struck dumb. At last Jamie rose, saying, "May I hold it?"

Wordless, she passed the carving to him. "It's very cold," he said, looking at her.

"Not as cold as it was last night, when it came out of Cailean's bony hand."

Jean could not help shivering. As an American, she wasn't on as familiar terms with hauntings as were the *Eilean Dubhannaich*, and could not deal with them as casually. She'd seen Jamie in action several times with the supernatural, and still had trouble accepting it all. Seeing was not necessarily believing.

Jamie handled the carving reverentially, turning it this way and that, muttering in the Gaelic, Darroch murmuring a comment now and then. At last Darroch said, "How old do you reckon it is, *a Sheumais?*"

"Old enough, older than Cailean Ferguson for sure. Made by one of his seafaring ancestors from ivory found on the other side of the world, and passed down through his family for generations. Now why would he have had it with him at the time of his death?"

"For good luck, perhaps?" suggested Will. "Because he was going to sea. I understand that sailors are very superstitious."

Jamie looked at him and nodded agreement. "Yes. I think you're right. A seaman's lucky piece, a carving of an albatross, a bird that's considered good luck on this Island, though it's bad luck elsewhere." He looked at Polly. "You can't keep it, you know, there may be, um, emanations that you wouldn't want in your life."

"Yes, I know, I've thought about that, too. And it's a genuine local artifact, as good as anything dug up in a bog or at the archaeological site, so it belongs here. I thought perhaps I would donate it to the Eilean Dubh Museum."

"Smashing idea," said Darroch. "Unless Jamie thinks that there may be unfortunate, umm, emanations occurring in the museum? Will it have to be, umm, exorcised?" He didn't look forward to having to ask Minister Donald to conduct a séance sort of thing; that gentleman was fiercely dismissive when it came to matters of the occult, and not even the Laird's involvement would sway him.

"No, it'll be safe there, among the other manifestations of the Eilean Dubh spirit, both real and imaginary. You'll have to think up an appropriate caption for the exhibit, Polly." Jamie smiled at her in a companionable way, which made her knees weak, and handed the carving back to her.

She recovered, and said, "I certainly don't want a sign saying that a ghostie gave it to me! We're just barely keeping a lid on the rumor I'm a nut case as it is."

"How about 'found on Eilean Dubh by Ms Polly Gillespie of the United States and kindly donated by her to the Museum,'" offered Jean. "You don't have to say where or how it was found."

"Or, 'Cailean Ferguson's knife, found by Ms Polly,' etc. Seems like he should get billing, too," said Darroch, with an actor's sensitivity about credit.

"Quite right," said Will. "Except what if someone asks Polly how she knew it was Cailean Ferguson's knife?"

"I'll say it was a lucky guess and smile mysteriously," said Polly.

"You'll be good at that," said Jamie unexpectedly. She blushed.

Màiri came bustling in the door just then, and the whole story of the lucky albatross and Peigi and Cailean Ferguson's ghosties had to be told all over again for her benefit. Afterwards, she turned to Jamie and said, "So, ectoplasm and ghoulies hugger-mugger all over Eilean Dubh once more, and you're not in the thick of it? How did you keep your clever self aloof?"

Jamie said, "The ghostie didn't come to me; it came to Polly, so I didn't want to interfere. Besides, she didn't need me. She did fine on her own." He had gotten involved, in a way, but he wasn't telling anyone about that. A tune had been haunting him, not giving him any peace, inspired by the girl and her ghostie. It was a promising tune, but it hadn't quite gelled. Jamie wanted his tunes to be perfect before anyone heard them.

He smiled at Polly, a conspiratorial smile, and she suddenly realized that when it came to the supernatural, they were kindred spirits, they shared similar powers. Spooks sought them out. Not many people could say that, she thought in awe. It was like being part of a family, an Eilean Dubh family. Oh, dear, the supernatural again; what would her mother say? She knew the answer to that one, but she refused to think about it now.

She was already looking forward to their return to the Island next summer, and had resigned herself to the possibility she might encounter more ghosties then, and that Cailean's appearance might be the start of a new career for her: ministering to spooks. Maybe she'd become Jamie's right-hand woman when it came to visitations. Maybe she'd become the Island's resident ghostie buster when he didn't want to be bothered, which apparently was most or all of the time.

But she didn't know much about ghosties; she needed to get training. Was there such a thing as a graduate school major in the supernatural?

No, there was no scientific basis for the supernatural; it would be like majoring in Santa Claus.

In whom she still believed. And Cinderella, too.

The Spirit of Eilean Dubh

G. Major (cheerful)

©2011 Sherry Ladig

Thirty-four

*It's what I always wanted to do, to show the laughter,
the fun, the joy of dance.*

Martha Graham

It was Friday, their last full day on the Island, and that night was the last *cèilidh* that Robert Burns, Will and Polly would attend on this visit. It was also the first *cèilidh* that R. B., Flora and Louise would experience on Eilean Dubh, though they'd been to many at Scottish festivals all along the Pacific Coast. So they knew what to expect. All three were adept at Scottish country dancing and looked forward to an evening of "cutting a rug," as Robert Burns MacDonald put it in his old-fashioned slang. They had not brought their ghillies, but Jean, Sally and Darroch had all offered to lend their spare pairs and between the three of them, they got the visitors successfully kitted out.

But the California MacDonalds and the *Eilean Dubhannaich* alike were surprised when Will ascended the stage and moved to the microphone, where he announced in his authoritative Scottish country dance teacher's way, "I'd like to have everyone here learn a new dance, one I've devised. If you'll take partners and form sets, I'll teach it to you."

Bemused, his listeners did as he instructed, and soon had themselves arranged in orderly lines of male facing female, in groups of eight up and down the dance floor. As she'd been instructed previously, Polly planted herself in the first woman's position in the center set, and waited for Will to join her as her partner.

"This dance is called "The Spirit of Eilean Dubh," and I'd like to dedicate it to Ms Polly Gillespie, whom I am proud to say has consented to become my wife," said Will.

There was an approving murmur and several people shouted out congratulations. R. B., Flora and Louise applauded, not realizing that was not the Eilean Dubh way. The Islanders looked at each other, shrugged, and politely put their own hands together to honor the visitors' custom.

Polly waved at everyone in thanks. She was no longer a shy wallflower, she realized, and she blew a thank-you kiss at Will because he had done so much to make her transformation possible. But a lot of it she'd done herself, she thought smugly, and smiled all over her face in pure happiness as he came to her side, having finished talking through the dance. The band struck up a new tune by Jamie MacDonald, written, at Will's request, to accompany the new dance. It was a bright and lively jig, and its bouncy good cheer made Will think of Polly's smile.

"The Spirit of Eilean Dubh" was satisfyingly complex, but intuitive and easily learned, as good dances are, and the *Eilean Dubhannaich*, all experienced dancers, picked it up quickly. Soon the floor was full of happy couples dancing the pas de basque and the skip change of step as the formations required.

Polly, as first woman in the first repetition of the dance, made a special effort to show proper technique and timing, until Will whispered to her, "You look so serious. Relax, honey, and have fun."

So she did, and she enjoyed herself very much. And after the dance

was over, she enjoyed herself even more accepting congratulations from the Dark Island residents who had become her friends.

It was a very satisfying evening on an Island that now seemed like home. She was going to miss Eilean Dubh and was already eager for their return next summer. Later, as she spun around the floor in Will's arms in the last waltz of the evening, she told him as much.

"Yes, it was a rare stroke of luck for both of us that we came to the Island," he said, forgetting that he had not wanted to come there in the first place.

"It wasn't luck. It was fate," she replied, and smiled mysteriously, just as she'd promised Jamie she would when confronted with inexplicable situations.

At the end of the evening, when the *cèilidh*-goers were packing up to leave, Jamie sat alone on the podium, humming quietly to himself. The tune that had haunted him was finally assuming its final shape. At last he took his fiddle, placed it under his chin and began to play. Polly, staring intently at him, felt the back of her neck prickle just as it had when she'd seen the ghostie, as she listened. It was a strange tune that made her glad the Hall lights were still on; it was about things best not thought of in the dark, odd shadowy forms and mysterious voices.

At the end of the tune, Jamie looked up from his fiddle at her. "It's called 'Polly's Ghostie,'" he said.

"Yes, I know," she answered.

They smiled at each other in perfect understanding.

The Spirit of Eilean Dubh

32-bar jig for 3 couples in a 4-couple longwise set
Devised by Lara Friedman~Shedlov
Tune: "The Spirit of Eilean Dubh," composed by Sherry Ladig

1-8 1C set and cast to 2nd place.

5-8 2C, 1C, 3C set and turn RH,
ending in the middle ready for

9-16 3-couple allemande, 1C finish facing 1st corners.

17-24 Set to corners and partner, i.e. "hello-goodbye setting."

25-28 3C, 1C, 2C turn RH half way with partner, then turning over RS, cast to partner's side ("half turn and twiddle").

29-32 All chase CW halfway.

Repeat having passed a couple.

Thirty-five

Live and work but do not forget to play, to have fun in life and really enjoy it.

Eileen Caddy

In bright autumn sunlight Eilean Dubh was beautiful, its burns sparkling blue, its thick grass cover a deep rich green, its snow-white sheep browsing contentedly on the hills, its fall wildflowers glowing in all colors like a rainbow. The cerulean sea crashed at the foot of the cliffs, and the high mountain *Beinn Mhic-an-Righ* lorded it over all below. Everything was as it should be. It was a perfect day on the Dark Island.

A myriad of birds warbled, saluting this perfect day, until their voices were drowned out by the whir of the blades of a helicopter. Murdoch the Chopper was taking the American MacDonalds back to Inverness where they'd make the first connections on their long journey home by taxi, train, and plane back to California.

Darroch and Jean, Jamie and Màiri, Sally and Ian, the children, and the wee dog Cèilidh, minus her recently adopted pups (and not missing the wee troublemakers at all), were there at the helicopter pad to say goodbye to their American friends. Polly and Will were there, too, but they were not going to Inverness on the chopper. They were taking the rental car on the Cal-Mac ferry tomorrow. Then they'd drive around mainland Scotland and see the sights, including a selection of grim and silent castles; Will looked forward to showing off to his beloved the places that previously he had thought boring. Polly looked forward to visiting the gardens; she was now toying with the idea of a career in garden design.

Then they'd be off to sunny California, to live in their own wing of the ranch house with the mile-long driveway, its cook, afternoon tea, and the MacDonald clan. Polly had gained so much self-confidence in the last few months that she felt sure she could cope with the eccentricities of her new relatives. She was, in fact, looking forward to being a part of a large and loving family. Besides, she had Will as support and back-up if she needed it.

She and Will would have a lovely autumn wedding on the ranch, and then they'd be off to graduate school someplace. They hadn't decided where yet but were leaning towards the University of Minnesota. Its College of Design included, besides Architecture, a program in Apparel Design and learning about designing clothing intrigued Polly. The entire subject of design fascinated her, and she even thought of asking Robert Burns to let her look over his shoulder while he worked in his newly returned-to career as an industrial designer.

And if they went to Minnesota, they would be close to Polly's mother and could build new bridges with her. Even if she disapproved of her daughter's lifestyle, Polly and Will would make an effort to reconcile their differing points of view, and they would start out by inviting her to the wedding. And if she came, they'd make her welcome.

Polly was so happy she didn't want to be at odds with anyone. Her friendship with Elspeth had shown her how pleasant it was to have an older person as a friend, and she hoped her mother would now fit into that role. It was worth a try.

The pair had made up their minds to chart a course that focused on leading a happy, productive life. There would, inevitably, be difficult and unpleasant patches, but they would do their best to face them with smiling faces and high hearts.

A quote from Robert Louis Stevenson that Polly ran across one day summed it up: *There is no duty we so much underrate as the duty of being happy.*

Polly and Will were taking that as their motto for the rest of their lives together.

Epilogue

The Spirit Departs

The lawn
Is pressed by unseen feet, and ghosts return
Gently at twilight, gently go at dawn,
The sad intangible who grieve and yearn . . .

T. S. Eliot

It was October 31st. It was Hallowe'en, it was All Hallows Eve, it was Hop tu Naa, it was *Nos Galan Gaeaf*, it was Allantide.

On Eilean Dubh it was Samhain. Summer's end, the beginning of the dark half of the year.

It was a time of divination, of gazing into a mirror to see a future spouse, of tossing an apple peel over the shoulder to see if it curled into the first initial of a future mate's name, of telling fortunes with stones and nuts and water. It was a time of bonfires and scary stories, a time when the boundary between living and dead stretched thin, thin enough to allow spirits to cross over into the human world, to allow themselves be seen and heard by a favored few of its denizens.

On Eilean Dubh it was a time when the human inhabitants of the Island buttoned themselves into their homes, pulled shades, locked doors, brought in the dogs and cats, and turned up the telly loud enough to hide strange noises from outside. That way they could pretend this night was like all other nights.

But it wasn't.

On *Cladh a' Chnuic*, Cemetery Hill, it was a time when the dead walked. Their voices, always faintly audible for those with ears to hear, like Jamie MacDonald and his daughter Eilidh, were loud and vigorous on this night, as the dead shared news and gossip, and shanachies, the storytellers, recited Island legends, lore and genealogies.

209

Cemetery Hill was packed with shadowy forms, weird wispy things, haunts, boggles, fairies, willies, and the Great Gray Man slinking around the outskirts of the Gathering, all of them talking, laughing and making music. And dancing, as ghostly pipers and phantom fluters struck up jigs, reels and strathspeys, and the shadows took partners and capered as though their vanished lives depended on it.

Not a human on the Island dared go near *Cladh a' Chnuic* on *Oïdhche Shamhna*, the night of the *cèilidh* of the dead. Spook Central, Polly Gillespie MacDonald would have called it.

As the evening drew to a close and the first rays of dawn appeared behind *Beinn Mhic-an-Rìgh*, the high western mountain, a nearly-transparent bagpiper climbed on top of the tallest tomb – that of a long-dead Laird Mac an Rìgh – and solemnly belted out "The Flowers of the Forest," an old Scottish lament for the dead.

Haunting voices joined in wailing the lyrics:
I've heard them liltin', at the yowe milkin',
Lasses a-liltin' before dawn o' day.
Now there's a moanin', on ilka green loanin'.
The flowers of the forest are a' wede away.

As the last notes from the piper died, the shadowy gathering prepared to disperse, their evening of freedom over. But there was one more ceremony to be gotten through before the sun rose, ending the night.

Cailean Ferguson, all bones and dripping fabric and flesh, appeared at the foot of the Laird's tomb, clasping his Peigi's spectral hand. He removed his hat and she curtsied, in farewell to their ghostly peers. Then they floated to the top of an old grave and hovered above it, heads bowed. It was Peigi's grave. There was no equivalent place of interment for Cailean, whose body had never been recovered from the depths of the cerulean sea in which he had been lost.

Cailean and Peigi took a step forward and down. And down and down and down, until they had disappeared into the depths of the grave, never to be seen again on the Dark Island.

Their souls were at rest, together, forever.

Author's Notes and Acknowledgments

Those of you who are familiar with my previous books know that I am very fond of cats and dogs, and have rejoiced in the companionship of one of the latter and several of the former. I am very sorry to have to tell you that our dear Teddycat crossed the Rainbow Bridge on May 6, 2013, a victim of oral cancer.

Teddy, a lilac point Siamese mix, was a rescue cat from the Heart of Minnesota shelter in Hutchinson, Minnesota, and Mike's and my beloved companion for nine years. He often warmed my lap while I worked at the computer, and in his quiet way provided inspiration for all things feline that I wrote about. In his later years he became adept at reading my mind, and I became almost as adept in reading his.

This is not fantasy; we did indeed have a psychic connection, and it is one of the many reasons I miss our Teddy so much. Left to hold the fort is Bailee, our sable Burmese girl, now an only cat, trying hard to walk in Teddy's pawprints.

How sad it is that we humans have such long lives, and our furry friends such short ones. To the memory of the world's best kitties, Twm Siôn, MacDougall, and Teddycat: rest in peace, little friends. We will always miss you.

As always, thanks to husband Mike for comfort and succor, to John the Computer Guru and to Carla for another fine cover, and Michael, Anita and Aaran, for being family.

Many thanks to Sherry Ladig for reading *The Spirit* manuscript and for offering unfailing encouragement.

Thanks to Lara Friedman~Shedlov for another spritely Scottish country dance, especially composed for this book.

Special thanks to Judith Palmateer and Chris Fayers for turning this book into reality, and for as always responding to my questions, worries and desperate cries for help.

Glossary

Arranged in order of appearance in the text.

All pronunciations approximate.

sgianan dubha – (skee-an-an duva) Plural of *sgian dubh,* the little black knife worn in the stocking of a kilt-wearer

an spiorad – (ahn speer-iot) a spirit

William Wallace – a Scottish landowner and leader defeated an English army at the Battle of Stirling Bridge, 1297, served as Guardian of Scotland until captured and executed by King Edward I of England

ceud mille fàilte – (kee-ut meeluh fal-tchuh) A hundred thousand welcomes

fàilte gu Eilean Dubh – (fal-tchuh goo ih-lan doo) Welcome to Eilean Dubh

Taigh a Mhorair – (ty uh vor-ur) The Laird's house

Rudha na h Airgid – (roo-uh nah air-git) The headland

Eilean Dubhannach – (ih-lan duv-ann-ack) A resident of the Dark Island; *Eilean Dubhannaich,* plural

ceart math – (kersh ma) Sure thing, okay

cèilidh – (kay-lee) A party with music, dancing and storytelling

haggis – a dish made traditionally of oatmeal, lamb's heart and liver, suet and onions, boiled in a sheep's stomach. Alterations have been made for modern tastes.

mo chridhe – (mo cree-yuh) My heart: term of endearment

Ian Mór – (ee-an more) Big Ian

taigh dubh – (ty doo) Black house; traditional Scottish Highland dwelling

ferrule crimper – a tool for bending a ring or cap (a ferrule) that strengthens the end of a handle, stick, or tube and prevents it from splitting or wearing

Scottish country dancing – traditional social dances of Scotland, given new life in 1923 when Mrs. Ysobel Stewart of Fasnacloich and Miss

Jean Milligan formed what became and continues to be the Royal Scottish Country Dance Society, for the preservation of SCD dances and music.

tha mi toilicht' d'fhaicinn – (ha mi tolleech-tch dech-keen) I'm pleased to see you

dè seòrsa rud a th'ann? – (jae shawrsuh root uh ha-oon) What sort of thing is it?

dè 'n coltas a tha'air? – (jaeng coltass uh hir) What does it look like?

A Dhia beannaich mi – (uh jee-a be-an-aitch mi) Lord bless me

Ameireaga – (amerruga) America

mo ghaoil – (mo gheul) My dear

feasgar math, a Sheanmhar – (fess-kurr ma, uh shen-na-var) Good afternoon, Grandmother

Bana-Ameireaganach – (ba-nah Ammer-ug-an-nach) American woman

mo fhlur – (mo floo-er) My flower: term of endearment

ni sin a' chùis – (nih sin uh hoo-is) That'll do fine

tha mi duilich – (ha me dooleech) I am sorry

A Pheigi? – (ah faeg-ee?) Oh, Peggy?

O mo Pheigi! Tha mi 'g iarraidh Peigi agam! – (oh mo faeg-ee! Ha mic eerie paeg-ee akam) Oh, my Peggy! I want my Peggy!

sann dhutsa a tha e. Mòran taing – (shann gut-sa uh ha eh, moe-ran ta-eeng) This is for you, with many thanks

Cladh a' Chnuic – (clav un hoo-nuik) Cemetery Hill

Oïdhche Shamhna – (uh-eech-yuh ha-oonuh) Halloween

The Scottish Island Novels

by Audrey McClellan

O'Leary, Kat and Cary Grant
O'Leary is a rescue cat, smart, nosy, and psychic. Kat Hennessey is a writer looking for the right cat and the right man. Cary Rodrigo Grant is the most eligible man Kat's met in a cat's age.

Kat has a lot of worries, like the Great American Novel she's writing that won't come together, the sneaky student slut seeking to steal her husband, the Faculty Wives Committee that wants her to get excited about evergreens. And the crack in the basement wall of her house, and what she and her Burmese cat O'Leary find when they go through it into alternative realities: everything from vampires to ancient Roman assassins to a two-headed fire-breathing Etruscan monster.

"The funniest book I've ever read." Reader comment.

O'Leary, Kat and the Fairy from Hell
Psychic cat O'Leary and his human, Kat, have shared many adventures in alternative realities, but they've never experienced anything like a seven-inch-tall, purple spiky-haired, mischief-minded figment of the imagination, a fairy named Zelly. She tricks Kat into inviting her into her home, and by fairy rules, once she's in, she doesn't have to leave until she's good and ready.

And Zelly is in no hurry to leave. Not when there are cats to tease, humans to torment, elderberry wine to guzzle and a baby to covet . . . She's here to stay and she's a major pain in the patootie.

How can Kat and O'Leary get rid of the infuriating intruder, and keep out any further proliferation of paranormal personages?

Westering Home
Jean Abbott leaves her unfaithful husband in Milwaukee for tiny Scottish island Eilean Dubh, where she finds music, friendship, and love with actor/laird, Darroch Mac an Rìgh. Bronze Medal winner, *ForeWord Magazine* Book of the Year awards.

The White Rose of Scotland
Will Jean agree to marry Darroch? Maybe, now that she has exciting news for him. Darroch, Jean, Bonnie Prince Jamie MacDonald and feisty wife Màiri become folk music stars, while the younger generation of Islanders try to sort out sex and love. Notable Book, *Writers Notes Magazine* awards.

The Devil and the Dark Island
When a smooth-talking money man arrives on Eilean Dubh plotting to develop its unspoiled coastline, can the Islanders resist the lure of big bucks tourism? What is mysterious Cornishman Zachariah Trelawney searching for, and why is wildflower preservation nut/newspaper editor Anna Wallace helping him? Small Press Contemporary Paranormal/ Futuristic Romance Award Nominee, *Romantic Times BookClub*.

Rosie's Cèilidh
A dog is in danger . . . and it's Rosie to the rescue. A little girl is in danger . . . and it's Jamie to the rescue. Waiting in the wings is another challenge for Rosie, a Dandie Dinmont terrier puppy as strong-willed as any little girl – even the Laird's daughter.
     Legacy Fiction Winner, The Eric Hoffer Awards 2011.

Magic Carpet Ride
Cape Breton Island is beautiful and so is *Québecois* writer Angus MacQuirter, the answer to a maiden's prayer. But Dorcas Carrothers' two previous lovers have left her love-wary and guy-shy. Can Angus break down her resistance? He certainly is going to have fun trying. A sexy romp set in Nova Scotia and Minneapolis.
     Gold Award Winner, *ForeWord Magazine* Book of the Year 2005.

Down by the Salley Gardens
What would you do if you won ninety-two million dollars and change in the lottery? Buy a new wardrobe? Buy a car? Buy a house? Quit your job? Wylie Kennerly happily tries all those ideas, but hits a romantic stalemate when she falls in love with Edward Jones, a passionate poet who doesn't want to be "collected" by a rich woman. Should Wylie give away all her money to win her poet's love?

The Woman Who Loved Newfoundland
Newfoundland. New-fun-land. Ever since she confused the two in fifth grade, Cleo English has wanted to visit the Canadian province known as the Rock. Now a twenty-nine year old teacher, she's off to spend her summer looking for some "new fun" in the Rock's Last Man Ashore Cove. Seductive B and B owner Max Avalon is more than ready to provide fun both new and old, when he's not dealing with mice in the kitchen, demanding guests, a combative Spanish housekeeper, and eccentric fellow Newfoundlanders. But Cleo, still traumatized by her husband's death three years ago, has an epiphany: are verbal sparring matches and madcap sex really all she's looking for?

Finalist in the Commercial Fiction category of the Eric Hoffer Awards.

Reviews and Readers' Comments on the Scottish Island Novels
"I cannot say enough about the novels – just that I felt I was right there, on the island, amongst friends – I felt I belonged!"

"A wonderful interplay of modern day American and traditional island culture, with a satisfying and plausible outcome."

"Audrey has written a book that has everything – romance, intrigue, mystery, danger, unexpected plot twists – suffused with a deep love of the islands of Scotland."

"*O'Leary, Kat, and Cary Grant* is a choice and very highly recommended pick for cat lovers." – *Midwest Book Review.*

"I have been devouring your Scottish Island books since I discovered them at a Highland festival . . . Your characters and description of Eilean Dubh are fabulous . . ."

"I have read, re-read, LOVE and own *Westering Home, The White Rose of Scotland* and *The Devil and the Dark Island.*"

". . . swirls with music and friendship and dance and, most of all, romance . . . A sweeping story."

(*Magic Carpet Ride*): "Beautiful, sexy love story . . . Angus tries to convince Dorcas that he's the man of her dreams by using funny, underhanded devices." – *Romantic Times Bookclub Magazine.*

Made in the USA
Charleston, SC
03 February 2015